Also by
Todd Michael Cox

Dizzlemuck
Love in the Time of Wee Folk

After the Death of the Ice Cream Man

Beast

For more information visit
toddmichaelcox.com

iowa

a novel

TODD MICHAEL COX

Sybil ✐ Press
Wisconsin

Special thanks to Troy Baumann for the wonderful cover painting. Check out more of his work here:

http://stinkerpaws.com/

ISBN: 978-0-9843661-2-5

Author's Note

Many works have attempted to capture the dirty facts and unsavory details of American politics, but a greater truth is the goal of a work like this, and therefore I have taken certain liberties with the various political and voting systems of this country. With this novel (the original composition of which dates to 2007) I was attempting to capture the *feeling* of modern American politics, an honest impression of what it's like to live in hyper-politicized and soured times, because that is the only way to truly arrive at the bloody heart of the matter... and the only way, of course, to exorcise the demons found there. If you're looking for a journalistic litany of facts (like a display of dried-out and soulless taxidermy specimens) you are advised to look elsewhere. Let it also be understood that the "Iowa" in this novel is not meant to be an accurate representation, geographically or culturally, of the Hawkeye state. Rather, the Iowa you will find in these pages is entirely a state of mind.

TmC
Aztalon, WI

Man is by nature a political animal.
--Aristotle

No man is wise enough to be another man's master.
--Edward Abbey

We have met the enemy and he is us.
--Pogo

No one for President.
--bumper sticker

iowa

Part I

Once upon a time, in a cluttered and vaguely stench-ridden little apartment in Milwaukee, surrounded by several dog-eared books, half-empty bottles of evil-looking liquids, and heaping piles of clothes in varying degrees of cleanliness, Jasper Callister woke to the sound of knocking. Knocking, gentle knocking, tapping at his apartment door.

He looked and felt like death itself, and for no reason, really. He wasn't hung-over and he wasn't sick... but there were other things that can make a man feel this way.

He was lying on his bed in nothing but dark green boxers, the tangled wrinkled sheets underneath him the same rough texture of his skin, the two pillows so flat and beaten as to look like roadkill. He opened his eyes, waited. The knocking stopped. He closed his eyes again. A strange semi-sweet dream of apple trees and—

The knocking resumed, a little harder this time, yet still polite.

Go away, Jasper mouthed. He didn't have the energy to speak, just wanted to lie there while the day slipped away and another night came on all beautiful and black. Perhaps whoever it was would be able to sense the off-putting radiance

2

of his aura and mood. Animals work this way, right? You can sense when they're not happy. Stay away, my cockles are up, bitch.

A few moments later there was more knocking.

"Who the living hell is it?" he called out in a voice both thunderous and phlegmy.

"Greg."

"Who the hell is Greg?"

"Greg Helter."

Greg Helter? Jasper ran through the names that mattered to him and couldn't place this one. Wasn't his landlord, wasn't his former boss, wasn't someone from the factory.

He stared at the ceiling, thinking. Do I know any Gregs...?

Outside the door there was a cough, then: "Helter *Skelter*?"

Jasper blinked once, twice, then turned his neck and looked at the door. There was a huge chunk of wood missing from this side of the door, the result of something thrown against it. A brick? A hammer? He couldn't remember. Perhaps someone or something had once tried to get out.

"Helter *Skelter*?" he asked.

"Yeah, Jazz, it's Helter Skelter."

"From school?"

"Yes from school. How many Helter Skelter's do you know?"

Good question. He had to think a minute.

"Let me in."

The answer was not many.

"Door's not locked."

A pause, then the door opened slowly, cautiously, and from his prone position on the bed Jasper saw a neatly put-together little man resembling a life insurance agent enter his apartment, sideways. This man was wearing a gray coat that went past his waist, he was nicely shaven, and his hair was styled in a standard nondescript white man's hairstyle... just like that of a life insurance agent. Another man might have had *not a threat* as a first impression, but Jasper Callister knew better, he knew this was the sort of person who could get you. This was *exactly* the sort of person who could get you.

"Helter Skelter from school," Jasper said. "I'll be damned." He'd lived in the dorms at Birnbaum University for two years and Greg Helter had lived up the hall. A good guy,

3

sociology major one week, poli-sci the next, but always quick to say yes to a poker game, the bars, campus streaking, or any of the other barely-legal midnight activities that keep college kids preoccupied between French and fucking. They and their crowd had been super tight back then, but still, Greg Helter was not a name he thought he'd ever hear again after he dropped out. People move on. Things happen when you're younger, bonds are formed and then easily fade, like snowmen. As far as he knew Helter had finished school, may even have gone on to post-graduate work. Straightened up, in other words. From college kid to... whatever the hell he was now. Perhaps he really *was* a life insurance agent.

"Nice place," said Helter, looking around nervously, with the door open to the greasy hallway behind him. "You hung over?"

"No."

"Depressed?"

"Pressed. How'd you find me?"

"Wasn't hard, you're not in hiding."

"Not yet." Still lying down, and making no effort to officially welcome his new guest, Jasper Callister turned his head the other way and looked at the set of three windows on the opposite wall. His was a small apartment, a studio, which had always suited him well: everything was within reach or, at the most, required just three full steps, what the hell need was there for several rooms stretched out over hallways and closets and bedrooms? Outside those windows, his only windows, the world looked faded and old.

"If you're here to hit me up for money," he said, "I'm a little strapped right now."

The other man laughed a little. "No, Jasper, I'm not here for that."

"If you're here to invite me to a college reunion, you should remember that I dropped out."

"I'm not here for that, either."

"It looks gray out there."

"It is."

"Cold?"

"Yes."

"Snow?"

"Not yet."

4

"Fuck. We need snow. Us, the farmers, the frogs and bears in hibernation. We all need snow." Jasper rolled his neck back the other way and looked at the other man. "So why *are* you here, Mr. Helter Skelter?"

"I want to offer you a job."

"Why are you standing in the doorway, are you afraid to come in? What kind of job?"

"Security."

"Really? Like at a bank or something?"

"No. Listen, are you sure you're all right, you haven't moved at all. Can you stand?"

Jasper frowned. "I believe so."

Helter stepped further into the apartment. He put his hands in the pockets of his gray coat and looked around, studied the floor, kicked at some clothes.

"I have a job that requires a good man, a man of special talents and a special sort of mind. You're the first person I thought of. Are you working?"

"No. No, as a matter of fact I am not. Laid off. Fight with upper management. Insubordination, crap like that. Which doesn't matter, really, since they're going to move the whole operation overseas one of these days anyway. India, China, wherever."

"So you need work?"

"I guess. What kind of security?"

Helter walked to the bed and turned his own neck sideways so he was looking at Jasper the right way, eye to eye, right-side up.

"Bodyguard for a Presidential candidate."

Jasper was silent for a moment, then nodded, like this was the most reasonable request in the world.

"Which asshole you working for?" he asked.

"Not one of the big ones. A third-party candidate."

"So... an asshole who's guaranteed to lose."

Helter shrugged. "That's one way to look at it. What do you say?"

"I hate politicians."

"He's not a politician."

"He wants to be one, that's worse."

"It's a job, and you need a job."

"What's the pay?"

"Minimal. But it'll be fun."

5

Fun? What the hell was *fun* anymore?

Jasper sighed. "So, like going all over the country, watching this dude shake hands and what-not? Make sure no one knifes him?"

"Exactly. With other duties as assigned."

"Right... it was other duties as assigned that got me in trouble with my previous bosses."

"This will be different. A casual operation."

Jasper sighed again and finally sat up, swinging his big legs off the bed and to the floor. He ran a hand through his hair, over his forehead, rubbed his eyes, looked at Helter... who was in turn looking at the scars on his chest and stomach, those ugly shiny things the size of nickels, each about three inches apart.

"You didn't have those scars back then, did you?"

Jasper looked down at them. "No. That was a few years after. A souvenir from Arkansas." He ran a finger over one of them. "Pitch-fork."

"What were you doing in Arkansas?"

"Trying to avoid pitch-forks."

"They're mean-looking." Helter studied them a moment longer, then made as if to cross the little room for the windows but found the going difficult, what with the clothes and books and bottles. He turned back to the bed.

"What's it been, ten years?" he asked.

Jasper nodded.

"And what have you been doing with yourself?"

"Working. Whatever."

"Why'd you drop out, anyway?"

"Listen, you're offering me work, you're not here to go over the old times. Right?"

"Right."

"So... what kind of guy is this loser candidate of yours?" Jasper asked.

"Name's John Bantam."

"Like the rooster."

"Sure, like the rooster. You'd like him, Jazz. He's not what you'd call a typical politician."

"No?"

"No, he's... different. He's real."

"He's real."

"Yes."

6

Jasper leaned back, stretched out his spine, gave his apartment a quick look-over (I live *here*?), then looked at Helter again.

"Will you be my boss?"

"Kind of, yeah."

"I don't want to answer to anyone other than you. And I don't want to answer to you. If some punk needs a head cracking, I want to be able to crack his head."

Helter was silent.

"Isn't that why you thought of me? Because I'm a good head cracker?"

"You're a smart head cracker. I like Bantam, and because he is who he is, and because he says the things he says, he provokes emotions... if it's ever the wrong emotion I want someone there who can protect him."

"What kind of things does he say?"

Helter smiled. "Think of everything a normal presidential candidate says, then think of the opposite. That's what he says." He thought a moment. "What are your politics, Jasper?"

"Angry. Those are my politics. Does this asshole Bantam want to send jobs overseas?"

"No, he wants to punish companies who do."

"Punish how?"

"Head cracking."

Jasper looked to see if the man was kidding, and saw a smile on his mouth.

"Is he for the little guy?"

"He *is* a little guy. Sort of. That's complicated...."

There was a car horn outside, followed by shouting and, unrelated and far off, the high whine of a siren.

"What about all these people?" Jasper asked. "What's he wanna do about all these *people*?"

"Negative Population Control. Listen, I need you, and if you're out of work you need me. I never forgot what you did for Susie."

"Susie?"

Helter answered with just a simple prodding look, a little raising of the eyebrows.

Jasper nodded and almost instantly felt an ancient pain in his knuckles. "Right, right." An old story, that. Best left forgotten. Outside the window there were more car horns, the

7

siren grew louder before fading off somewhere to the west, and that gray sky still did not look like snow.

"All right," he said. "Sure, why the hell not?"

Helter smiled. "That's one of his campaign slogans: Why the hell not."

Jasper laughed a little and shook his head. "Man, this guy *wants* to lose."

The two men shook hands, sealing it.

*

One week later he stood cross-armed and stone-faced outside an ancient VFW building in a cliché Ohio small town, freezing his ass off and trying to look as friendly as a security man should while viewing everyone who was shaking Mr. Bantam's hand before entering the crumbling old block of a building as a potential Chapman, Oswald, or Hinckley. Not even a month earlier and he was making tractor parts. Life is funny, though. Like a driverless train gone off the track and into the Great Unknown. Hilarious.

Where would he be if not here? Back in Milwaukee, bored in his apartment, job-hunting with the other bums, maybe looking up certain other old friends who, honestly, he would have been better off avoiding.

Ah well, the train goes on. As the last of the guests arrived Jasper took the time to study this guy, this John Thomas Bantam. Here was a man who—

"Mr. Callister?" Bantam said, glancing over to him.

"Yeah?"

"You freezing to death out here?"

"Not at all." Always lie to the man signing your checks. And when lying no longer works, rip off their goddamn heads.

Bantam nodded. "Right. Me either." But each man practically ran inside as soon as they could.

Ohio in January, and everything you've heard about Ohio in January is true. The mean temperature might be twenty-five, but it was eighteen this day, and it had been eighteen for the past *three* days. Eighteen and with this odd blustery wind that came out of the north every twenty minutes or so, tearing at your neck and face and keeping parts of your skin the same shade of pink as a properly cooked prime rib. With this wind

8

added in, the temperature was closer to zero than anybody really wanted to think about. Demonically cold.

A few minutes later Jasper Callister stood at the back of the room and watched as this guy Bantam was introduced. It all seemed like childish madness to him, this desire for a job in which every freedom you've ever known would be taken away. President? Who the hell wanted to be *President*? Little nerdy boys and shrewish little girls, that's who. Teacher's pets. Overachievers.

"You know the sorts of people who want to be President?" Bantam asked, the microphone spitting out a jagged run of feedback. He looked out over the gathered crowd (maybe twenty-five people total) as if he was actually awaiting an answer. "I'll tell you: only assholes and the arrogant."

Interesting, thought Jasper.

Bantam continued: "It's a terrible job, the only good thing about it is the pension."

So why the hell do *you* want to do it? Jasper wondered. Which are you, arrogant or asshole?

"So you're asking yourself why the hell would *I* want to do it?"

Exactly.

Bantam stood tall behind the podium and smiled. "Let me be perfectly clear: I don't care if you vote for me or not. I'm not doing it to win, I'm doing it to be a pain in the ass to the guys who *do* want to win."

Jasper frowned and looked at the crowd, seeing a few confused looks from some of the older folks. Then he looked back at Bantam. Why the hell would someone *admit* to such a thing?

"Why?" Bantam asked, still calmly surveying the people before him, unconcerned with some of the looks he was getting back.

Why? Jasper wondered.

"For that oldest of reasons: because someone has to do it. Someone has to speak the truth to these people and it might as well be me. I'm in a unique position, because I can say whatever I want to them and they can do nothing in return. They like to attack their enemies, they like to go after those who tell the truth. But they can't hurt me. There's nothing a politician can do to me at all, and that gives me a moral

9

obligation to go up to them and tell them how the real world works. I'm their worst nightmare: I'm untouchable."

Jasper heard the wind kick up outside the door behind him, a sudden swelling of the air which just *sounded* cold, bitter cold, like it could kill you. He looked around at the people gathered here and wondered if they were thinking the same thing he was thinking. Which was:

So long, buddy, it's been good to know ya.

Helter was twelve when he first flipped off a figure of authority, a local cop who was being a little too rough with a stray dog. A good age, too, to discover the power of a well-timed and well-placed *fuck you*. Unfortunately, the beating he'd gotten from his father afterwards had stifled any repeat performances, and poor little Gregory Helter slipped back into the role of meek conformer, Don and Sarah's boy, the nice gangly kid with the big ears and the flat feet. Gonna play basketball like your father, little man? Yes sir. And he did play basketball, for two years of high-school... until his old man died and he finally found himself freed from expectation. His Junior and Senior years were marked more by sloth than anything else, and he coasted to graduation with a very low B-minus average. Whatever. It was enough to get him into Birnbaum, where he marked his time with even more sloth, plus more than a hint of melancholy... which made him no different than any other kid his age. It was an era of sloth and melancholy. At least three ragged wars were huffing and puffing in far off and insignificant corners of the world, like dying beasts gasping for last breaths, and though everyone felt reasonably safe here at home there was,

11

nevertheless, a sense of doom and gloom, like things were definitely ending and it was only a matter of time. And not ending as in Apocalypse, but ending as in *wasting away*, a slow and steady fade. In a way it was nice to be there at the end of everything, always cool to be present at the death of a world. So, open up that whiskey and pour us all a shot, my good man.

"Ever visit your father's grave?" Lisa would ask somewhere outside of Davenport... Lisa with her reporter's notebook and her reporter's questions.

"I did once. I went to piss on it, but I didn't have to go."

"Are you always this bitter?"

A question worthy of contemplation.

Other than the overbearing and mildly-abusive father, and the mother whose sole full-time job appeared to be keeping out of the way, hovering mouse-like in the corner of the kitchen or livingroom, his was not at all a bitter childhood. There were the standard American childhood scenes of backyard water-balloon fights, or playing cowboys and Indians and having great wars that covered whole neighborhoods (he remembered hiding under bushes, waiting what seemed like hours to ambush Billy or Rick or Terry), or making jumping ramps for bicycles out of old one-by-sixes and bricks, or drinking awful and yet awfully-delicious grape-flavored soda and sitting out on the grass as the sun set and the night settled down with an explosion of stars and planets. There were, too, winter afternoons wasted making snowmen or having snow-ball fights, and great sledding adventures down the big steep hill at Creekview Park. There were many bloody noses, dozens of bruised legs, a thousand-and-one little fights with Billy or Rick, each leading to the final end of those friendships... until enough days had passed and they were hanging out again, losing themselves in the madness of childhood. You didn't stay bitter as a kid, you got over things. Maybe it would take a sharp hard punch to the elbow just to return a relationship to equilibrium, but you understood this instinctively, the way a puppy understands when its mother violently nips it to keep it in line. One single good solid blow to the elbow, and a new bruise to go home with, and you were back hanging out with Billy like nothing had happened, like you were the best friends in the whole world and nothing could ever tear you apart.

So, not a bitter childhood at all. Rather Rockwellian, in fact. Yes, again, there was that father, but he had learned the fine art of staying out of the way from his mother, and though he couldn't do it as well as she did (the old man seemed to gain pleasure from outright ignoring her) there was enough simple pleasure in his life to make the occasional outburst from Daddy bearable.

Nevertheless, it was a sheer joy when the guy died.

So where did his bitterness come from? He thought about that, and as he did he began to wonder if its basic premise was even true: *was* he bitter at all? Did understanding the benefit of a well-placed *Fuck you* qualify one as bitter?

"You know what I think makes you bitter?" Lisa asked, and she would sound less like a reporter and more like a pseudo-therapist from TV.

"No."

"It's that you still feel like you're staying out of the way. You still feel like you're following a prescribed role for yourself, laid out by someone else. You still feel the need to live up to expectations. In other words, you might understand the need for a well-placed *fuck you* but you don't feel you actually have it in you to say it."

"Fuck you."

"Not to me, that's too easy. To the world at large, and to what it wants out of you."

"This is a stupid conversation."

"All right, then. Tell me about when you first heard the name."

"Bantam? That was a thousand years ago…"

*

It was mid-November and there was little snow on the ground in Dreary, Illinois, just the ugly and thin remnants of what came down the week before, all of it melting slowly… a slow death by struggling November sun. They were calling for it to get even warmer over the next few days, but there would be even less sun, with a heavy cloud-cover like a wet gray woolen blanket sitting over a good chunk of the Midwest for the foreseeable future. Expect a dreary oppressive Thanksgiving, they said (with no pun intended), but that was what he always expected. He sat in his little office and looked out past the old decrepit bank building next door to the sliver of barren frosted field that lay on the outskirts of town. There was

13

a thin unhealthy growth of trees at the far side of that field, and when he left work in the afternoon he could hear the distant reports of rifles. It was deer season. Time for the chosen to die.

For a time Mary Anne Wilkins, his co-worker, had the radio on, but it was all talk about the recent midterm elections, during which nothing had changed but the status quo. That's right, one status quo had become another status quo. How is that possible? you might ask. Welcome to the weird and wonderful world of American politics.

"Can you turn that off?" he asked Mary Anne, when he could no longer stand it. The female voice on the radio was going on and on about some Senator Leroy out of Arkansas, but what she was saying was nothing no other talking head (or disembodied voice, as it were) wasn't saying. Senator Leroy, the latest liberal-conservative to be elected on the Republicrat ticket. Yes, yes, dear sweet status quo. He was both for and against a woman's right to choose, wanted to both shoot off guns in the street and corral them all up in a top-secret bunker. He wanted to cut off federal funds for "obscene" art, while wishing to have the government pay for some giant marble pudenda in the veranda of the Capitol. Or something. Who knows? Who cares?

Mary Anne made a face (she was always making faces) but she half-stood from her chair and leaned over toward the radio. She hesitated there, in a pose that a normal man might have found sexually thrilling (bent over like that, expectantly, her eyes big and round and *waiting*). "Can we have music?" she asked.

"That's a good question. *Can* we?" He sighed. "See if you can find something resembling music, and then we'll talk about it."

She found a country station, which he nixed on principles of good taste, a hopping urban channel pumping out hyper-repetitive bass lines designed to make idiots dance, which he nixed on nausea principles, a polka channel she didn't even really stop on (one wonders who in the world *does*), a channel featuring two very clear and deep macho voices discussing, without benefit of intellect or facts, various social ills, which he and Mary Anne both agreed was worse than country, and then, at last, the sweet and gentle trills of several violins backed by oboes and cellos. Classical, yes, always go for the classical.

14

She settled back in her chair, returned to work. They had each started off with a six-inch pile of papers on their desks, but she was almost through it all and he had yet to make a real dent. He blamed it on that moody sky out there, those thick depressed clouds hanging ominously low, like they might fall down and suffocate everyone. He worked better in sun, something he had only recently come to realize. This made him think he would have done better if he had moved out west. California maybe, or the desert. What vitamin was it the sun gave us? B? D? He should know these things.

The muted light through the window, and that thin sugar-coating of old snow on the yards and field, made it look colorless outside, and though he should have continued working he leaned back in his chair and stared mindlessly at it, thinking how perfectly the music on the radio fit the scene. Was this something Russian? he wondered. Sounded Russian. Bleak and dreary. Once upon a mid-day dreary, while I pondered bored in Dreary....

Minutes went by, then the song reached its soft anti-climactic end and a gentle woman's voice said:

"We here at WWJD would like to remind you to seek counsel in the Lord and Savior, Jesus Christ, in whom all things are—"

"Jesus Fuck!" Helter yelled.

Mary Anne looked over to him. "What's wrong?"

He was pointing frantically at the radio, one arm out like he was trying to tell her the office was on fire. "That... turn... turn it, turn it!"

Mary Anne cocked her head, heard the woman—

"—and blessed are the sheep who—"

"Turn it!"

— then she understood and half-stood again to change the channel. It was a small radio, they found it in a back closet when they first came to the building, and in her nervousness to flip the channel she pushed it off its precarious position on the shelf and it fell to the floor. There was the sound of something small and plastic and newly liberated rolling away.

"Son of bitch," he said, leaning back with a sigh.

"Sorry." She stood to retrieve the radio.

"Forget it." He looked out the window. This was how all his days went, gray into gray into blue-gray into black.

15

A moment later there was the sound of static. "It still works," Mary Anne said. "I think." She flipped through the channels, finding, again, country, then rap, then classic rock, then talking, then....

"Forget it," said Greg Helter, still looking out the window. "It doesn't matter."

"But I think I know a good station." She was standing there spinning the dial, producing a weird rhythm as she alternated between static and music.

"I for one am not a sheep," he said to himself as he stared out at his bleak corner of the world. His head was back on his chair, his mouth was open, his eyes were glazed. "I am not a sheep."

The words might have meant something if he hadn't felt so penned in. Sheep or no sheep, follower or not, he knew it didn't matter, he wasn't going anywhere anyway.

The sign on the door outside was small and unassuming and said: UNION SERVICES AND LEGAL COUNSEL, LOCAL 170. Not to be confused with the actual union headquarters in Waukegan, nor (he would think in his more down moods) a real law office. What it was, basically, was a very poorly located and little-used resource for those few who were still hanging in there at Dreary's sole sheet metal outfit and any nearby places that still had a union presence. And, truthfully, it was rarely that, because there were actual honest to goodness professional spots where experts and other truly knowledgeable folks did the real work: what he and Mary Anne did was dot the i's and cross the Ts, make sure the staples are good, and offer local guys a place to walk in after work and talk to a living breathing human being... which they rarely did.

"You've picked a hell of a place to live," his good friend Hamm once said. They were talking on the phone one day and Hamm had just looked up Dreary on the internet. Hamm had a real office in a real town out East. New York, in fact. "Population twenty-thousand, average income thirty grand... no healthy industry since the late sixties. A bedroom community, everyone commutes to... where?"

"Bloomington. Champaign. A few of the real wackos go all the way to Springfield."

"Land of Lincoln."

"Yeah."

16

Hamm paused. "We need another Lincoln like we need a hole in the head."

Helter sighed. "I should pack up, go out by you."

"Tough crowd out here. Different kind of union."

"The union in Chicago is tough. Ball busters. Head crackers. Mafioso, too, maybe." He was thinking about New York, the great American tradition of starting over. Just pack up, bid that young biddy Mary Anne goodbye and hit the road, go to the big city, take a bite out of the Big Apple and if there's a worm then dammit swallow it down. See Hamm, hang out with him for a while. Good old Hamm.

"Hamm?"

"Yes Helter?"

"You think I'd survive out there?"

Pause. "What kind of a question is that? What is that place doing to you, buddy? I thought the heartland was supposed to build toughness, determination, grit. Of course you can survive, *anyone* can survive here, it's designed for survival. Cheap food on every corner, taxis willing to drive you anywhere you want so long as you speak basic beginner's Arab. Museums for your mind and bars galore for your soul."

"Yeah... if I can make it there I can make it anywhere."

Hamm sighed. "You'd find work. You're a good worker. You'd find something."

"I have a terrible resume, it's pathetic, full of holes."

"No. Let's hear it."

He hadn't really thought of it in a while. Four years of Birnbaum, a doomed internship with the ACLU in Chicago (they actually wanted someone who was going to pursue a higher degree), nearly two years slave labor as a Bloomington Civil Servant (maintenance), then, lucking out, this gig here processing complaints and human resource crap for the local Metalworker's Union.

"And how'd you get that job?"

"I was dating the daughter of a top union guy. This was when I lived in Bloomington."

"Ah, good old nepotism. Listen, you're good at it, right, you have good references?"

"Sure, I guess." Did he? He had no idea.

"Then get out here, come see some action. Wouldn't you like to just once know what it feels like to get good and loaded in a place called Sal's Tavern, then wake up the next morning

17

with some nice piece of New York City ass? These girls out here are like models, man, I swear to Jesus."

"Don't. People who swear to Jesus make me nervous."

"I swear to Allah, Mohammad, Buddha, Richard Nixon, Richard Simmons, George W. Bush, George Jetson, whatever you're into."

It sounded intriguing, he had to admit it. A nice piece of New York City ass, it had a good ring to it.

"Some cliché Jewish princess," Hamm continued. "Black hair, black eyes, soft sweet skin, she'll cradle your matzo balls all—"

"All right, enough. Maybe I will."

"Maybe you will what? Come out here?"

"Sure. Maybe. What the hell."

"You have the matzo balls for such a move?"

He shrugged but said: "Of course. I'm a heart-lander, I'm a man of grit and steel and iron."

"You are the salt of the earth."

Yes, maybe he was, but he'd always detested that phrase. If good honest working folk are the salt of the earth it's only because they're sweaty.

"Don't let life pass you by," Hamm said. "Get out of that rut, move out here, see some action, live a little. Are you coming? Mr. Helter, Mr. Helter Skelter, are you coming out here to see some excitement and do something worthwhile with your life?"

"Yes," he said, quite definitively, but he knew he'd have to think about it.

He thought about it very little over the next week. One day in the office, while Mary Anne was busy decorating for Thanksgiving (she saw this as one of her duties, to brighten up the place in case any union members wandered in), and while the radio was playing a *real* classical channel, the front door suddenly opened and a man stepped inside. A very unassuming young man, slight of build, with a thin scruff of what was supposed to be facial hair sprouting like dried-out August weeds from his chin and upper lip. He looked tired, too, like most of the guys who wandered in here. Hard workers, all. This guy had a greasy baseball cap low over his forehead, a faded red t-shirt, and surprisingly clean carpenter's jeans. He trailed the distinct odor of recently welded metal.

18

"Hey," he said, walking first to Helter and then, seeing Mary Ann there, changing course and going to her.

She gave him a pretty smile. "Hello, how can I help you?"

"I was told to drop these off," and he handed her two manila envelopes with a hand that was scarred and scabbed enough to belong to a man forty years older.

Up close, Helter could see how at odds that harshly marked skin was with the boy it belonged to: the kid couldn't be more than twenty, he still had baby-fat cheeks, and despite or because of that weak growth of sad beard his face looked innocent and young. Those hands, however, were thick and large and marked with the passage of rough, hardworking times.

He looked over at Helter for a second, nodded, and then back at Mary Anne, who was opening the envelopes. His eyes went right for the small bit of cleavage she was revealing.

"How's the weather out there?" Helter asked.

The kid shrugged. "Not too bad. Could be worse."

Helter nodded. Then he saw the button that was pinned to the side of the kid's cap. The top and bottom of the button were solid black, and across the bar of white through the middle, in red letters, all caps, were these words:

BANTAM FOR A FUCKING DIFFERENCE.

Helter frowned. It certainly looked like a political button of some sort, possibly for a union office, but you didn't see "fucking" on just every political button, that sort of thing is usually frowned upon.

"Okay," Mary Anne said, looking up and smiling. "Everything's here. Anything else?"

"No ma'am," he said, and actually tipped his cap at her, all polite and cowboy-like. He gave her a smile, then nodded at Helter and turned to leave.

"Wait," said Helter. He stood from his chair and leaned over his desk toward the kid. "I have to ask you something."

The kid frowned. "Sure."

"That button, on your cap."

The kid's frown deepened and he reached up to feel for it, as if he hadn't known it was there. He said cautiously: "Yeah...."

"What's that all about? Is Bantam a candidate for union president?"

"No sir."

19

"I just thought it was a little strange that—"

"He's running for President."

Helter frowned now, blinked once or twice. "That's what I meant, running for a union position with that word on there is—"

"No, he's running for *President*. Of the United States."

Helter stood tall, considered this a moment. "Oh."

The kid looked nervously at Mary Anne and then back, shuffled a bit like he was itching to leave.

"I've never heard that name," Helter said.

"John Bantam. He's from Wisconsin, I think."

Helter took a stab in the dark: "Third-party?"

"I guess... he ain't a Democrat or Republican."

"Independent?"

The kid shrugged. "Independent ain't the word."

"Oh. Okay." Helter tried to smile like the kid answered all his questions. "Okay, thanks." He was still thinking it odd to use profanity on a political button but now he figured this Bantam was from something a little off the deep end, like the FUCK YOU PARTY, or whatever. A joke. Hundreds of people run for President, all sorts of crazies and jokesters. He knew of an American Nazi Party, the Communist Party USA, the Natural Law Party, the Prohibition Party, the Pansexual Peace Party (Wiccans, of a sort), and somewhere out there you just *know* there's a Party Party.

"He's actually coming here next week," the kid said. "You should go hear him."

Helter smiled politely. "Maybe. Why's he coming here, of all places?"

"That's one of the things he does, he goes to all the little shitholes, the places everyone else avoids. He gives talks at VFWs or whatever, for whoever will have him."

"Where's he talking here?"

"The lie-berry."

"Really?"

"Yes sir. You should go. He's something different."

"I'm sure."

The kid looked at them both, then nodded again. "Well, you guys have a nice day." He turned and left.

"*Guys*," Mary Anne said with distaste when he was gone. "I hate that. I'm not a *guy*. He was doing all right with that whole *ma'am* and *yes sir* stuff. But *guys*...."

20

"He's just a kid," Helter said. He sat back at his desk and looked out the window, catching a glimpse of the boy as he climbed into a beat up old Chevy pickup. Something that looked like a yellow lab greeted him warmly, all wagging tail and hyper puppy ass. "He doesn't know what he's saying."

*

And how did Helter come to find himself at the Dreary Public Library that fateful night the following week?

It was a woman.

Jennifer LaClare was a pretty, plump, vine-ripened sort of woman he'd met earlier that previous summer when they both volunteered for some trash-collecting work at the Dreary Memorial Park. She'd had a nice smile, enticing, and though he preferred gals of a bit more exotic nature, he was intrigued by Miss LaClare because her outward look of Midwestern "normality," perhaps even ordinariness, conjured in him long lost feelings of home and security. She was, he believed, the sort of woman his mother would like to see him with. Mrs. Helter (now happily Mrs. Ellison) had not always approved of the girls he'd dated, and though she had never expressed this dissatisfaction with him it had been apparent from certain looks she'd given him and little things she'd said. Is Marsha coming with you? she might ask a few days before Christmas vacation in those long lost days of college. Yes, she is, he would answer, and her response would be: Oh.

He knew what it was, too. All of the girls he was interested in had about them a very definite aura of modernity. They were all quite obviously young women of their times, quick of humor, a few of them even downright vulgar, and several sporting a cynicism he found fresh and thrilling at the time. His mother, happily liberated from her oppressive husband, refused to see the world as anything but bright and beautiful. You'd think she might be jaded after all that time of being relegated to the status of non-entity, but she was quite the opposite, quick with a smile, happily whistling and singing around her home, a fluttery little bird of joy practically dancing from room to room. When he brought home the aforementioned Marsha, or Debbie, or (perhaps the worst of them all) Kat, each with their sharp little jabs at contemporary life, it was just a matter of course that she should dislike them.

21

And what do your parents do? she had asked Kat (which was not short for anything, she insisted) one Easter weekend.

My dad is a corporate manager, so I guess what he does is screw over the workers beneath him. And my mom is a nurse in an ICU, so she helps people stay alive and in pain. You know, makes them a robot tied to tubes and hoses and strange liquids, when what they really need is to die like a human being, peacefully and quickly. That sort of thing.

But Jennifer LaClare was exactly the sort of woman his mother would embrace. She radiated an aura that was old-fashioned and innocent. Not that she was naïve, but you could tell, looking at her, that she would grow up to be one of those women who could bake a good loaf of bread or fix you up a huge bowl of soup. The sort of woman who would take you into her arms, press you against what was certain to develop, through her middle-years, into an ample bosom, and make you feel all better.

Almost in spite of himself, he found her exciting. They'd struck up a friendship, had gone out to dinner a few times, but nothing had ever developed. He felt like a high-school kid, afraid to tell her what he felt because he might ruin their friendship, so he simply put up with the ache he felt whenever he was around her. She looked so clean, so goddamn *nice*, her eyes so bright and warm, that he just wanted to press close to her, kiss her, take her passionately some soft and rainy night.

It wasn't raining the night John Bantam came to town, but Greg Helter had found himself sitting in Miss Jennifer LaClare's apartment, buzzed on white wine, with a belly half-full from her attempt at Chinese stir-fry. He hadn't meant to go over to her place, but they'd met by accident in the grocery store after he got out of work, and she'd invited him. I'm making a stir-fry tonight, she said. Come over and help me eat it.

So he did, and it was fine food, if a bit bland. Nothing the wine couldn't help with.

I've had this bottle for a year, she said. My sister gave it to me when I moved into this place. Is it any good?

Delicious.

What's your favorite wine?

The closest.

After they ate they sat there on her couch digesting. She had changed from her work clothes (a reddish, knee-length

22

dress) into sweats and a t-shirt. Her apartment was hot and he was wishing he'd changed out of his own wrinkled old suit before coming. That was the thing with apartments, they were either freezing or hellish.

Are you all right? she asked.

I'm boiling.

She leaned over to him, reaching with one delicate hand to grasp his tie. Take your tie and jacket off, she said. You look uncomfortable.

Which was when he kissed her.

It would have been better if she'd slapped him or something, but instead she slowly leaned back, sitting suddenly upright and stiff, and looked at him like he'd just told her he was an alien. Shit, he thought.

Shit, he said. I'm sorry. I....

Greg, she said slowly. Greg, listen... I like you and all, but....

Old story, familiar to far too many. He apologized, said it was an instinctive reflex, whatever that was, and she said it was okay, he just had to understand that she didn't like him *like that*. He stayed another fifteen minutes, another awkward fifteen minutes, and then mumbled something about work the next day and needing to prepare something and she said fine, she understood, she had things to do too, and he left her place without ceremony, and without knowing if he'd ever be invited back.

There's a reason high-school kids worry about ruining friendships: it's because friendships get ruined.

So there he was, walking back to his own place across town on what was an unusually warm November evening, trying not to think about what just happened and what it might mean and instead taking in the fresh air, the quiet night, the placid insularity of this little Illinois town he'd found himself living in.

It was purely by coincidence that he passed by the Dreary Public Lie-berry, having taken sidewalks nearly at random. But there it was, a smallish building of considerable charm. It was, once upon a time, the Courthouse, but now the real Courthouse sat further north, an all-modern building with economy and no style, the single newest construction in Dreary.

The Old Courthouse, though, radiated an aura of old-time style and ruggedness, all brick with a sharply angled roof that

23

poked against the sky like a church steeple. He saw the lights, a few cars in the parking lot, and then the sign out front:

JOHN BANTAM CANDIDATE FOR US PREZ 6:00pm.

People were coming out of the library with armloads of books… simple books, ordinary books, nothing unusual about them at all. Young mothers walked their little children out by the arms, whispering harshly that they will never act *that way* in the library again. Solitary men came out looking pleased with their reading selections. It didn't seem, to Helter, like this Bantam guy was attracting much of a crowd. The library's business as usual was still going strong, and if even half of the cars in the lot were actually for *him* (doubtful) then he might have managed to gather a crowd of five, at the most.

Which did not surprise Helter, of course. He remembered the union kid's button. There was a reason such things as the word *fuck* were frowned upon in political circles: it did not generally endear one to the voting public.

Still feeling a bit stung and out of sorts from the Jennifer incident, Helter decided, what the hell, might as well check this kook out. Dreary didn't get too many loonies from the outside, you had to go gawk at them when you could. The same with carnies and two-headed cows.

He went into the library to see the show.

*

Lying wide wake in bed somewhere in Iowa months later, Greg Helter, Campaign Manager for John Thomas Bantam, would think about that November evening and realize that that pretty much summed up the world of politics, as far as he could tell: it was all carnies and two-headed cows in this business. What was new was someone actually *admitting* that's what they were, actually owning up to their mutant status. Imagine that interview on *Face the Nation*: I'd like to state for the record that I am, in fact, a hideous sideshow freak.

Is that what I am now, he thought, suddenly bolting up in bed. Is that what I've just become, a ringleader in this particular traveling circus? Or something with even less power, something like….

Jesus, he thought. I'm the barker out front, that's what I am. Step right up folks, and come see the pickled punk.

24

There was no sleep for him that night. Same with every night that followed.

Her apartment sat high above the city, with a great view of everything to the west… that is, every building top, alleyway, bird-shit-smeared window ledge, swirl of smog haze, traffic-infested side street, and gargoyle there was to see. Had it faced the other way she at least would have had a semi-decent view of the lake, so distant it looked like its waves were barely moving, a single giant sheet of blue-gray plastic. Not that she was complaining, since it was for the most part quiet up here, away from the sirens and screams and paranoid shouts of homeless men. Indeed, the only sounds she ever needed to worry about were the people in the neighboring apartments, at least two of whom were into serious hardcore drugs and one couple whose loud fucking was the stuff of legend. There was, too, the woman who seemed to have a new man in her life every week. I'm not a goddamn hooker! she was screaming just the other night. I'm not a goddamn hooker! Then there was the sound of heavy footsteps retreating down the hall. Crazy shit, but this is what she came to the city for, to get enmeshed in just this sort of thing. Her friends from back home thought she was absolutely insane, and maybe she was, but… well, life is short, baby.

Her name was Lisa Yates, and on this evening she sat before her window and stared out at the building across the way, dreaming of other Yates-folk far off, back on the farm, wondering what they were doing right now at this very moment. Uncle Marty would be bringing the cows in for milking, while Aunt Theresa would no doubt be trying to corral Jimmie, who had been overflowing with something very like evil energy since the day he was conceived. Her other uncle, her mom's brother Billy, would probably just be getting off work at Bob's Engine Repair and heading over to the Fall Inn Tavern for the night's festivities. And what about her mom? Well, sweet frail old Ma Yates would be settled in front of the television watching sitcoms and reality shows and whatever else she used to keep her mind from her troubles.

Lisa grimaced. What kind of a girl are you, leaving your mother in that state? Dad was most likely a skeleton down in the Shawnee Forest somewhere, and nothing like closure had yet to settle over his wife of thirty years. Why hadn't anyone stumbled on the old bastard yet, or found a shoe, a wallet, a bone, *anything*? It had been nearly ten goddamn years! Life was full of mysteries, and you can't ask these sorts of questions too long before you start to really go crazy. Why had no one yet found hide nor hair of Jack Yates? Simple: that was just the way this little story went.

You go, Lisa's mom said when she announced her plans to go to the city. Don't worry about me, I'll be fine. You have to live your life, you have your future to think about.

You know, she said it so sweetly, so innocently, that it was possible to think she wasn't laying in a little guilt there, too, but Lisa could sense it, she'd grown used to her mother's subtleties. And maybe the older woman didn't even know she was doing it, and maybe she would have been horrified at the thought, but it was there nonetheless, built right into the tone of her voice, an old habit, a deeply-embedded family trait. Gramma Yates had been the same way.

All around the building next door were little lion-like gargoyles, and as the light slowly faded over the city Lisa studied them. She knew there were books on Chicago architecture, whole libraries of them, and she supposed there were hundreds of studies of these gargoyles, but she wondered if anyone had ever taken the time to just sit and look at them, to just sit there like she was doing, dressed in loose flannel

27

pajamas while a supposedly prairie-scented Yankee Candle burned in the background and the soft sounds of beautiful but oddball music blurped and blipped and droned from the stereo, and just *look* at them. After a time they didn't look like simple architectural ornamentation, or even anything like talismans to frighten off evil, but more like the benevolent—

—you *are* going crazy—

—true denizens of the city. And maybe not so benevolent. They looked down on all of us with their amused and bemused faces and there was indeed a certain smugness to them, a look that suggested they might someday come down to reclaim all that was rightfully theirs. Or maybe it wasn't rightfully theirs, but maybe we created them and set them up there to absorb all the city's shit, the crime, the pollution, the hustling bustling impersonal energy, and some day it just might bring them to life with bitterness and anger.

Crazy.

The lion directly across from her sprouted from just under the top-most ledge of that building, and though it was essentially the same design as the other three on that side (one every fourteen feet or so) it looked different because it had long ago lost a chunk from its forehead. She had always wondered what had happened to it. What could dislodge a chunk of granite like that? A bird? A fragment of meteor?

On her own building were bird-like figures, each with the muzzle of a dog and little knuckles that appeared to swell from the brick to grip their perches tightly, holding strong against the wind. She didn't much care for them because they looked newer, less organic, more *designed*, than the lions. Those lions looked at ease up there, they looked natural. The bird-dogs looked over-planned, and therefore sort of lifeless.

She felt a chill and brought her knees up to her chest. She was sitting on a large cushion, her arms folded on the window ledge and her chin in turn resting on her arms. Classic pose for a lonely city girl. This would be the part of the movie where the heroine sits sighing and thinking about a lost love. Harry Connick, Jr. would be playing, and there'd be a slow zoom into her face with its deep and sparkly eyes.

Lisa Yates did indeed sigh, but the music from the stereo was now into a seriously fuzzy and static-like drone section, like a heavily distorted radio signal tuned between channels (neither of them light jazz), and she was not thinking about lost

28

love. She was thinking about gargoyles coming to life and raising hell in the city.

One by one streetlights and headlights came on down below, all silvery and pulsing, but by the time she noticed any of them it was too late. Night was really here and she'd wasted another day.

*

She heated up some left-over Chinese and watched the news, and you know you're in trouble when you resort to watching the news. She sat on her futon spilling noodles and sweet and sour sauce down her front and staring at the pretty talking head on CNN as if she were caught up in an exciting movie instead of just the same old blah blah blah you always found on these channels. War was still raging on the far side of the world, the best place for wars. Keep wars on that side, those people are used to them, we'd all freak out if they came this way. *Raging* might be the wrong word, though, since almost everyone agreed that the three main conflicts were in actuality limping sadly along, not quite to the degree of being *quagmires* but close. More people might have cared if American troops were involved in more than one of them, but as it stood we, as a nation, were only financially supporting the other two, sending equipment and (one assumes) good wishes to our current favored side. And what else was new, this was the way it had always been, we pick sides and then stand back like the over-smart but geeky kid who stays out of the way as his friend fights the playground bully. Nothing new here at all.

After a few requisite shots of tanks and distant bombs exploding over dusty crumbled neighborhoods they switched to yet another story of yet another missing kid. It seemed as if hundreds of kids were going missing every day, and as she watched this latest one (his name was Derrick and there was an Amber Alert for him in the Miami area) she wondered if this symbolized anything. It was perhaps not too nice to think of those poor kids in abstract terms, but it seemed to her there was indeed a symbol here: more and more of us go missing every day, in every meaning of the term. It hadn't begun with her father and it certainly hadn't ended with him, either.

She finished her food, set the plate on the floor by her feet, stared open-mouthed as some sheriff department spokesperson

29

gave descriptions of the vehicle and suspect. The lighting in her apartment was low and she felt lonely. Something about this damn missing kid story and her lack of decent lighting and the bleak Chicago night that was melting in its slow burn outside her window made her feel broken down, spiritless. She knew she should turn off the news, for godsake *turn off the news*, but she couldn't, you never knew what was going to come on next, might be something good. Look, Israel and Palestine were in peace talks again, that was good. And look, studies have found that the level of arsenic in the water supply is less than previously thought. Good.

Shit, how bad are things when you're happy there's not quite as much poison in your water as you'd been led to believe? Shouldn't *any* poison be cause for concern, for anger, for outrage? And what about that Israel-Palestine thing? Is it cause for celebration that two countries have decided to scale back the level of their killings? And that was exactly what they'd decided, that they wouldn't bomb each other quite so much over the next month, just to allow some breathing room for those peace talks.

How bad *are* things? Pretty goddamn bad, if you believed the news. And was there reason to believe the news? How the hell does anyone know if those people are lying to us, it was way too much work to verify anything, and that left us with nothing but trust. Trust? *Trust?* Why in the world would anyone willingly give themselves over to so ephemeral a thing as trust? Look at this guy, this square-jawed quasi-human in the dark suit, not a single blemish on his forehead, a supposed man of color and possessor of the world's worst sense of humor, why would anyone believe a single thing he said? Why would anyone believe *any* of it? How do we really know there's a kid missing in Florida? It could be nothing more than an elaborate lie designed purely for entertainment purposes. Starting tomorrow there would be nearly round-the-clock coverage of the incident, complete with its own dramatic theme music and a definite arc to its narrative, ending in rescue of the kid or the discovery of a body... either would do, either was fine, and either would spawn its own spin-off stories in the days to follow, more goodies to entice the viewer, to lure them in, to keep you glued to their coverage.

Yet maybe that was too much work, all that lying, hiring those actors to play sheriffs and parents and suspects. What

30

was easier, and more practical, was for the news organizations to do what they *really* did, which was to pick and choose their stories. When shit came over the wire there had to be someone standing there to point with an index finger like Caligula picking concubines and say "yes, no, yes, no." So who were these people, and by what right did they get to pick what us regular Joes saw on the news?

Lisa sighed again. If you think about it, whoever those bastards were it was *they* who were deciding how we viewed the world, and that was way too much power to give to anyone.

She knew these thoughts were not original, but they had never quite come to her this way, and she felt them physically in her gut, squirming around in there with the Chinese.

If we have a negative view of the state of the world it was entirely due to those faceless geeks who decide what stories to put on the television or the news page of goddamn Google. And of course they'd pick the most dramatic stories, that was what we all wanted, wasn't it? We like drama, we like a good story... and that's what they call these things, *stories*. Not exposes, not investigations, just stories. Little tales.

Was the world really so bad as we believe, or was it all due to being fed this kind of crap?

Shit, Lisa, what do you want them to do, just pick stories about sunshine and daisies and puppies getting rescued and old people learning how to play the guitar at ninety? That too would be a distortion of the world. The world is not all roses and breezes, just as it was not all wars and rapes and famines. What was needed was balance.

I should have gone into journalism, she thought. I'm a good writer, I'm doing nothing but wasting my talents with rancid technical writing, perhaps the lowest form of writing next to poetry and... well, journalism. Still, as a journalist I would have had at least *some* say in shaping what passed for news. But no, technical writing it was, slaving for a place called LaDell that published medical journals... spending all day in my little white-walled office reading about tumors and diseases and head wounds. Oh my.

Feeling more than a bit disgusted and frustrated with the whole thing, she sat back on the futon, wishing she had the energy to turn the TV off but also sort of fascinated with what they were showing... morbidly fascinated, the way she sometimes felt as she watched people on the L. Right now they

31

were doing a story on a whole family who died from carbon monoxide poisoning, and they were urging people to get detectors *now*, because this was evidently a huge problem that will kill us all if we're not careful.

There was the sudden sound of sirens on the street below her apartment. Another family, DOA.

The CNN anchor was saying: "When we return, the campaign season is underway early, but it's not just the major parties who are out there. We'll tell you what some of the minor contenders are doing and saying to garner attention... including attacking yours truly."

Then they cut to a jumpy shot of a man in a brown coat, obviously filmed by an amateur. He was standing outside of a neat and clean office building, apparently having been stopped and asked a few questions by a non-journalistic type... just a regular civilian, from the looks of him.

"Well, you know," the man in the brown coat was saying, "these people control how you and I view the world, just by the stories they pick to show us. I don't know if idiots like Bryan McBryan have any say in it, but he's always doing stories about how... I don't know, how there's a hidden cancer risk in your carpeting, or something. They want to keep us in a state of fear or... or even worse, uncertainty. They want us to actually think they know what they're talking about, but listen to them, just listen: it's obvious they don't. It's *very* obvious when the teleprompter goes dead."

They cut back to the aforementioned Bryan McBryan (raceless, sexless, humorless), who smiled smugly at the camera and said, very sarcastically:

"Always nice to get name-checked by the next President of the United States. We'll tell you who that agreeable gentleman was, and more, when we return."

Cue the commercial for laundry detergent.

Lisa leaned forward now, turned her head to look out the window. Interesting that her thoughts had been mirrored by that guy, whoever he was. She knew she'd have to stay tuned to hear more but it was tough, she was tired and her stomach was upset and she just wanted to lie down, crawl under a blanket, slip away. Presidential politics, at either the major or minor level, never interested her much, but she wanted to hear this guy, felt she owed him at least that much just for that quirky little lining up of their thoughts.

32

It wasn't to be, though, because just then, from next door, came the sounds of violent fucking, a hard-core Metallica-rhythm pounding against the wall, with the expected moans and groans that always accompanied it. Those two have to be into serious bondage play, with a bit of rape-fantasy scenario thrown in for good measure, she thought. The sound was so distracting, and so further upset her tummy, that she had to flick off the television and do nothing but sit there waiting for it to be over... which it would be, in approximately six minutes. Then there would be a cease-fire for another twenty before it all started again. This would happen three times, and each time the pounding would last a little bit longer. You can't screw like that without losing some sensitivity.

You can't *live* like this without losing some sensitivity, she thought as she sat there. She heard the voices of her friends back home:

You're crazy, they said. Why would anyone in their right mind want to live in the city?

For just this sort of thing, she told herself. For just this sort of thing.

*

It was fucking cold in Iowa this time of year. If you were rolling with the Democrats or Republicans you had access to top-notch cold-weather gear... namely, high-quality winter-wear, and big SUVs and buses with real honest-to-goodness working heating systems. If you were rolling with the Green Party, the Peace in Our Time Party, the Return of Disco Party, the Guns in Every Hand Party, or any of the other freak shows, you had to make do with whatever old tattered coats and hats you could scrounge up, and old Ford Econoline vans whose heating might work but which also just might rattle and groan like death itself and end up pushing out nothing but a cold hissing whisper. This was dangerous on a whole host of levels, chief among them being the risk that chilled supporters and campaign people might choose to spend their days inside hotel rooms instead of driving here and there to various campaign stops, freezing their asses off just to spend fifteen minutes with a bunch of people who may or may not be voting for your candidate. So, mixed in with the big-time main party candidates and their excited and perhaps overly-enthusiastic

33

(certainly overly-optimistic) minions, on every street corner in nearly every Iowa town you'd run into very disgruntled folks of definite energy but also very definite bitterness. It's one thing to want to change the world, quite another to keep a smile on your face when you're trying to save it at five above.

In a coffee shop in Cedar Rapids, Greg Helter stood shivering in his long gray coat, waiting for the girl behind the counter to get him his black coffee. They had to make more, she said to explain the wait. Lots of folks ordered coffee today.

Yes, he saw them, all his hotshot colleagues in the major parties, getting their coffee first because they all traveled in big groups that dominated, alpha dog-style, every single place they went, moving like hyenas across the plains of this state… or, better yet, like army ants leaving swaths of desolation behind them. Well, whatever. Bantam was already off to Davenport and it didn't matter what time Helter got there, he could stand here and wait for his coffee. It would be hot and black and fresh, at least, not like the warmed-over remnants the others had gotten.

"Greg Helter," someone said behind him. He turned and saw a man dressed very similar to himself, though his tan pants and long gray coat were newer and of much higher quality than his own. He knew who he was right away, of course, the guy was a major player on the national scene. Just last week he'd been on Meet the Press defending his man, Senator Parsons from New Mexico.

"Ted Meredith," Helter said, holding out a hand.

The two men shook.

"Enjoying this stuff?" Meredith asked.

Helter shrugged. "I'm used to the cold."

"Ah yes, that's right. Illinois man. Educated at good old Birnbaum U. Sociology degree, with some dabbling in poli-sci, I believe."

Helter frowned but tried not to show any emotion. "You do some research?"

"A little."

"A little is right. I never got a sociology degree. And why the sudden interest in me, anyway?"

Meredith smiled. "Let's just say some people are impressed with you, how does that sound?"

"Frightening."

Meredith laughed. "Your coffee," he said.

"Huh?"

"Sir?"

He turned and saw that the girl behind the counter was holding out a white paper cup. He took it with a smile and turned back to Meredith.

"That stuff will be your best friend before this is all over," Meredith said. "You'll find you can't live without it. When will that be for you, do you think?"

"When will what be?" He tried to sip the coffee but it was ridiculously hot. He held the Styrofoam cup to his mouth and blew through the sip hole.

"When will this be over for you?"

"I don't understand. When will it be over for anyone?"

Meredith smiled again. It was a charming smile, but full of thought, the sort of smile that was up to something.

"Greg, listen. You're a smart guy, you know Bantam won't get very far. His campaign is a joke. Or," seeing the look on Helter's face, "at least so highly unorthodox as to be always on the fringe. Hopeless, in other words, no matter how noble its intentions. You must see that."

Helter said nothing, just kept blowing.

"So how long do you think it will go? We'll pick a nominee, the Republicans will pick a nominee, and maybe the Independents… and, I'm sorry to say it, there's no way you will ever get into the national debate. It just won't happen. You'll always be on the fringe, that's just the nature of the game. So…."

"So what?"

"So how long before you decide to jump ship and join a real campaign?"

The coffee was cooled enough to sip, and he did so, a long, slow sip that allowed him time to think about what Meredith was saying and also relish the sensation of the hot liquid going down his throat, warming his core. At last he lowered the cup, smacked his lips, and looked the other guy in the eyes.

"You want me to join you, is that it?"

Meredith's smile now was actually a pleasant one, no malice in it whatsoever. "We're going to nail the nomination. That, too, is a fact. It will be Parsons and Keith, just watch."

"So why in god's name would you want me? And to do *what*?"

They had walked over to the coffee shop door now, and were both looking out at the frigid day.

"Like I said, people have been impressed with you. You came out of nowhere and yet you seem to have a natural instinct for this sort of thing. We could find something for you to do."

"What if I think Parsons is a schmuck?"

"You'll have to do better than that."

"What if I think he's an asshole?"

Meredith laugh. "He might agree."

"What if I think he's a man so without convictions that he'd let his gramma drink strychnine if it would get him just one more vote?"

Meredith turned to him. "You'd know that's not true. He's a good man, and he *will* be the one to go against Keith. Now *Keith* is an asshole and a schmuck and a dangerous, dangerous man, I'm sure we agree on that."

Helter thought about this for a moment, took a few more sips of joe, looked out at Iowa. Gray skies seemed to be squatting on the Midwest... had been following him from Dreary, in fact, and he was getting sick of it. He looked back at Meredith and leaned in a little, lowering his voice to just above a whisper.

"They still have rattlesnake roundups in New Mexico?"

"Huh?"

"Do they still roundup snakes and kill them for fun down there?"

Meredith's turn to frown. "You know as well as I do that the Senator has no say in—"

"Isn't his brother the Governor?"

Meredith said nothing.

Helter held his coffee with one hand and used the other to pull his collar up around his neck.

"If it was something cute and cuddly you people would give a fuck," he said, and then he walked out.

There was of course something invigorating about this sort of weather, and it really wasn't that bad, anyway, as far as the Midwest goes: twenty degrees, with only a moderate wind pushing the temps down to the low teens. It has certainly been worse. Yet you wonder why someplace like Florida or Hawaii can't be important primary-wise. Sunshine and beaches and tan-lines are more than American, they were great symbols of

36

hope and optimism. But *this*, gray skies and godawful cold, this was a symbol of depression. Black hearts. Blacker souls. Suicide.

You're being too hard on Iowa. Yes, he was, and he'd been told as much just that morning.

"You're too hard on Iowa." It was Hamm's sister Scarlett, traveling along with the clan as extra-credit or something for college... which made no sense, since she was an art-major, but Helter hadn't given it too much thought. She was there until the next semester started and then she'd be gone.

"Hard on," Hamm said with a laugh.

She shook her head. "Idiot."

Helter sighed and looked out the window of the tin can that was their automobile, a Toyota Corolla they were renting from a car salesman out of Des Moines who was sympathetic to Bantam, and who just happened to be their largest campaign contributor thus far.

They were on a long and monotonous stretch of desolate highway in the tedious northeast of the state, nothing around for miles but fields and farms and the little pockets of civilization that had sprung up over the years to serve them. Some of those fields looked beautiful, empty and flat vistas covered in lovely snow, but the others were more sparsely covered in powder and looked dirty and worn-out. He'd found himself sitting in the backseat of the shaky little rice burner, his forehead against the cool glass of the window, and watching as the landscape seemed to morph before him into a dreamland. He started wondering about the people who lived out here, the guys who owned those grain silos, the women who milked those cows. He started thinking about campaigns and politicians and voters and that old Simon and Garfunkel song about going out to find America.

"Is this America?" he asked aloud.

Hamm had been driving, with Scarlett in the passenger seat. Helter was sharing the back with their luggage and briefcases. They couldn't use the trunk because it didn't open, a fact that had led them to speculate on whether or not there could be a body inside it. The Des Moines guy had certainly looked like the type who might use them as scapegoats. Imagine the press *that* would get, said Hamm. *Presidential candidate John Bantam's staff found with corpse.*

37

Scarlett turned and looked back at him. She was pretty in a faded sort of way, with very black hair that had been cut ear-length and bowl-style, a complexion like a porcelain doll, and eyes so inquisitive and intelligent they were intimidating.

"What?" she asked simply.

"Is this America?"

She looked out the window, her chin now resting on the back of her seat. "Is what America? Iowa?"

"Yes. All of it, all of *this*, is it America? These people always claim to be the heart of the country, this is where the *real* America is, like nothing else was part of it. So... is it? Is it America?"

She looked out the window again for a while before turning her eyes back to him. "You're too hard on Iowa."

And while she and her brother had their little back and forth Helter sighed and thought about what he was asking.

"I'm not saying it's a bad place," he finally said. "I'm just... is it America? Is this really... is it America?" He pulled his forehead from the window for a moment before returning it and sighing.

"You should get some sleep," Scarlett said. "You're starting to burn out on us. Dork."

"What's wrong with him?" Hamm asked.

His sister turned back in her seat and shrugged. "He's burning out. Like a dork."

Hamm flicked the rearview mirror down so he could look at Helter. "You burning out?"

"No."

"No?"

"No."

Or maybe I am, he thought. He was certainly too hard on Iowa. He liked the state, he really did, it reminded him of where he grew up. He was a Midwestern boy, after all, born and bred in the center of the country, and he felt at home in small towns and flat landscapes. Nevertheless, the big problem with such places was they were all the fucking same, there was very little difference from one mile to the next. Especially on a trip like this, traveling the interstates and never taking the time to stop and maybe see something interesting. You can't see anything from the interstates, they had no soul, no depth. You had to take strange roads, back streets, dead ends. You had to get lost. Then and only then could you find the real life

38

beneath the placid facades. He figured they probably passed a dozen murder sites every day, little towns with dark secrets they wanted to keep hidden, evil little corners and crannies where someone had chopped up forty people back in 1965, or where someone's uncle went nuts and sliced up his wife for supper. Little wooded hills where just last year they found all those bodies....

Is that your idea of the soul of the country? he'd asked himself at the time, and of course to that there was no answer.

Now, as he walked down the street sipping his coffee he looked for that damn Toyota. Hamm and Scarlett were supposedly eating at some place called Krauski's Cafe but he saw no such place. They had probably been in such a hurry to meet up with Bantam in Davenport that they'd left him behind. He'd have to go find Meredith and ask for a ride. Shit.

After ten minutes of walking he decided to call them. He ducked into a doorway and pulled out his cell. He dialed and listened. It rang and rang and rang.

"No fucking way," he said.

"Excuse me, sir?"

He looked up, expecting Meredith, and instead saw two men. The first was middle-aged and wearing a large white and orange winter coat. There was an ugly light-green wool hat on his head and he looked like a local. That is, he looked absolutely comfortable, and not in a hurry to get anywhere in particular.

The other man, standing slightly behind the first, was wearing a longer coat the color of heavily-creamed coffee, and his head was bare, displaying a high forehead with a receding hairline. He was younger than the older man and looked uncomfortable.

Helter sighed, snapped his phone shut, and looked at the first man.

"Can I help you?"

"Yeah," the man said. "Yeah, you can. You work for that guy?"

"What guy?"

"That guy... that Bantam guy."

Helter swallowed casually, tried to gauge the level of threat here. There was certainly a distinct tone to the guy's voice that made it clear he wasn't about to whip out his checkbook and give them a donation. He decided to play it confident.

"I do indeed," he said.

The guy nodded and did not blink. "I don't like what I've been hearing about that guy. The radio's been talking about him and I don't like what I hear."

"Me either," the younger man said.

"The radio, huh? And what qualifies the radio as an expert?"

"Spelling's been talking about him. He said he's just another liberal fool, comes into a place like this and starts spouting all this bullshit."

"Potts says he's to the extreme of the right-wing," the young man said.

The man in the orange and white coat sighed. "*Potts,*" he hissed. "Potts doesn't know his ass from a hole in the ground. Bantam's a lib-tard."

"Spelling barely graduated high-school. Bantam's a fascist."

"Is that what Spelling and Potts say?" Helter had no idea who Spelling or Potts were but figured they were some local talk-radio nut-jobs, members of the useless and far too common lip-flapping fraternity. People who talk, talk, talk, and never do anything. What do you do for a living? I talk. I comment. I have loyal listeners who tune in during their commute and listen mindlessly to me. I am Muzak for my particular choir. They all agree with me and they all listen as I speak their thoughts. They need me to tell them how to feel.

There are talkers, Helter knew, and there are listeners. And unfortunately, these days both types are made to feel like they are part of the process, that they are actually contributing something to the national debate. They are not, of course, but sometimes one does envy their fantasyland existence. The real world with its real problems can be so cold and hard sometimes. Like Iowa in Winter.

Helter took a sip of coffee and looked at the men before him.

"What do you fellows do for a living?"

The older guy cocked his head and shifted his weight a bit, like he was preparing for an argument or a fight. "I run a front-end loader for an asphalt plant."

Helter tried not to smile. "Bantam worked on an asphalt road crew for ten years. Quade Asphalt, out of

Wisconsin. He always says it was the single best job he's ever had."

The guy shrugged. "Is that supposed to change anything? I don't like the guy, he says—"

"I'm a teacher," the other man said.

"Of course you are," the first man said with a sigh. "Push any progressive bullshit on your kids today?"

"If by progressive bullshit you mean teaching them how to think rationally and use their heads for something other than football helmets, then yes."

"Shouldn't you be in class? Is my tax money letting you take days off in the middle of the week?"

"If you'd raise your kids right we wouldn't—"

"Gentlemen, please," Helter said. "You're hurting my brain."

"I suppose you'll tell me Bantam's a teacher," the teacher said.

"No. His father might have been, though. It's never been very clear."

"Look," the front-end loader guy said, "I don't care what anyone does for a living, all I know is this Bantam guy is exactly what's wrong with the country today."

"We agree on something, then," the teacher said.

Helter sighed. "Did either of you see him speak?"

"I don't need to hear him speak, I—"

"I think you should hear him speak. He's not the kind of guy you think he is. Either of you. Even more to the point, he's not the kind of guy this Spelling and Potts *want* people like you to think he is. Be careful where you get you information. Everyone has an ulterior motive."

"I heard he was your typical anti-gun and pro-flag burning and—"

"Racist homophobic gun-loving anti-intellectual—"

Helter stepped out of the doorway. "You should come hear him speak. It might not change your mind, and that's all right, but it's not good for men with your smarts to believe what others tell you to believe and not see the facts with your own eyes. It's all right to hate Bantam for what he says, he would have no problem with that, but to hate him for things he *hasn't* said... now that's just not right. Right? Now, it was nice chatting with you, but I'm looking for some friends who may have left me behind and—"

41

"Is he, though?" the older man asked.

Bantam frowned. "Is he what?"

"Is he anti-gun?"

Helter sighed. "Hard to be anti-gun when you're packing all the time." He tapped his left side, just under the ribs. "The bulge, look for the bulge."

"I knew it," the teacher said with a roll of his eyes. "A gun-nut."

"Yeah," Helter said. "The kind of gun-nut that wouldn't mind shooting a redneck-homophobic-poacher-asshole in the head if given the chance. In fact, I think he'd get a kick out of it."

He started down the sidewalk and found Hamm and Scarlett sitting in the Toyota half a block down. He slipped into the backseat, still sipping his now-cold coffee.

"Turn your phone on," he said to Hamm. "And take us out of here."

*

"...and they frame it in such a way as to make these divisions. I'm telling you, if you went up to anyone on the street, anyone who wasn't some crazy mush-brained idiot, and asked them if they wanted clean air and water, they'd say yes, of course, who the hell doesn't? *That*, my friends, is called being an environmentalist. But *they* use the word to mean... hell, I have no idea what they mean when they say it. Someone who would rather save some goddamn oak tree in some doomed little wooded lot than... I don't know, than pour water on a burning baby. Whatever they mean by it, that's not what it is. Clean air and water, and saving our last remnant wild places and the wildlife that live there, that's what it means, and that's what an environmentalist does. Why? Because that's what we're *supposed* to do! Anyone who wants a country of parking lots, subdivisions, strip malls and oil derricks is a narrow-minded ignorant un-American asshole."

Helter could hear these words but was out in the lobby, admiring the taxidermy. The good thing about Bantam was he did not have a stump speech, so if you were traveling with him you didn't have to hear the same damn thing over and over, said exactly the same way every time. He'd heard other guys who were following the Dems and Repubs complaining about

42

this, saying it made them feel like they were in a constant dream state, their minds turning slowly to soup with each stop because they knew just exactly what was going to be said and how, could even mouth the words along with their candidates. *Mind-numbing tedium* was a standard description. He couldn't imagine what that would be like.

Nevertheless, Helter had a pretty good idea of what his guy was going to say because the man spoke what he felt, and what he felt never changed from town to town... nor did it change depending on who he was talking to, which was not the case for most politicians. That last bit there, about the meaning of the term "environmentalist," was no different, at its essence, than what he would say tomorrow at that sportsman's club, Whatchamacallit Gun and Rod, or whatever the hell it was called. He had no written speech, but the meaning would be the same. What the fuck did he care who he was talking to? What the fuck and what the hell. You say what you mean or you say nothing.

So, while Bantam spoke before this Conservation Club in No-Name Iowa, Helter took the opportunity to wander around the building, stretch his legs, give his mind something to think about other than images of the endless stretch of asphalt it had already been forced to study for several hours that day. If he needed to he could draw that scene from memory: flat gray-black lined with gray and white, and maybe, just maybe, a dead deer or two rotting on the shoulder.

The building was little more than the large front lobby-room and the larger meeting room where Bantam was speaking. In the front room were a series of displays on the local flora and fauna, including the taxidermied specimens he was admiring. He walked over to the largest of these, a white-tailed doe that was standing and gazing off into the unseen distance with large black glass eyes. She'd been a beautiful girl when she was alive, her coat that deep red-brown of deer in Autumn, her ears alert, her face inquisitive... though this all could have been merely the results of the taxidermist's artistry, of course. He studied her for a long time, and his thoughts led him from the living animal to the dead one to the taxidermist who did the work to the whole strange idea of making dead things look alive... ending, almost naturally, at a vision of Norman Bates' shriveled old husk of a mom.

43

"*Norman*," he said in a croaky old woman's voice while bringing a finger up to tickle the animal's nose.

"You losing it?"

He jumped, then turned and saw Jasper Callister sitting across the room next to the coat rack.

"Shouldn't you be in there?" Helter asked.

Jasper shrugged. "Some bird-watcher gonna take his head off? They're loving him, he's saying the things they feel."

"True." From inside that big room, in fact, came laughter and applause. Helter left the deer and walked over to Jasper. The big man was sitting on a metal folding chair, which he had turned so he could look out the windows near the front door.

"The real danger is out there," Jasper said.

Helter looked, saw nothing but the dormant skeletons of trees and a street of white-sided houses.

"Where?" he asked.

"Everywhere." Jasper closely watched a squirrel scamper across the front yard, even leaned forward a bit like that squirrel might be trouble, then leaned back and looked at Helter. "So... are you losing it?"

Helter smiled. "Never had it. You?"

Jasper shrugged. "I've been on worse trips than this. I can handle it. Sure beats moping around back home."

"What will you do when it's all over?"

Jasper shrugged again, his broad shoulders moving up and then down with a slow-motion rhythm that suggested natural forces: tectonic plates shifting, mountaintops birthing avalanches, the breathing of an elephant.

"One day at a time," was all he said.

Helter nodded, looked out the window again, then turned and walked over to a tree branch that had been nailed to the wall and on which was perched a stuffed owl. The owl stared down at him judgmentally. Next to it was a nice display on Creatures of the Night, with photographs of other owls, moths, and bats.

"Is he good to travel with?" he asked.

Jasper looked over. "Bantam? He's fine. Reads a lot... though now and then he likes to talk about music I've never heard of. Occasionally he hums a strange tune, now and then makes up lyrics about things we're passing. He sang a whole song about cow-on-cow humping the other day."

Helter smiled. "He's an interesting guy."

44

"Presidential material, though?"

Helter turned back to see what sort of look was on Jasper's face, but he couldn't tell, no emotion or thought registered there... just an honest inquisitive gaze.

"I think he makes an interesting candidate," he said. "And right now that's all that matters."

Jasper nodded. "Hey," he said, his mood changing, "hey what's it like in your car?"

"Fine."

"Got a girl with you guys now, huh?"

"Hamm's sister."

"She nice?"

"She's all right. She's a female Hamm."

Jasper winced. "Not enough women on this ride."

"You have a woman back home?"

"No. You?"

"No." He thought of Jennifer LaClare. "No, I apparently repel females. Must have sour pheromones."

Jasper laughed, then stood and stretched. He stood at least six inches taller than Helter and when he looked down at him it was intimidating. But that was why he was along, of course. A head cracker.

"I'm glad you offered me this job," he said. "It came at the right time."

"I owed you one."

The big man looked for a moment like he didn't get it, then he nodded. "Your sister? That was nothing."

"It was something at the time."

Jasper shrugged and walked over to the door that led to the big room. From behind it came brief applause.

"Everything's something at the time," he said. "What we need is something that is something *forever*."

A smart head cracker.

A couple seconds later Helter's cell went off and he reluctantly answered it. It was Marco from back in Washington. Apparently some freelance journalist had called and wanted to know if they could hook up with the Bantam campaign for a quasi-in-depth story, a real behind-the-scenes thing full of blood and glory and grit and gristle, to be published at a later date, after the election... if at all. Sounded like a college kid, said Marco. Someone looking for a kick, a little fun. Should they accept?

45

Helter thought of the press they had been getting so far, these little half-serious mostly-tongue-in-cheek references at the bottom of page-nine stories. "The *alternative* candidates," they'd say. Or "the third-parties." Or "candidates come out of the woodwork." Or "and here are some other loser psychos with delusions of grandeur."

They needed good, solid press, someone to take them seriously. Aside from that, when it was all over there would need to be some sort of document, something that captured, accurately and honestly, what this had all been about. Some no-name freelancer with something to prove and the energy and edge to bring it off would be nice. It certainly wouldn't be Hamm, or Helter, or Bantam himself. Might as well be some college kid. Still, you had to be careful, it might not be a college kid that shows up at all... might be a spy or a nut-job.

"Call them back and give them my number," he said. "I want to know who we might be dealing with." What they didn't need was some fat pervert from *Whack Off Weekly*, or *Bazoombas*, or any other weird magazines or ephemeral internet sites looking to get in on a "real" journalistic gig. One imagines that a good and honest piece of literature by a former editor of *The Fetish Freeman* or *Celebrity Flesh* would really be of no use to anyone.

Across the room Jasper was studying a stuffed skunk. Wasn't there a political joke about a dead skunk? Helter wondered. If there wasn't there ought to be.

A sudden burst of loud applause from the other room, sustained and passionate, and he knew the talk was over.

"We need to secure our borders, yes, but we must also ensure that the good and honest people who wish to come to this country and contribute to its economy, escaping war and poverty in their own countries to pursue peace and happiness here, are able to do so, and they should understand that we welcome them."

This was a standard line from the stump speech of Senator Parsons from New Mexico, a sentiment he repeated in roughly the same words during every television and print interview he gave.

At a rotary club gathering, where barely ten people stuck around to hear him speak after the major guys left, and where Parsons had said that exact thing not forty minutes earlier, John Thomas Bantam had this to say:

"We need to cut off immigration completely. Illegal or legal. From anywhere and everywhere. I don't care if you're a poor workingman from England or a Professor of Science from Sweden, or a stoner college kid from Italy or a desperate teenager from Mexico… we need to prevent you from coming here. There are too many people in this country as it is, we can't afford any more. Sorry if things are bad in your own country, but I say stay there and change them, be a man and stand up for what you believe, challenge your governments and the corporations that control them, strangle the dictators, charge the capitols and throw out the fascist regimes. Do what you have to do, but for the love of god don't think you can just abandon your homeland to come here and take up our air and water and open spaces. *Homeland* means something, and all people everywhere should fight for theirs."

Likewise, Senator Keith, the Republican front-runner, said this:

"We as Americans must understand the role that God has played in our success. We can't shun Him, or push Him out of the public debate. We need to keep Him alive, as not only the Creator of the Universe but the guiding light behind the existence of the United States of America. If we allow the Godless Left to attack religion, to push the Almighty out of the schools and the public debate, we will lose everything. If God is no longer in the equation, anarchy and immorality will reign."

And Bantam said this:

"I myself am an apatheist. Simply put, I don't care if there's a god or not… a god or gods or goddesses or a goddamn all-powerful computer floating somewhere in deepest space. I wouldn't change a single thing I do either way. If I was shown proof that there was no god, would I suddenly start smashing in the heads of babies? Of course not. Certain people put way too much emphasis on 'God,' whatever their idea of it is. Religion plays little to no role in the daily behaviors of everyday folks. If you think the world would suddenly spin into chaos and immorality without it, then you have a very sad view of your own grasp of right and wrong."

*

"This is John Bantam."

Greg Helter extended his hand, which was taken warmly, firmly, in a good manly Midwestern way, by the man before him. Bantam had just gotten done speaking to a very small crowd at the Dreary Public Library, where he had said, among other things, that homosexuals should be allowed full marriage rights because choosing to spend one's whole life with someone else is among the most noble and sacred acts a person

48

could do ("these people are staying together for decades anyway, so let's give them all rights under the law. Anyone who opposes this is meaner than a retarded rat and twice as stupid," was one quote). He also said that not only should American citizens continue to be allowed to possess guns, but that anyone who *didn't* own a weapon was not living up to their obligations to protect themselves ("and not only from the government but from each other. We know who the enemies are, and rarely are they the bureaucracy: usually it's your neighbor").

The eleven people sitting in the Library meeting room, a place that just the night before had hosted the local Quilting Club, looked at once confused and intrigued by him. It was a look Helter would come to recognize intimately.

There had been thirteen people there when Helter walked in, but two elderly women had walked out with the first curse word that had come from Bantam's mouth (it had been *bullshit*). Which was fine, because they freed up two seats, one of which Helter had been able to take. He had come in a little late, while some gray-haired guy in horn-rimmed glasses and loose fitting treehugger-style clothes (uber-casual khakis, trail hikers, and a dark blue button-up shirt) was introducing Bantam, so he had been forced to stand at the back of the room like an idiot. He felt more than out of place, he felt like an intruder, gawking at something the way any outsider does. Of course, most of the other people gathered were doing the same, but none of them were standing.

Of those eleven people remaining, five were younger folks, a mix of men and women who looked the neo-hippie part, with longish unwashed hair and skin so pale and badly complexioned as to suggest more time spent with a pot-pipe than outside hugging trees. Two were a middle-aged couple that looked like they could have owned a llama farm somewhere, he with a big gray beard and the rugged body of a real workingman, and she with the tough posture and warm eyes of a woman who could chop wood and then take you in and fill you up with good homemade soup. Two others were your more standard political-gawkers, most likely Democrats… and, in fact, yep, after he was able to sit and see them from a better angle he saw the buttons they each wore (*Friends Don't Let Friends Vote Republican*, and *If you Want a Republican to Care About You, Stay in the Womb*). One was a demure-

49

looking younger woman of slight build but well-designed face, the sort of woman who might be pretty if she only ate a little more. And the last was the young union guy Helter had met the previous week. He caught the guy's eye once and they each nodded in recognition. Helter had to assume the thin girl was the kid's woman. If she wasn't she ought to be, they looked perfect for each other.

"...now, the man who, if the world was right and sane, would be the next President, Mr. John Bantam."

Bantam had been leaning against the wall by the doors, and when his name was spoken he seemed to sigh almost out of boredom and push himself straight. The man who introduced him turned, offered his hand, and then went and stood at the very back of the room. There was polite clapping, nothing passionate, and Bantam looked slightly disturbed by this... not by the lack of passion, but by the very presence of any applause at all. Later Helter would learn that he just didn't like the sound.

Bantam was wearing something very similar to the man who introduced him, but mixed with the wardrobe of the llama-farm guy: a dark blue shirt with the top three buttons undone, revealing a sliver of the white T-shirt below, and heavy and well-worn carpenter's bluejeans, the sort with lots of pockets. Helter couldn't see the shoes but he could imagine them, scuffed brown stompers with thick-soles and maybe more than a few scars from the trail.

Not the wardrobe of a man seriously running for the Presidency of the United States. Shit, even Nader wore suits... wrinkled, ill-fitting suits, but suits nonetheless. Bantam was dressed like... well, if not like a farmer, at least like a man who did business with farmers. A seed salesman, perhaps. Or a guy pushing tractors.

There was, though, that most cliché of things: *something about him*. It was in his face, in the earnestness you saw there. He was three days late for a shave, and the stubble on his cheeks and chin made him look weathered and handsome, a rugged forty-something man who could leave this place and go climb a mountain somewhere. The stubble also seemed to bring out his eyes, which were deep and kind and intelligent. They were remarkable eyes, and Helter didn't feel like less of a man for noticing: they were eyes that belonged to someone who did a lot of thinking, yes, but who wasn't afraid to *act*.

50

Absolutely clear and bright eyes, animal-like in their focus. High-lighting them were a series of light wrinkles at their corners, and a forehead well-lined with thoughtful creases and what looked like a few minute scars well-placed here and there to give character.

Helter thought: put this guy in a standard suit and tie and give him a close shave, and he would not have looked out of place on either of the major party tickets.

However, there was still that *something*... and it kept coming back to the eyes, and the way the man used them. Thoughtful eyes, yes, but there was also a very strong suggestion of decisiveness behind them. And strength, too. Conviction.

You'd follow this guy, Helter thought. Maybe not to the polls, and maybe not as Commander in Chief, but certainly into the woods, up a cliff, into the desert.

"Ladies and gentlemen," he said, "my name is indeed John Bantam, and I have some things I'd like to say...."

*

The union kid's name was Chad, and he introduced his wife as Kara. She had a pretty smile marred only by what looked to be a dead tooth on the bottom left side. When it fell out it might lend her a certain charm, like an Appalachian beauty queen. Helter shook their hands but kept his eyes on Bantam. He was amazed at the audacity of the man. He had not spoken like a candidate, no, but rather like someone of much greater seriousness. Candidates speak like commercials. Bantam spoke like the actual show. He was forthright and honest and vulgar and coarse and full of life. All meat, no fat, as Helter's dad used to say. You could sit around a campfire with the guy and solve all the world's problems by the time the embers burned out.

The man in the horn-rimmed glasses who had introduced Bantam was talking to him as the other people filed out of the room. Bantam shook hands with all of them, receiving polite smiles and a few half-hearted "good lucks" in return. When the last person was not even quite out the door the kid, Chad, stepped up to Bantam and shook his hand.

"Thanks for coming," Chad said. "It's awful cool of you to accept our invite."

51

Bantam smiled. "How could I pass it up? When someone says they want you to come and try to wake up their stupid little town, you kinda have to accept, just out of common courtesy. I'm quoting you, of course. I would never call this a stupid little town. It looks too much like the place I grew up... which actually *is* a stupid little town, now that I think about it."

Chad laughed nervously, then remembered Helter. "Oh, this is...."

"Helter, Greg Helter," Helter said, stepping forward and offering his hand.

"This is John Bantam," Chad finished, saying it just as the two men's hands met. "He's gonna be President."

Bantam shrugged. "Or piss off some folks trying, more likely."

"Is that why you're running?" Helter asked. "To piss off the establishment?"

Bantam's smile was sly and strangely reserved. He looked at Helter like Helter had seen through to something, something private and hidden. It was a Harry Lime smile.

"There are worse reasons to run for President, aren't there?" he said.

Helter nodded. "Almost every reason might be worse. I've always wondered what sort of people actually think they not only *can*, but actually *should* lead others. Most of them are egotistical jackasses. I have much more respect for a gadfly."

"Gadfly?" Bantam's face lit up. "That's perfect. I hadn't thought of that. I may have to use it."

"It's yours."

"What do you do, Helter?"

"Union rep. Legal services and things like that. Mostly, though, I sit and dream of adventure, like any Midwesterner."

"Ah, and what sort of adventure does a union rep from Dreary, Illinois dream of?"

Helter thought a moment. A good question. And how honest should he be here, in front of Chad and Kara and the guy in the horn-rims, who was still standing in the doorway? He hadn't planned on coming here tonight, let alone baring his soul for these strangers... but maybe it was the wine from earlier in the evening, which was still buzzing gently, sweetly, in his mind. Maybe it was boredom.

"I've always wished I'd done something with wildlife. You know, like in Africa, with lions and crocodiles and snakes and—"

"Snakes?" Bantam's face lit up again. "You like snakes?"

"What's not to like? I caught and kept garters when I was a kid, and kept a few corn snakes in college, too. Snuck them into the dorm. My roommate had a Columbian boa." He hadn't really thought of that in years, but now the images of them keeping dead mice in a little freezer and sneaking bags of aspen chips up to their room came to him vividly. Wonderful stuff, those memories. Hey, an RA said to them once, what's with all the wood chips? We smoke it, they answered. Oh.

Bantam stood tall, nodding now as if in satisfaction. The smile on his face was no longer the Harry Lime sort, but warmer, even wistful, birthing kind wrinkles at the corners of his eyes.

"Sounds like me when I was younger," he said. "I've always thought the love of the less cuddly animals was a sign of something good and noble."

"It's the mark of a truly enlightened man."

Bantam nodded. "Be ye therefore wise as serpents, as Jesus said. Probably his best advice."

Kara shivered. "Snakes...."

Bantam glanced at her and then back to Helter. "Hey, here's a joke: what's the difference between a snake and a politician?"

"A snake serves a purpose," Helter answered.

Bantam's smile was wide, toothy, and he reached out and clapped Helter playfully on the shoulder, not phony-salesman-style but with meaning and warmth, like they were old friends. He was taller than Helter but he didn't loom, he was just *there*, sharing this particular little space with him at this particular little moment in this particular little town.

"Hey," he said, "you know a place where a guy can get a beer?"

She said her name was Lisa, and though she probably said her last name too he couldn't for the life of him remember it. It was only the "Lisa" that stuck with him, the voice on the other end of the phone alluringly soft and with a tantalizing over-emphasis on the S, like some sort of speech impediment, the opposite of a lisp.

Lisa.

He had never liked the name much, it was safe, white-bread, but the way she said it, on a voice with that uniquely feminine combination of fragility and toughness, made it sound like the most exotic name in the world. *Lisa.* She sounded young, too, and there was no denying the attraction of that element as well.

She was not a typical journalist, she said so right from the beginning. She was, in fact, just embarking on this career and had absolutely no credentials to her name other than a few writing awards in college and the fact that she currently worked as a technical writer in Chicago. Not much for credentials at all, she admitted, and then she said: About as many credentials for journalism as Bantam has to be President.

And he'd laughed, of course, because right then he knew that she was the perfect person to cover this campaign from the embedded journalist's perspective. It would not have fit the Bantam campaign to have some sweaty, seasoned, bored fat-ass from New York or Washington traveling with them and trying to capture the essence and energy and excitement of what they were trying to do, he just wouldn't have produced the right tone. But Lisa, now... she was something else.

Lisa. The way she said it made him think of incense, beads, all sorts of exotic oils glowing warmly in the soft sweet liquid light of candles. Why? Why not?

Come to Iowa, he said. You have full-access to the campaign of John Thomas Bantam.

*

Late one afternoon Senator Keith was answering a few questions from the local media. Simple stuff, nothing earth-shattering, mostly just the same questions he'd been answering for months. A few items in the news came up, namely the most recent anti-American flame-up in Iran and something Parsons had said about Keith's integrity on energy independence. In regards to the last topic he said this: "I am the only one running in this race who speaks openly and honestly about their past, their feelings, and their thoughts. I hide behind nothing. Yes, I have ties to oil and gas, and I've been forthright about that. Name me someone else who has been so open and honest."

Which was meant to signal the next question, but from the back of the little crowd of reporters came a timid little man's voice:

"John Bantam."

Now, Keith's people had been aware of the presence of Bantam all along, but they had wisely decided that the best thing to do was ignore him. If they answered any of his challenges or even acknowledged him at all they ran the risk of giving his campaign the aura of legitimacy. The best thing to do was completely pretend he didn't exist, and then the media would do the same... or, at the very least, he would continue to be seen as just another loony fringe candidate, good for a side-bar and a humorous quote but not as a serious subject.

Maybe Senator Keith was tired this day, or maybe he just hadn't gotten the memo to ignore all mention of the name Bantam (and in this case it certainly would have been ideal for him to say "never heard of him"), but he looked up, almost right into the face of the only television camera present, and said:

"John Bantam's only reason for existence is to come out like a... what do you call them, one of those clowns that come out and dance before the king and queen... he wants nothing more than to come out, say a few jokes, sprinkle in a few swear words, try to appear all real and earthy, and make the rest of us look processed and fake. But we're serious people of substance, with many years of experience, and what does he have? There's no substance there. I bet if we were sitting together and honestly debating the issues he wouldn't have a thing to stand on."

*

"Son of a bitch," said Helter when he saw the paper the next day, the headline of which was: KEITH TURNS ATTENTION TO THIRD-PARTY CANDIDATE.

"The word he was looking for is *harlequin*," Hamm said absently. "Jester also would have been acceptable."

Helter looked up. "You know what this means?"

They were sitting in a little diner named Molly's, which was like every other diner they'd ever been in, right down to the color of the tables and chairs. The coffee was exceptional, however, and the smell of the food heavenly. Helter and Hamm had each ordered omelets. Scarlett had ordered French toast.

"Means we're getting under their skin," answered Hamm.

"That, and a whole lot more. He's basically made us more interesting to people who were either ignoring us or hadn't yet heard of us. Jesus, he points out the differences between him and us in almost the same exact way *we've* been doing it. Christ, he really opened his mouth. Even sort of compared himself to a king, if you think about it."

"Kind of puts us on the map," Hamm agreed.

"There's something else, isn't there?" Scarlett asked. "Doesn't it mean he wants to debate Bantam?"

Helter's mouth dropped, his eyes widened. He read the quote again... and son of a bitch, there it was: *I bet if we were sitting together and honestly debating the issues....*

He looked up at Scarlett.

"Good catch," he said. "If we ask to be a on a debate, he can't really say no, or it would look like he's scared of something."

"He's basically saying he would *love* to debate him," she said, adding sugar to her coffee. "If he's so confident in the idea, why would he back out later?"

"Why do you add so much sugar, you ruin the taste," her brother said, a look of disgust on his face as he watched her open a second pack.

"Fuck off."

Helter leaned back in his seat and sighed. There was a big smile on his lips of the sort he hadn't felt in a long time, and though it was still promising to be another gray-skied day he could almost believe in blue again... couldn't it open up a little later, couldn't the clouds part for just a little while and let sweet pure blue come down to warm his heart?

His cell phone rang. He answered. It was Bantam.

"Yeah, we caught it."

Scarlett made a sound.

"*Scarlett* spotted it first," Helter added with a sigh. "Yeah, I know. Yup. Should I say we're getting under their skin because they know what we're saying is... yes, I know. Sure. Umm, soon, I hope. All right. Yes. Bye." He hung up, put the phone away.

"Big man happy?" Hamm asked.

"Our official comment will be: we're ready to debate the integrity and honesty of our campaign anywhere, anytime."

"And the unofficial comment?"

Helter picked up his coffee, blew at the steam, took a sip. "Bantam said Keith is a douche bag."

"Shit," said Hamm. "That's not unofficial, that's what he told the *Register* last week."

Right after the food came Helter's phone rang again. He pulled it out and looked at the caller ID.

"Yes," he said. Then: "Greg Helter here." Pause. Pause. "Yes, we do have a comment, in fact: John Bantam is ready and willing to debate his integrity and honesty anytime, anywhere. He looks forward to open and honest discussion

57

with Senators Keith and Parsons, or anyone else, and is glad they're acknowledging the presence of other voices and views in this campaign."

"Nice touch," Hamm said when Helter hung up.

"Cute," said Scarlett, with no real feeling in her voice. "You're good at this dorky shit."

"Thank you."

*

"You know what I like about beer?" John Bantam asked. "It's like a democratic inebriant. It's fit for kings and paupers alike. You can make beer in your basement, in a closet, anywhere... but, say, wine now, wine requires vineyards and orchards and...."

"Bees?"

"And bees. Now where the hell can a pauper get *bees*?"

Greg Helter started to laugh, and Bantam joined him. They were sitting in one of Dreary, Illinois' finest establishments, the Dew Drop Inn, and other than an older man who looked like he was slowly fading away into the ether (not a single drop of meat on his old bones anymore, by the look of it) and the bartender (a droopy-eyed middle-aged woman who looked like she'd seen better days and didn't want to remember them), they were alone. The old skeleton of a man was down at the opposite end of the bar, and the bartender was reading through a magazine by the peanut rack. Something that might have been jazz was on low in the background.

Bantam held his bottle of Central Waters up and examined it. "Beer," he pronounced, "is the drug of choice for Everyman."

Helter laughed, then studied Bantam for a moment. Closely. "You are out of your mind," he finally said. Then he held up his own bottle in a toast. "John Bantam, the candidate of choice for wackos."

"Hey, how about: the candidate of choice for Everyman?"

"How about John Bantam: why the fuck not?"

They fell into loud laughter, making even the old man look their way. The bartended glanced up only long enough to see if they needed more drinks.

"Hey, listen, Helter," said Bantam, quieting and turning in his stool to face his new friend. "Listen, listen...."

58

"I'm listening."

"Listen, what do you say… why don't you…."

"I say *Hey! Ho!*" and he raised his arms and did a half-assed hip-hop dance.

"No, listen now. Why don't you quit this monkey business here in… what's the name of this place?"

"Dreary."

"Yes it is. Quit this bullshit and join me."

"Join you how? In holy matrimony?" He laughed again. Drunk, goddamn are we drunk….

"Listen…."

"Beer requires hops and malt and all that, where can a pauper get *hops*? Fields of *hops*? Your theory is *crap*."

"No, join my campaign. Come on. You're smart, you're insane, you like to drink beer… you're everything I need. Join up, give us some help, and let's change the country."

"Change the country? Jesus man, you've had too much, time to cut you off. No offense, but you're not going to change the country."

"No?"

"No, because… because you can't change *this*," and he made an expansive gesture with his arms. "Change the country? You're too rough around the edges to change anything. Shit…."

"Join me and let's die trying."

Helter looked into the other man's face, saw how serious it was… then promptly burst out laughing again. Bantam joined him for a moment, then turned to look at the bartender. "Hey Sweetie, you think I'm rough around the edges?"

"Leave me out of it," she answered without looking up. Probably hadn't heard a word of what they said. Probably didn't care.

"Listen," Bantam continued as he turned back to Helter. "In all seriousness, I need smart people. I need people who aren't coming from the world of Washington and the media. I need people who aren't tainted by how everything works. I need fresh people, honest people, *real* people. People who haven't been poisoned."

"People like me."

"Yes, people like you. People like Gregory Helter from Dreary, Illinois."

"I'm not really from Dreary. I'm from Dickwater."

59

"Dickwater, then. Gregory Helter from Dickwater: I need you."

"Because I'm real and honest?"

"Yes. Aren't you?"

Helter shrugged. "What would I be doing? And more importantly, what would I be paid?"

"You'd be... some sort of coordinator. You're a good talker, you can do phone stuff, write up letters, keep information flowing. You know anything about starting a website?"

Helter lifted his bottle to his mouth and finished it. He sighed and looked at Bantam, searching for something in the guy's eyes that might suggest insanity, looniness, even irony... but there was only a deadly earnestness that was even more frightening. When John Bantam looked at you goddamnit he really *looked* at you.

"You're really serious about all this? You wanna be President?"

"I want to say things. Things that need to be said but haven't been said yet. The Presidency isn't the point."

"What if you get elected?"

Without pause: "Then I get elected."

Helter nodded. "So what's the pay?"

"Minimal."

"Minimal?"

"It's a noble cause."

"Maybe a lost one...."

"Maybe. Aren't all noble causes lost ones? Aren't all lost ones noble?"

Helter shrugged and looked over to the bartender, tried to get her attention. He needed another beer. *They* needed another beer.

"Helter," Bantam said. "Listen to me."

Helter looked at him.

"What do you have to lose?"

60

Part II

"Lisa Yates, John Bantam."

This was her first time meeting the candidate, and she was nervous, for reasons she couldn't explain. It wasn't like he was famous or something… and it wasn't like he actually stood a chance in this thing, either, so she really didn't feel like she was standing before *the next President of the United States of America.* Nevertheless, there had been a little bit of buildup toward this first meeting and build-ups always started her nervousness a-fluttering. Maybe it was, too, the way Greg Helter had looked at her when *they* first met just an hour earlier. It wasn't predatory, no, nothing so vulgar. It was more the way a husband looks at his wife of thirty years… which was *way* too comfortable for the circumstances.

John Bantam did not look like the wild guy she thought he'd be: he was handsome, kind in the eyes, and rugged. From some of the things that had been quoted from him she had half-expected a drugged-out or otherwise wild-eyed lunatic foaming at the mouth and screaming curse words at the top of his lungs. But no, nothing so interesting.

"So you're gonna cover us from the ground up?" he asked her.

62

"That's the plan."

"And then what? Write a book about what you see, hear, and learn?"

"Sure."

He nodded and smiled down at her. "I'd buy that book. I'd like to know what this was all about, myself. Maybe I might realize what I was supposed to learn from all of it."

This meeting took place at a VFW in some town south of Dubuque. Twenty minutes later they were headed *back* to Dubuque for what Bantam had called a "bird-watcher's luncheon."

"All we do is drive, wait, listen to Bantam give a talk, and drive some more," Helter explained to her. "It's maddening."

"You're getting better press lately," she said. "That's gotta be nice. And what exactly is a bird-watcher's luncheon?"

"We keep getting invited to speak to these conservation groups. Bantam has a huge conservation agenda, and... snakes, you know, if you get him talking about snakes he's your friend forever."

"Snakes?"

"He loves snakes. I'm fond of them myself. We're Midwestern boys."

"Midwestern boys like snakes?"

"The smart ones do. What about you?"

"I'm a Midwestern girl."

"But you don't like snakes."

"I never said that."

"So you like them?"

"I never said that, either."

Helter smiled. "You should pick a side on the issue so we know where you stand."

"I'll give it some thought. By the next bird-watcher's luncheon I'll tell you what I've decided on that and other important topics."

"I think," and he was going through a little notebook now and not listening to her, "this one is for something called the Society for Iowa Skies, or something. A clean-air group."

"So, can it be said that Bantam is an environmentalist candidate?"

"Sure."

"Isn't that Parson's thing, too?"

"Sort of, but Parsons only goes half-way. Which is fitting, because in many ways he's a half-wit."

She was already writing stuff down in her own notebook, working quickly, concentrating.

"John Bantam is not part of the Left-wing," he said.

"What? What was that?" She looked up.

"He's not Left wing."

She frowned. "He's pro-choice, pro-labor, pro-environment, pro-gay rights... isn't that the Left?"

"He's anti immigration, of all sorts, he's pro-gun to a degree that can be scary, and he's pro-capital punishment. On all of these things, by the way, he's an extremist. He'll be the first to admit that. However, it's his stated belief that so are the vast majority of American people. He has a quote from Ed Abbey he likes to use: 'The bird of truth flies with both wings.'"

She wrote that down. "Abbey, you say?"

"Yes."

"Not Albee, Edward Albee the playwright?"

"No."

He watched her work for a moment, then, again out of the blue, said: "He's against NASA, too."

She frowned once more. "Why? What has NASA ever done?"

"Exactly."

*

At the bird-watcher's luncheon the topic of NASA did not come up, but the heavens (so to speak) did. Bantam said:

"Skies and sky-watching are... can we say this as adults and not feel like blithering idiots? Watching the skies, just the lazy play of clouds over a pure blue sea of air, is one of the most important things a person can do. It's certainly one of the best things a person can do... beats almost anything else, I'd say. You can't be stressful when you're watching cloud formations. You can't rob somebody, rape somebody, screw over someone's life... you just can't. But when I look up there I have to tell you, I don't think of space and aliens and other planets. Not even at night. When I look up there I think of *us*, this planet right here, and how fragile it is. It's the only planet we'll ever know, and the only planet worth a damn."

64

Which reminded Lisa of something... a little ancient history all her own.

There were always blue skies over the farm, it seemed, and though this might have been simple romanticizing of the past on her part, she honestly could not remember one single memory of rainy days or gray afternoons in all the time she'd lived there. It was all brilliantly clear skies smeared with only the barest of thin clouds or the laziest of fat-assed cumulous moving so slowly overhead it was like they were falling asleep as they went. And down below it all, the farm itself, lit afire by the sun, the beams of the barns a deep gray full of character and stories, and the fields around them stretched tight with green and amber, the color of hay, or the dirty-yellow of old cornstalks. There was work, yes, much work, but she also remembered whole days wasted dreaming in the corn, or lying on top of the hill that overlooked the far southern side of the farm and watching those lazy clouds drift past, telling stories in their shapes, transfixing her with their slow beauty. It seemed everything was clean then, even on the dirty shit-smeared animal-infested environment that was a farm. Everything was washed in silver and gold sunlight. Perfect childhood.

When she brought friends home from school to spend the weekend she always took them to that southern hill, made them lie down and stare at the sky. I thought we'd be milking cows,

66

they might say, and she'd hush them. Shhh, just watch. And they'd watch, seeing first the blue, then the clouds, then—

"See?"

It might be a hawk, it might be turkey vultures, soaring silent as thought overhead, making concentric circles as they came lower and lower, highlighted or backlit by the sun. It was mesmerizing to watch the birds, hawk or vulture alike, a hypnotic stillness even in the simple motion of soaring, wings tipping for balance, those arrow-shapes like symbols from dreams coming lower... and then, just like *that*, rising back up, catching a breeze and letting it take them away to the North. Just wait, she'd whisper, and soon enough the birds would be back, lifted by thermals and following another breeze, eyes surveying the landscape for the movement of a mouse or mole (the hawk) or the sight of something dead and rotting in the far corners of the fields (the vultures).

Is this what you do? her friends might ask. Lie here all day like this?

And she would say yes. As far as she was concerned there was nothing better to do anywhere than lie and stare at the sky. If she stared long enough she'd lose herself entirely inside of it, or in the fat morphing shapes of the clouds. Years later, living in the city, caught fast in the smell of exhaust and sewage and *people*, she would often think back on not only the clean and clear look of the sky but the feeling of the grass on her back as she lay there, that southern hill so rough and dry her skin would be pocked when she stood. On days when she was stressed at work, when the very idea of something called "technical writing" was threatening to drive her mad, or when she was overwhelmed by the sheer number of all the people pushing and breathing on the L, she would drift off on memories of those times and use them to calm herself. To think there had once existed a period when all you had to do was waste entire days lost in the beauty of skies and clouds. The clouds tell stories, Dad had once told her. They change shapes and tell stories, you just have to know how to read them. He himself had been a great watcher of skies. In fact, it was he who first brought her to that little hill and set her down on her back to watch some huge blue-bellied clouds drifting overhead like whales. See that? he'd asked. Looks like you could reach up and touch them....

She was thinking of her father, and the great mystery that was his absence, and how deep and dark it must be in certain sections of the Shawnee Forest....

*

"Where did Bantam get the money for his campaign?" she asked. It was a question that had been bugging her for some time. "I don't mean *now*, because I assume you get donations, but like when he first started? What did he do before? How could he just up and quit and start a campaign?"

Helter listened to her carefully as she spoke, nodding a little, his eyes occasionally finding themselves fixated (absently, to be fair) on her breasts. She'd been wearing a heavy winter coat when they'd met but now, riding in the car, she had taken it off. She was a good-looking healthy young woman... a distraction, really, like all good-looking healthy young women. But a distraction in a different way than Scarlett Hamm had been. There had been something predatory about Scarlett, something full of nerve-endings and instinct. Lisa Yates had something else going on, something deeper, something more elemental.

"That's one of several mysteries," he finally said, realizing what he was doing and turning his head to look out the window.

"Isn't he required to reveal that by law?"

"No. I don't think so." He thought for a moment. "Maybe. I don't know."

She wrote this down, then looked up. "You guys must have some suspicions," she said, looking from Helter to Hamm. "Of where the money came from, I mean."

"We try not to think about it," said Helter.

"Yeah," Hamm agreed. "We like mysteries. Mysteries are good. Give me a good mystery to dwell on all day and I'm a happy man. Like... what the hell do people do for fun out here?" He meant the flat open farming areas of Iowa. "What can a bored little farm kid do for excitement?"

"I'm a farm kid," she said.

Hamm regarded her with suspicion. "Really? You don't look like it."

"No? And what does a farm kid look like?"

He thought about that as he drove, turning his head to look her up and down, and shrugged. "Thick in the thighs, I would

68

imagine. You don't look thick in the thighs. You don't look thick anywhere."

"I think you're thick," she said. "Thick in the head."

Helter laughed.

Hamm laughed too, and then pretended he was nauseated and covered his mouth with his hands. "I think I'm gonna be thick...."

"This is going in my book," Lisa said. "I'll do a whole chapter on your thick head."

"You should mention my Uncle Bennie," Hamm said, "now there was a guy with the thickest head in the world, would literally pound a nail into it at parties, like one of those—"

"Hey," Helter said suddenly, sitting forward and practically pressing his face again the glass of his window. "Hey, stop!"

Hamm looked in the rearview mirror. "What? What for?"

"Just stop!"

"What's wrong?" Lisa asked.

"Just... stop the car, turn around!"

Hamm slowed the Corolla as he pulled onto the shoulder, then checked the traffic (of which there was absolutely none, save the tiny black shape of a vole crossing the asphalt) and pulled into the opposite lane.

"What are you looking at?" he said, frowning. Both he and Lisa were frowning, their eyes searching excitedly for whatever Helter might be freaking out about.

"There," said Helter. "Pull over!"

Hamm pulled onto the shoulder, and even before the car had stopped moving Helter was out of the backseat and starting for the field they were next to.

It was a cornfield, and remnants of last year's stalks sprouted from it like bamboo, four feet high and the color of old bones. Ghosts of the season past. Helter entered the field and started crossing it, headed for an old tractor that was sitting right in the middle, a vestigial-looking old chunk of machinery that might possibly have been red or green when it was new but which was now a deep and dull flat gray, the color of raw metal.

The field was hard and therefore not muddy, but Hamm and Lisa were reluctant to enter it.

"What's wrong?" Hamm called out. Helter didn't answer.

"Is this a common occurrence?" Lisa asked.

69

Hamm shrugged.

"He's flipped out," Lisa said. Then she pursed her lips and entered the field herself, followed a few steps behind by a sighing Hamm who was mumbling about how he could have stayed in nice clean field-free New York City, eating dirty-water weenies and making time with hot and desperate Jewish princesses. This is the last noble adventure I ever go on, he said.

The wind was harsh as it blew across the field, and a light snow was starting to fall, just a few weak dry flakes on the air, little more than flotsam. Lisa, who had had the foresight to grab her coat, looked back at Hamm, who was shivering in his turtle-neck sweater. Idiot. Thick-headed idiot.

By the time they caught up to Helter he was already at the tractor. There was a man lying on the ground, his eyes open, his chest rising and falling steadily.

"You all right?" Helter asked.

"Never better," said the man. He looked to be in his seventies, a tough and rugged old farmer who nevertheless possessed a thin body of the sort you rarely saw on old folks. He looked like an old greyhound that had been put out to pasture: worn and used, perhaps, but still fit from a lifetime of physical activity. He was wearing a deep-blue coat buttoned to his neck, dark jeans stained and smeared with a variety of farm-related substances (oil, mud, cowshit, blood), and ancient boots as rough and leathery as his face.

"What happened?" Lisa asked. She was speaking to the old man but it was Helter who answered:

"He fell off the tractor."

"What?"

"I was just looking out the window and I saw him fall."

Lisa knelt down by the man. "You sure you're okay?"

"Never better."

"Anything broken? Can you move?"

"Sure," he said, just as calmly as can be. "Sure, I can move just fine."

She waited. "And...?"

He didn't answer, just kept staring up to the gray sky. A few of those dry flakes of snow landed on his eyelashes and lips and immediately melted.

Hamm came up. "Holy shit... heart attack?"

70

Helter ignored him, instead asked the farmer if he could get up.

"Sure," was the response.

"Do you want to try?"

The farmer said nothing.

"What happened?" Hamm asked.

"He fell off the tractor," Helter said again.

"How do you fall off a tractor?" Hamm looked down into the man's eyes. "How do you fall off a tractor?" he asked loudly.

"He must have hit his head," said Lisa. She was still kneeling over him, and looked like she wanted to touch him and check for injuries. Her hands fidgeted but didn't quite know what to do with themselves, making her look like she was casting a voodoo spell on him.

"What, you just look out here and happen to see him?" Hamm asked, but Helter wasn't listening.

"Gotta be a head injury," Lisa kept saying.

"Listen," Helter said, leaning over the old man. "Want us to help you up?"

"No, no thanks. I'm fine."

"Sure?"

"I'm sure."

"Like fuck he's sure, we have to help him up!" said Hamm.

Helter stood tall and shrugged, staring off across the field to the nearest farm a mile or so away. "He says he's fine."

"What were you doing out here?" Lisa asked.

"Driving the tractor," the old man answered. He had not looked at any of them yet, just kept staring heavenward.

Lisa stood and examined the tractor, which was idling weakly. She jumped up on it and killed the engine.

"So you *are* a farm kid," said Hamm.

"Thick in the head," was all she said. She jumped down and walked back to the old man. "Want us to call home for you? Have someone come out?"

"Nope."

She sighed. "Listen, are you *sure* you don't need an ambulance or something? Why don't you get up?"

"Don't make much difference," the old man said. "Lie here, lie there, the work'll get done."

"What does that mean?" Hamm stage-whispered to Lisa, like she was a translator.

71

Lisa sighed again and knelt by the old man once more. She took a more aggressive approach, reached down to touch his arms, his legs, then carefully put both hands on either side of his head and turned it right, then left.

"Can you move your arms and legs?" she asked.

"I reckon I can."

"Then… *can* you? Right now, move your legs."

"Don't make much difference," he said again. "The work'll get done."

She sighed and looked up at Helter. "My work made us all take CPR but I… shit, I can't remember anything!"

"I don't think he needs CPR, he says he's fine."

"Bullshit he's fine, he won't *move*!"

"Move or not, the work'll get done."

Hamm's turn to sigh. "He says that one more time I'm gonna kick him."

"Come on," Lisa said, tugging on Helter's pant leg. "Get down here, help me get him up."

Helter took his eyes from the farm across the field, studied this little scene for a moment, and then relented and knelt down next to the guy, on the opposite side from Lisa. They each put their hands underneath him, high on his back, and looked at each other.

"Sure," the old man said. "I'm fine."

"Ready?"

Helter nodded.

They started to lift the farmer up and he immediately made a horrible little gurgling sound, thick with phlegm. The sound struck something visceral and elemental in the other three: their guts understood that noise even if their minds did not.

They slowly set the old guy back down to the earth. His eyes were still staring skyward but his chest was no longer rising or falling.

"Shit," said Lisa. She looked at Helter, then put her fingers on the man's neck.

"Well?" asked Hamm.

"Nothing," she said.

"What do you mean *nothing*?" Hamm asked. "There has to be *something*!"

"Nothing." She tried it again, even put her ear to his mouth, though hearing a breath above the wind would have been impossible. "Nothing."

72

"Oh for fuck's sake," said Hamm, stepping back. "This is… this is great. Are you telling me he's *dead*?"

Far across the field a cow mooed. For whatever it's worth, the sound was deep and lonely and sad.

*

If I'd known I was going to be a chauffeur *and* security I don't know if I would have taken this gig, thought Jasper Callister. He wasn't uncomfortable with the boredom, or the constant sameness of the places they drove to, but being a big man his legs tended to get cramped if he sat behind the wheel too long. The only thing that made it more than bearable was Bantam.

Bantam had invented this game wherein he kept throwing out various assassination scenarios for Jasper to comment on. It had started with the simplest: what would you do if someone took a punch at me? Then it was: what if they pulled a knife? What if they pulled a gun? Progressing ever upward to: what if they tossed a grenade? What if there was a bomb? What if a group of them came at me when I was speaking? What if a car came out of nowhere right now and tried to run us off the road?

For each of them Jasper calmly elaborated on what he would do, taking no more than a minute or two to come up with a detailed and effective policy. The latest one, more subtle than the others, had him slightly stumped:

"What would you do if someone decided to poison my food?" When Jasper took longer than usual to formulate a plan Bantam settled back in his seat and said: "You go ahead, take your time, think about it. I'm going to take a nap." And he did, slipping into sleep easily there in his reclined seat, even snoring a little. Jasper just stared out at the highway, which seemed to stretch and stretch and stretch vainly for the old unattainable horizon.

Earlier Bantam had asked him why Helter had picked him for this detail, driving all the way up to Milwaukee and not knowing at all if he'd be able to locate him. Why would he think of you? Bantam asked. An old college buddy he hasn't seen in a decade or so?

Jasper just shook his head. No need to go into that. Water under the bridge. All he said was: I'm a big man, maybe I'm the biggest man he's ever known.

73

Bantam was smart enough to let that be the last word, which said a lot about him. Lesser men might pry, but Bantam was an expert at reading subtle little animal-like hints, little changes in skin tone or the glint of light in the eyes. Which was admirable, and which was one of the first things Jasper had liked about the guy: they each shared that sort of instinctual understanding of bestial body language and movement. Not many people are tied in to things like pheromones or the subtle and subconscious quivering of lips and eyebrows. We are a dying breed, thought Jasper. Us humans have separated ourselves from all that. We are removed from our original natures.

As Bantam slept Jasper thought about these assassination questions. Being so connected to that ancient animal nature, was it possible that the man knew something about his fate? Was he thinking about these things because some fundamental and primal instinct told him there was danger ahead? Were his mental cockles up, was that it?

Jasper glanced over at the man. He himself was getting no feelings about it either way. He couldn't see an aura, couldn't sense a future Death on the guy, didn't feel any strange electricity in the air, couldn't smell the stench of Fate. There was only this car, this highway, these endless days. And that question:

What would you do if someone decided to poison my food?

I'm not going to start tasting his food before he eats it, absolutely no fucking way. So, what would I do if someone decided to stick arsenic or anthrax in with your fries or your steak or your hamburger or your root beer?

What *could* I do? I'd sit back like everyone else and watch the show.

It's strange, this risking your own life to save another, all for the sake of a paycheck. It was good money, though, no doubting that: 500 a week to do little but stand around and look mean, like a good old-fashioned head cracker. And driving, yes, we can't forget that. Five hundred bucks to drive this guy around from event to event and *then* stand around looking like a head cracker. Definitely worse things to do for a living. Like making tractor parts, for example. He wondered how all the guys from the factory were doing, wondered how upper management was feeling. Cross big old mean Jasper Callister, will they? Treat good ole Jazz like common dirt? No way.

74

They might *think* they got the last word, but all they got was a reprieve. Someday he'd go revisit that little scene, pay Mr. Beakins and Mr. Taylor a little of the attention they deserved. Someday, but a day far in the future. There was always time for planning and thoughtfulness when it came to justice and revenge. Always room for thinking through every last goddamn detail. Let them get good and comfortable in their pathetic little lives, let them forget all about Jasper Whatsisname... let them feel safe and secure back there in their little cubbyholes, their corner offices, their pissant little factory. *Then* imagine their surprise when he walks in someday... or, better yet, meets them in the proverbial back alley. Yes, that was better... the back alley. Lots of back alleys in Milwaukee, the place was fucking *made* for head cracking.

But all that was for later, and there'd be plenty of time to formulate a good solid plan. It was probably best not to dwell on that old bitterness right now, driving a Presidential candidate (however much a long-shot he might be) down some benign old highway in Iowa. Iowa? Christ, first it was Ohio, now Iowa. Soon enough they'd all be headed up to New Hampshire, following Keith and Parsons around like little dogs, yapping and nipping at their feet. That was essentially what Bantam was up to, of course, nipping at the big dogs' feet. A hell of a way to spend your time, and a hell of a way to spend your money. Until he'd met Bantam, Jasper had never known another grown adult who would have even considered such a thing. Much to admire in that, of course. Worse ways to pass the time. And the guy actually seemed to view it as a duty, a sacred duty he absolutely *needed* to perform, and not like a lark or some strange perverted feeding of an out-of-control ego. The guy was totally *serious* about this, you could see it in his eyes. He was absolutely and totally serious about being a thorn in those guy's sides. And he was good at it, and getting better every day. Again, there was much to admire in that. In fact, the very first time he'd met him he'd—

"What are you thinking about?" Bantam mumbled from the passenger seat, his eyes puffy slits.

"That's a woman's question."

Bantam mumbled something else and shifted his long legs to get comfortable.

"Why don't you sleep in the back?" Jasper asked, but the man was already out again. Snoring a little, even. Maybe dreaming.

Jasper sighed, shifted his own weight, and looked out at Iowa as it passed by, trying hard not to start thinking again about revenge and plans and dark back alleys in the middle of the night....

*

"Jasper Callister, John Bantam."

Bantam was looking at him with a huge grin on his face. "Holy shit, Helter was right: you're a big son of a bitch." He put out his hand and Jasper took it, gave it just enough squeeze to show the potential of his strength but not enough to be uncomfortable for the guy. The handshake he received back was exactly the same.

"You should see my father," he said.

Bantam's eyes widened. "No shit, really? Bigger than you?"

"Bigger'n all of us."

Bantam was roughly the same height as him, but Jasper was solid, the proverbial brick wall, with broad shoulders and a chest like the side of a mountain. He didn't just look like he was as strong as an ox, he looked like he could kick an ox's ass. For pleasure.

He was well-shaven for this meeting, and his neck showed it: his skin was red and angered from an apparently rough meeting with the blade. He was wearing nice khaki pants and a dark blue shirt buttoned all the way save for the top two buttons, and there was a white shirt underneath. He hadn't given his choice of clothes much debate that morning, since these were really the only decent things he owned. Job interview clothes. Well, he *did* own an actual honest-to-goodness suit, but it had been tossed violently into the back of his closet and was probably so wrinkled as to be unbearable. Plus, it was full of blood stains. Long story.

"Helter seems to think you'd make a helluva security guy."

"I guess."

"What do you think?"

Jasper shrugged. "I think... if I was being paid to protect your ass nothing would ever happen to you that I didn't allow to happen. That's what I think."

The left corner of Bantam's mouth trembled with a smile withheld, and he stared deeply into Jasper's eyes. Both men shared the same animal instinct for detecting motivation and intent, and a deep concentration could be seen gathering and focusing in each of their faces. Helter would later say it was like watching a rhino and an elephant sizing each other up, looking deep into each other's souls to see what might be found.

"I believe you," Bantam said finally. "So tell me, what are your politics?"

"Angry."

Bantam smiled. "Good. Welcome aboard, then."

Another handshake sealed it.

*

Sometimes he was amazed that he could keep his various angers in check. In fact, sometimes it scared him. A person who felt the things he felt, who harbored the anger and hatred he did, should not be as calm with that anger and hatred as he himself often was. But it felt entirely natural to have those things coursing through his mind and heart, and indeed, on the rare occasions when he felt none of it, when he felt at ease with the world and his place in it, those were the times he felt agitated and uncomfortable, not himself at all. But what was worse, *that* agitation, or the idea that some day all of his venom might show itself, might finally bubble and broil over and come spewing out to poison and pummel every mind and body within range? He wasn't sure, wasn't even sure this was a good and healthy thing to be thinking about, but what was the other option? Further contemplation of these highways and fields and small towns and cars and dead deer and broken gray skies? Or, even worse, thinking about *why* he had all of that anger and hatred in the first place? No, not that, never *that*.

Bantam stirred and mumbled in his sleep. Sleep in the backseat, you fucking idiot, Jasper thought. He himself took a glance in the rearview mirror, checking that seat out, staring at it longingly. Lots of room back there for a man to stretch out, drift off, forget the world and everything in it for a while.

"You want to pull over?" Bantam said, startling him. His voice was rough, cracked.

"You gonna be sick?"

"No. Pull over, get in the back, take a nap. I'll drive."

Jasper frowned, said nothing.

"I saw you looking back there. Pull over. I've slept enough."

He pulled over, got in the backseat, took his nap. Dreamt.

*

Jasper the Friendly Ghost, they called him as a kid. The nickname Jazz never really stuck, and was taken up only by a rare few, becoming more common as he got older... but only half-heartedly. Usually, when someone was *really* talking to him, they called him Jasper, simply Jasper. Never adding "the friendly ghost," though. Never ever never.

Jasper, Jasper, the Friendly Ghost, he's the one we hate the most. Some neighborhood kids had taken up that chant. Jasper, Jasper, the Friendly Ghost, he's the one we—

You have to learn to ignore those things, his mom told him. You just encourage them when you get mad.

He looked at his bloody knuckles as she swabbed them clean with warm water and then sprayed Bactine where the skin was fresh and raw. Even at that age (twelve) he knew it was probably not good to go through life breaking noses and splitting lips, but it was so hard to hold himself back. And he wasn't even a big kid yet, that wouldn't come for a few years, just before high-school, when he'd suddenly sprout like a son of a bitch (to use his father's phrase) and pack on fifty pounds seemingly overnight. Nevertheless, he was a bruiser of a kid, tough as leather, very physical and not afraid of anything. All of which might have endeared him to others his age were it not for the *other* part of his personality, the other side of the Jasper Callister coin: the part that kept to himself, that would rather sit and draw pictures of dinosaurs at recess than join in the others' games, that made him the quietest kid in or out of the classroom, never a peep out of little Jasper the Friendly Ghost. Some thought he was stupid because of this, a dumb block of a boy who would likely drop out of school by his Junior year, the kind of boy who would grow up to live a simple life of quiet (or otherwise) desperation fixing cars or driving heavy machinery. Look at his father, after all. Look at his father.

Which was why, when high-school did finally roll around and his growing physical attributes were starting to become obvious, some of the older folks in his life began to take an interest in him. Like Coach Hartman, who likely saw in the boy's size both a chance to help the kid out of a cycle of silence and solitude *and* an opportunity to put a big and tough tackle on his football team.

"Why do you want me?" Jasper had asked him.

"It'll be good for you."

And it was... it was in fact one of the best things he could have done at the time. Here, with this simple but rough full-contact game, was the perfect outlet for his natural aggressions, and the perfect antidote to any bad feelings those aggressions might have caused: he was being asked to legally hit other kids as hard as he could, and there was no moral or ethical quandary about any of it. It might not be good to split lips out on the sidewalks and in the classrooms (regardless of how it *felt*), but there on the gridiron it was the only thing that was asked of him, the only task that was required. The harder he hit an opponent, the more the crowd (and the coach and his teammates and his father) appreciated him. There was something lovely in the simplicity of that arrangement.

But it had to end.

Some talking head douche bag on CNN was complaining about the sudden publicity John Thomas Bantam was starting to get. This was a former chair of something called the Foundation for America, which was at its essence a Catholic organization designed to push the Catholic agenda.

"This marks the very lowest point in American politics," he was saying. "This is nothing but catering to the lowest, vilest, most vulgar impulses of society. Will it have an effect on anything? If it does, it will be a negative effect. We're lowering our standards by even talking about this guy."

To which the other person on this "panel," a lowly on-line pundit affiliated with nothing in particular, replied: "I've been out there to see the people who are coming to hear him. They're normal, average, ordinary working folks. When asked, they say they're interested in him because he sounds like they do. More than anyone else in the history of American politics, he sounds like they do. It's not pretense or acting, it's real. They say that about him, too: he's real."

The moderator of the program said: "But do they honestly think he has a shot?"

"Well that's the thing, and they'll tell you right up front: no, they don't. But winning isn't everything."

*

Jasper Callister woke from a good and solid nap of the sort he hadn't had in years, his big body aching but his mind pleasantly lulled into something like peace by a series of dreams he could only feel, not recall. They sat over him like a buzz, or the pseudo-orgasmic tickle that follows a good massage. He sat up, rubbed his cramped legs, and looked at the figure of John Bantam in the driver's seat. Bantam was swerving ever so slightly as he drove, the car threatening to slip over the yellow line every now and then, and Bantam would have to gently swerve it back the other way, just as casual as could be.

"You drive like an asshole," Jasper said.

Bantam flinched a little. "It's awake." He smiled into the rearview mirror. "Actually, I drive pretty good when I'm not on the phone." And sure enough, his left hand was holding his cell to his ear.

"Stop talking on the phone, then."

Bantam clicked off the cell and set it on the passenger seat. "I can't get a hold of Helter."

"I'll alert the media."

"I don't know if we go straight to the union hall or to the hotel first," Bantam said. Phone or not, he was still swerving, only now he was able to stay within the confines of his own lane. Still, all that back and forth, toward the center line, back towards the ditch, toward the center line, back toward the ditch... it was sickening.

"I pray it's the hotel," said Jasper.

Bantam frowned. "I think maybe it's the hall."

Jasper sighed. "Another fucking union hall...."

"Would you rather it be a bird-watching group?"

"At least there I can stop pretending I care about your life."

"You think none of those people could kill me?"

Jasper frowned, thought about it, shrugged. "I suppose anyone could kill you, if they had half a mind to."

Bantam laughed. "And *that* is today's pleasant thought, ladies and gentlemen." He picked up the cell again, tried Helter one more time. "Where are they?"

81

Jasper was staring out the window. "What kind of man," he wondered aloud, "starts driving down a highway without any idea of where he's going?" *A Presidential candidate*, he answered to himself. Shit.

Bantam looked at Jasper via the rearview mirror again. "You wanna come back up here?"

Jasper shook his head.

"What if I was getting tired... what if I fall asleep and go off the road? Could you save me from myself?" He suddenly looked excited, his eyes all wide, and sat up straight as a board. "Hey, there's a good one Mr. Callister: could you save me from suicide?"

Jasper didn't hesitate: "Why would I want to?"

Bantam laughed. "Why the bitterness, Jazz? Wasn't it a good nap?"

"It's not that. If a man wants to kill himself, he's got a right to. Why would I stop him?"

"Because you're getting paid to keep him alive."

"I'm not getting paid that much."

Bantam kept smiling. "It's an interesting question, hey? What right does a bodyguard have to keep someone from killing themselves?"

Jasper rolled his eyes and kept staring mindlessly out the window. It wasn't that interesting a question, he didn't think, but let the guy have his fun. Right now Mr. Bantam was up there with his mind just *jumping* at this question, examining it from every angle, salivating over it, titillated and tickled by some perceived conundrum within its very center. Look at the guy, he was like a kid. His face had gone distant with happiness, his mouth half-open, his eyes wide. At least he was staying in his own lane, for now anyway. And what the fuck and what the hell.

It seemed to Jasper that this campaign crap was all an evasion of something else, a classic example of avoidance. A man or woman *runs* for office, so what does running imply? You either run to or away from something, and though it could be argued that the politician is running *to* the elected position, Jasper didn't think this was quite right, in a psychological sense, and it was the psychological sense he was interested in. If you looked at the sort of people who actually did this kind of thing you'd see an obvious and disturbing similarity: they were all desperate for attention, egomaniacal little kids crying out to

82

be looked at, to be taken seriously, to be *seen*. And shit, isn't that what people like Helter were always saying, that such and such an activity was a great way to "get seen?" Bantam here might be a unique sort of candidate, one of big mouth and little political instinct, one who spoke not only what he thought but what he *felt* (and there was a huge difference between the two), but in essence he was still a classic example of a candidate, one desperate to get his "message" heard, one who was, by the very nature of the activity he was engaged in, egotistical enough to think others should elect him to the highest office in the land. A *real* alternative candidate, thought Jasper, would be one who did the exact opposite of this, one who was content to stay in the background, who preferred to hole up in his own basement rather than go out shaking hands, kissing babies, chatting up all sorts of desperate and fringe social groups. Hell, the *real* alternative candidate was one who wasn't even running at all.

But back to psychology: look closely at all of these political folks and you'd see people with messed up backgrounds full of deep emotional wounds (lots of divorced and/or alcoholic parents) and more than a few physical ones (whether suffered in foreign wars or at the hands of disease or abusive dads). It really looked for all the world like they were trying to attract attention to themselves in order to make up for whatever part of their past was plaguing them. Classic over-achiever syndrome. My daddy beat me in drunken rages so now I will go out and try to be the most powerful person I can be. It made Jasper wonder what sort of shit lay in Bantam's past. So far the man had not spoken much about his life prior to the campaign, other than vague little comments here and there, a spare detail or two, a hint, an impression. What was your life like back there in Wisconsin? Jasper wondered, looking at the guy. Jesus, Bantam trailed questions the way an overfed goldfish trails shit. But why was no one asking them? Why did it seem no one cared?

"Are you rich?" he asked, surprised to hear his own voice. He hadn't meant to speak, it just sort of came out.

Bantam glanced in the rearview mirror. "Compared to who?"

"Compared to me."

Pause. "I suppose."

"Compared to Helter."

"I guess."

"Compared to Keith or Parsons."

No answer.

Jasper asked: "And where did you get your vast wealth?"

"It's not vast. Hey, look at this. Fifty-seven Chevy." A canary-yellow hotrod flew past from the other direction, and Bantam followed its progress in the rearview mirror before glancing again (nervously?) at Jasper. "Maybe fifty-five."

"So where'd you get your not-vast wealth?"

"Are you writing a book?"

"I have a right to know about a man who's running for President."

"Do you?'

"Yes."

Bantam said nothing for a moment, just watched the highway ahead of him unroll. At last he said: "You're very talkative today. I liked the old Jazz better."

"You're making me nervous, avoiding my questions like this. You got something to hide?"

"*Everyone* has something to hide. Except for me and my monkey."

"A man running for President can't have secrets. Right now there are hundreds of folks looking into your life, I bet. Swarming around your hometown, sniffing into the old Bantam childhood home, digging through your parent's lives, maybe right now going through your underwear drawer, looking to find out who exactly John Thomas Bantam is."

"I don't wear underwear."

"Sock drawer, then."

Bantam shook his head. "They won't be doing any of that."

"You're naïve."

Bantam fell silent again, let nearly a mile go past before speaking again... and when he did his voice was low, flat, cold, like he was speaking to himself:

"They won't find anything," he said. "There's just nothing to find...."

Which Jasper took as the end of the conversation, and which he was glad to see happen. It wasn't like him to ask so many questions, let alone questions of that nature. He sat there in the backseat half watching Bantam and half looking out at Iowa as it slid past. Imagine being a trucker, and seeing *this* sort of thing day after day, all day: highways, farmland, distant houses, a half-dozen nervous deer scampering across fields, cars approaching and cars fading away, that endless run of yellow line leading there and there and there but never *here*. It should drive a man crazy, and maybe it did. He tried to think if he knew any long-haul truckers and couldn't name any... though he was familiar with the guys who drove the semis that picked up tractor parts from the factory. The factory, the goddamn factory... not that again. He desperately pushed those thoughts away (later, remember, save them for later) and looked at Bantam.

"I could go for a beer," Bantam said.

"You want me to drive while you suck down a six-pack?"

"Let me think about that." A moment or two later Bantam picked up his cell-phone again. He pressed a button, listened, hung up. "Still no Helter. Where the hell *are* they?" He glanced at the rearview mirror, saw Jasper looking back. "Can I ask you a question, big guy?"

"I suppose."

"Would you vote for me?"

Strange question, thought Jasper. Kind of inappropriate. "What's in it for me?"

Bantam shrugged. "Peace and prosperity. The return of common sense and integrity and all that kind of crap."

Jasper laughed. "Yeah, right."

Bantam smiled. "I am totally goddamn serious."

Jasper settled back, looked out his window, and decided not to say anything more. Stupid conversations. Next thing you know the guy would ask about—

"Really, what right does a bodyguard have to prevent a suicide?" Bantam said.

That again. Jasper sighed. "If you see a gas station, pull into it. I'm gonna get you that six pack, maybe it'll shut you up."

"Isn't that illegal?"

"What the hell isn't anymore...?"

"Ahhh... spoken like a typical angry Midwesterner, the poor powerless workingman at the mercy of forces greater than him... all that bureaucracy, all those regulations, all those government types." Bantam was looking out at the surrounding countryside as he spoke, formulating a theory as the miles sped past.

Jasper said nothing.

"You know what's wrong with that sort of thinking?" Bantam asked. "It's the thinking of people who've rolled over already, who've just put their hands up and surrendered."

"I thought you were on the side of people like that."

"I could never be on the side of people like that. People who feel that way need to realize that the only way to get over oppression is to fight back."

"The system isn't set up so a workingman can get a say," Jasper grumbled.

"Who said anything about using the system? I'm talking about using force, if necessary. A government can't oppress a people if the people are unwilling to be oppressed. If you refuse to take something, they can't make you take it."

"They'll squash your ass. When civilians rise up, the government slams down on them. Look at Ohio State. Tiananmen Square. Chicago in '68. Any major city last year...."

Bantam nodded and looked in the rearview mirror again. "I didn't say you'd make it out alive. Death, too, is a form of victory. You can't oppress the dead."

"The dead are useless in a fight."

"I don't know about that, big man. Ghosts make good allies."

"We don't need martyrs."

"Not martyrs. Ghosts."

"No such thing as ghosts."

"I mean real ghosts. Sorry if you've never met any."

Jasper thought about his old nickname and wondered if that little sing-song rhyme (*Jasper, Jasper, the Friendly Ghost, he's the one we hate the most*) ever got into the heads of his old classmates. He hoped so. He liked the idea of it driving them nuts as it looped around in their sad little dull minds in the middle of the night, keeping them from sleep and their sad little dull dreams.

A SHELL sign became visible in the distance. Bantam slowed and pulled into its parking lot, raising a hand in greeting to a grizzled man in a giant beat-up old Chevy pickup who was pulling out at the same time.

"See that guy's face?" Bantam said. "That's a real, honest, strong face. A face like that could scare the crap out of any politician in Washington."

"Does it scare you?"

86

"I'm not a politician in Washington."

Jasper laughed. "That's right, and you'd better get used to it."

*

In actuality, he agreed with Bantam: when a people dislike the direction their leaders are headed, they always, always, *always* have the right and goddamn obligation to rise up, storm the palace, strangle the soldiers, break the heads of the heads of state, hog-tie the queen, terrorize the First Lady, prey upon the President. In most such oppressive regimes there was really little choice. Take America, for instance: what's a poor downtrodden man to do, take out a loan, form a political action committee, or become a lobbyist, spend every waking hour lurking about the halls of Congress, whispering creepy little Rasputin secrets into the ears of whatever creepy little politician he could corner? No shortage of willing ears in Washington, of course, but the system was set up quite nicely to keep people like our poor downtrodden worker (say, a factory man) from having access to anyone who might be able to help. The oppressors like to keep the oppressed in a nice state of dependency, to keep them from ever being able to take even a single day off and go look up a Senator or Congressman and tell them their troubles. The day common men and their wives and children are able to march into Washington D.C. in one big righteous parade will be a day to make even the most powerful politician piss his pants. Imagine the authority they would command, millions of working men and women marching down toward the Mall, beating on drums, playing guitars, brandishing monkey wrenches and hammers and about a thousand feet total of good solid hangman-quality rope. The meek might inherit the earth, sure... *later*. But it's the aggressive and angry who get it *now*.

In the Shell Station there was a stack of newspapers on the counter. The *Des Moines Register*. One of the front-page headlines read:

PARSONS AND KEITH UNITE AGAINST GADFLY.

Bantam picked one up and stood by the counter reading it while Jasper paid for two six-packs of Leinenkugel Red Lager (the only thing even half-way approaching good beer in the place), several sticks of jerky, and a bag of Cool Ranch Doritos.

"You don't have any fruit?" Jasper asked the dumpy-looking woman at the register.

"We got what you see. You have gas?"

"No."

"Listen," Bantam said. He read the following out loud:

"For the first time during this whole campaign the two main candidates have found common ground: each of them has made recent statements expressing disappointment and anger at third-party candidate John Thomas Bantam. Bantam has been called "John the Vulgarian" by the Washington Post, because of his free use of profanities, but he has also made what Parsons considers "inappropriate comments that do not take into account the feelings and beliefs of others." For his part, Keith has called Bantam "an agent of evil, a low and coarse-minded clown whose only goal, it seems, is to bring down the level of debate in this country." Greg Helter, campaign manager for Bantam, told the Register via phone call that Bantam "talks like an honest man. He's a man with the bark still on him, a great example of a classic American archetype, the sort of guy you don't find anymore, the kind of man people like Keith and Parsons try to render extinct with pussy-footing and political cowardice." Parsons and Keith, who normally have very little in common, are both calling for an investigation into the legality of Bantam's campaign, and have looked into whether the things he has said are open to lawsuits. For example, last week Bantam called Keith "the worst sort of right-wing [expletive], one who says things he doesn't truly believe in order to rile up the passions of poor misguided Bible-belt idiots too poor and stupid to realize eighty-percent of the things they think are untrue." He has also openly said that he thinks Parsons "was breastfed until he was fifteen."

"Isn't that just terrible?" the woman at the register said as she handed Jasper his change.

Bantam folded the paper up nice and neat and set it back down on the others. He gave her a very charming smile. "Yes, ma'am it is," he said. "And very disingenuous. I doubt if any woman has ever let Parsons get anywhere *near* her breasts."

She nodded, not really listening. She was already turning her attention back to the *People Magazine* she'd been reading when they came in.

88

Jasper picked up one of the six-packs, handed it to Bantam, and then picked up the paper bag that held the rest of the stuff.

Without further words, they left the place.

*

"We should leave this place," Hamm tried to whisper, but the other guy had come back into the room and, besides, neither Lisa nor Helter were listening to him.

They were sitting in the small, cluttered, claustrophobic livingroom of a farmhouse that smelled of woodsmoke, manure, cigarettes, and old woman perfume. And cluttered was an understatement: every horizontal surface in the room (indeed, in the whole house) was occupied with some offensive little bit of crap, knick-knacks from long-forgotten vacations, ancient pictures in frames, dried-flower arrangements, cassette-tapes (who has *cassette* tapes anymore?), magazines, stacks of mail, envelopes, and other so-called decorations. Two bookshelves sat in this little closet of a livingroom, floor to ceiling bookshelves that held nothing even remotely resembling a book. Instead, there were family pictures, at least a dozen ashtrays, and a small village of Hummel figurines that looked more than haphazardly placed, they looked like refugees from some disaster in Hummel-land, gathered together in gentle chaos to await a drop-off of government relief. On the wall opposite the largest of these bookshelves stood an ancient Franklin Stove, above which was mounted the head of a beautiful eight-point whitetail buck. The antlers of this deer were covered in tinsel, and from one tine hung a red and white Christmas stocking.

"Ma likes to decorate for the holidays, but it takes her a while to take it all down." This was a ragged man of dark complexion and hollow cheeks named Ricky. He was standing in the doorway that led to the kitchen (at least, it looked like a kitchen, though it too was swollen fat with *stuff*), and must have caught one of them looking at the mount. "Last year she kept the tree up till May. Kept it green too, I have no idea how. Kept givin' it water, takin' care of it, and up it stayed. Then one day Dad came in and couldn't take it anymore, he took it down himself. You know, in all my forty-two years I never heard them argue, but they argued that night. Ma was cursin' up a storm."

89

"Ma don't curse," said a female voice from the kitchen.

"She did that night, she did, she said *shit*, I shit you not." He smiled. "You thirsty?"

"No thanks," said Helter.

"I'm fine," said Lisa.

"We got some Milwaukee's Best out in the garage, if you'd like a beer. Water, we got water. Kool-Aid."

Hamm looked at the other two, who were shaking their heads. "I'll take a beer, if you don't mind."

"Why would I mind?" answered Ricky, and quick as a snake he slipped back through the kitchen.

Hamm shrugged at the other two. "Might as well have a beer...."

Helter was sitting on the couch in front of the window, and when the man was gone he turned and looked outside. A beaten and battered old Ford pickup that might have once been yellow but was now so faded it looked damn near white was sitting there behind the rented Toyota. An older woman with a body like a small ox was standing at its back end talking with a slightly younger man. The woman was dressed in formless jeans and a formless blouse (white with a blue flower-shaped print), the man in darker pants and a white t-shirt. As they talked they were looking down into the bed of the pickup.

"What are they doing?" asked Lisa, looking up from her notebook. She'd been making furious notes ever since they'd come to knock on this farmhouse door and tell the people inside the old man was dead, and Helter assumed that should the Bantam book ever actually come to fruition *this* particular chapter would prove to be the most interesting. He wondered if there was some political symbol to be found here and hoped not. A man drops dead in his field, that wasn't the sort of symbol you wanted for your campaign. And while we're at it, let's think about that campaign: here in this ordinary home, surrounded by the claustrophobic but very real and honest trappings of everyday American folks, the campaign seemed alien, comical, an escape from reality. Like college. And, as a matter of course, it began to look like what it might very well really be: a pipe dream. Bantam had once spoken of it being a noble cause, only to say that all noble causes were lost ones. As Helter sat there in this Iowa farmhouse that smelled of woodsmoke and perfume and cigarettes and manure he began to wonder if it was all pointless. Would Bantam win? *Could* Bantam win? And Jesus, *should* Bantam win?

"I don't know," he said, answering Lisa.

"Are they gonna bring him in?" asked Hamm, leaning forward a bit and lowering his voice. From the kitchen they could hear the sound of dishes clinking, water running, footsteps on a creaky floor.

"How should I know?"

"Well, keep your eye on them. If they start to bring him in I'm out of here."

"We can't just leave," said Lisa.

"Watch me."

"It'll be rude."

"Rude? Rude is plopping a dead man down on a couch, *that's* rude."

It didn't look to Helter like they were about to bring the man inside. The old lady and the younger guy in the black pants were just talking, that was all. In fact, now they were gesturing off to the East, and were apparently heavily absorbed in a debate of some kind. After some strange hand movements by the younger fellow the woman nodded and looked toward the eastern sky, her face thoughtful.

A few moments later Ricky came back. He was holding two beers, and after he handed one to Hamm he opened the other and took a deep drink.

"It was real nice of you folks to do what you did," he said. "How the hell did you happen to just look out and see him like that?"

Helter shrugged. "Luck, I guess."

The man sighed and shook his head. "He might still be lying out there right now. Coyotes could have come and made a meal of him. Woulda been funny, seeing as Pa hated coyotes."

"What's wrong with coyotes?" Hamm asked.

"They're sneaky and they're up to shit."

"Oh."

Helter was still looking out the window. "Is that the coroner?"

Ricky walked over to have a look. "Nope, that's Uncle Jim. Lives a few miles North."

"Has anyone called an ambulance?"

Ricky looked like he hadn't heard a stranger question. "What for? Ambulances can't help the dead."

"Doesn't he need to be, you know, pronounced?"

"Pronounced?"

"Pronounced dead."

"No, I don't think so."

"What about the law? Doesn't he need to... I don't know, be looked at by someone?" This was Lisa.

"What for?"

She frowned. "I don't know... the law? Isn't there a law?"

"Pa died on his farm, he's gonna be buried on his farm. Don't need a law to tell us that."

"Oh." She settled back in her chair, taking this in.

Helter looked up at the guy. "Is that legal?"

Ricky sighed. "Legal? Shit, what's legal mean? Legal means some other man says it's okay, that's all. It was always Pa's idea to get buried on the farm, back up on the hill looking over Flotsam Creek, the one with the quiet little oak woods behind it." He said this like they would know what he was talking about. "If that's what Pa wanted, that's what's right. Right?"

Helter nodded but said nothing. He was thinking about death certificates, legal paperwork, lawsuits, investigations.

"Here, here," said Hamm, raising his beer in salute. Ricky returned it and they both took deep drinks.

"Are you planning on burying him today yet?" Lisa asked.

Ricky looked out the window, studied the scene there for clues. "I reckon. Can't really put him in the freezer, I don't suppose. Got a quarter side of Tucker beef in there already."

There was the ringing of a phone, three full bleeping trills with a fourth cut off half-way.

"Word'll be getting around," said Ricky.

A moment later a young woman appeared in the doorway to the kitchen. Ricky's sister, the spitting image, in body and face, of the older woman outside. Pretty but overworked, her skin already tough from labor and life, her hands scuffed and big as a man's. She was in a similar outfit as her mom, though her blouse was a solid salmon, and a thin silver chain with a cross on it was hung around her neck.

"It's Tapper," she said. "He wants to know if we need anything."

Ricky answered quickly, without thought, looking back out the window: "Some good shovels and some strong hands."

*

"All right, check this out," said Jasper.

Bantam was in the passenger seat sipping with relish from a bottle of Leinenkugel Red Lager, his second. The two six packs sat on the floor by his feet, and the bag of Doritos was in Jasper's lap. The jerky was already gone.

"I'm listening," said Bantam.

"If you were really of a mind to kill yourself I don't think I, as a bodyguard-slash-security guy, would have any right or obligation to stop you."

"I'm listening."

Jasper shifted in his seat. "I think that any man that comes to that conclusion probably deserves the right to carry it out with dignity. And he probably isn't worth saving in the first place."

"Interesting," said Bantam with his mouth at his bottle, causing his voice to sound hollowed, ghostly.

Jasper thought about further elaborating but decided against it, instead reached down and took another handful of Doritos and stuffed them in his mouth. Who made this evil shit? he wondered. Probably some poor saps like me, just waiting to get in trouble with upper management for saying, loudly and clearly (and, okay, within inches of a manager's face) that those goddamn "duties as assigned" were really nothing more than a clever little way of keeping employees relegated to the status of indentured servants. Oh hell, fuck it, *slaves*. Duties as assigned? Duties as *assigned?* Christ. What that meant was no one had the safety of possessing a real job description. Hell, the head of human resources might end up cleaning shit off the walls of the bathroom some day. The accountant might have to soak up puke with that red sawdust crap. Duties as assigned was another way they had of fucking you over.

Bantam sighed and contemplated his second bottle of beer, now empty. "Should I have another?" he wondered aloud.

"Have another."

"Will you have one with me?"

"Jesus... where the hell are we headed, anyway?"

93

"That way," said Bantam, gesturing ahead as he reached down for another bottle. "That a way." He came up with one, cracked it open, and took a drink.

Jasper watched him for a second, then shook his head. "How long have you had this problem?"

"What problem?"

Jasper sighed.

"I only have a problem when I don't have any beer," Bantam said. "Whose quote is that?"

"Malcolm X."

"Bah...."

"Orel Roberts."

"Orel Roberts... that's funny."

"John Bantam."

"No, that one's not mine. And anyway, for the record, I don't have a problem. I do, however, have several beers that need drinking, and there's nothing wrong with drinking that isn't also wrong with medicine, religion, sports or politics. Everything in moderation, you know. Too much of any of those things will kill you. Here, have a beer."

"No thanks. You put that bottle in my lap and I'll break your head open."

Bantam laughed. "That doesn't sound like fun. Hey, listen, you went to college, right?"

"Not wholeheartedly."

"What the hell does a man like you major in? I mean, a big head cracker like yourself? What was it, weight-lifting? Physics? The fine arts?"

"The fine arts, that's right. I was a painter."

"Really?" Bantam appeared to think about this a moment. "You're messing with me, aren't you? I could see you as a sculptor, though. One who works in metal, like David Smith. Come on, have a beer. All right, then, just hand over those Doritos."

This Jasper did, but he found he had spilled enough in his crotch to satisfy any lingering hunger. He scooped up the crumbs and stared ahead at the road out there. The road ahead. A well-used phrase in political slogans and speeches, of course: *the road ahead is paved with danger and hope*, and all that sort of bullshit. But was the future really like that distant spot on the highway up there, was Time really like the highway itself, unrolling steadily, inevitably, onward and onward and onward?

94

It sometimes seemed to Jasper that it was anything but, that all things that had ever happened were still happening right this instant, and that all things that were yet to occur were occurring now, as we speak. Why did it seem this way to him? Because he felt the weight of everything he had ever been through as clearly as if it had happened just a moment ago. Every betrayal, every abuse, every broken heart. All of it. And the good stuff, too, but as any sane man knows the bad stuff has much more weight and gravity than the good. We gain more from the bad, it affects us the most.

"Here's the thing with Keith and Parsons and what they symbolize," Bantam said.

"Jesus, is that really your *third* beer?"

Bantam considered the bottle before him but ignored the question. "The thing with Keith and Parsons is this: people like that will say anything, absolutely anything, to gain and hold onto a position of power. An obvious observation, I know, but I don't think too many people actually *think* about what that means. Think about it... I mean, even those people who agree with what they're saying must understand that it's all lip-service. Now why, I ask you, would a sane and reasonable and supposedly grownup man or woman sit and listen to someone like that *knowing* full well that they were just being used, that the words coming out of those mouths were lies, half-hearted bullshit, the attempt by a wily politician to cater to an audience? Who the hell would whore themselves... no, *humiliate* themselves that badly? Everyone knows all politicians are liars, so what does that make the person who stands there and nods and applauds when the lies are told? I put this question to you now: what kind of man or woman thinks so lowly of themselves?"

Jasper shook his head but did not answer, figuring it was a rhetorical question.

"So here's what Keith and Parsons symbolize," Bantam continued. "They symbolize our willingness to accept crap if it sounds like the crap we *wish* were true. In other words, these two big ultra-modern politicians stand for the whole big illusion that we've created out of our modern society. Modern life is all about illusion, perception, distraction. Religion might be *an* opiate of the people, but it's far from the only one, there's also TV and movies and football and basketball and porn and music, *bad* music, like country and modern R&B and rap and... are

95

you following me? You know the *biggest* opiate don't you?
It's politics itself.   Modern politics is a deceitful illusion
designed to mislead the common man from the truth, from
reality, from cold hard facts. It's not that it doesn't matter, it's
that it doesn't matter in the way they want you to *think* it
matters. They want to get you to come to the voting booth not
because of what they've promised you... like Parsons with his
amnesty for illegals nonsense, or Keith with his God-loves-
America crap.   Those issues are the handkerchiefs the
magicians want you to focus on while the *real* trick is done
over there, behind your back, or right in front of your eyes,
under our goddamn noses. All I'm offering people is raw
honesty, absolutely no illusions, just a completely visible thing
for them to look at and judge. No tricks, no distractions. No
magic. When I talk, what I'm talking about is *all* that I am
talking about. I don't say 'keep our air free of poisons' and
really mean 'I can't wait to cash in with my buddies in the oil
industry.' That's what I'm offering people, a free and open and
honest campaign. That's it."

He tilted his bottle back and finished it, then tossed the
empty into the backseat where it rattled around with the other
two. Jasper checked the rearview mirrors. There was a car
back there but it was too far away to tell what kind. He was
imagining all sorts of scenes, most of them having to do with
getting pulled over by the local or state pigs. Which wouldn't
have been too big a deal, really, since what the hell did he care
if another mark went on his record? *Open intoxicants* was
better than *driving under the influence*, he supposed, but either
way... whatever. It was Bantam who was drinking, and Jasper
wondered what that might mean to the man's campaign. PREZ
CANDIDATE DRUNK IN CAMPAIGN CAR, would be the
headlines. Not a good thing, probably. Well, it might endear
him to a few loonies across the nation but would likely peg him
as more than a bit wild and unpredictable and troubled and... oh
Jesus, was that the man's *real* intention here? For all that big
talk about openness and honesty and no distractions, was
getting caught out here in the middle of Iowa drunk off his ass
with a car full of empty beer bottles part of his plan? Was he
hoping it would further cement his reputation for being just a
raw-minded regular guy? Was his intention to wait until a cop
was behind them and then just reach over and grab the wheel,
get the attention of Mr. Pig and then, when they were pulled

96

over, cause a scene, dancing around like Pacino in *Dog Day Afternoon* while arguing that the passengers in a car had every right to drink beer, since they were free goddamn American citizens? Certainly another feather would be added to his bad boy cap, and wasn't that what the man was going for, to look like the complete opposite of safe plastic pseudo-people like Keith and Parsons and anyone else who'd ever run for President?

Jasper glanced over, expecting to be looked at in return, but Bantam had his head turned the other way and was staring out the window, interested in something out there.

Jasper checked the rearview mirror again. The car behind them was closer now, and gaining steadily. Could be a cop, it was still hard to tell. Maybe that's what Bantam was watching, too, staring into the side mirror and waiting to see bubble lights.

If he even *tries* to reach over and grab the wheel I will split him open like a Thanksgiving turkey.

A mile or so down the road the car was close enough to pass them and did so quickly, just a small little import driven by an acne-infested young punk with a cell phone at his ear. He flew around them and sped ahead, disappearing slowly into the coming horizon. Bantam kept staring out his window. Nothing out there but fields, a sudden thick run of forest, an old fence running on the far side of the ditch. He never looked once at the car fading into the road ahead.

Jasper sighed. The road ahead, he thought. My fellow Americans, the road ahead is filled with peril. But we will persevere and thrive, because we have the good old all-American can-do spirit, and we've been tested before, and we've always come out on top, and—

"I should try Helter again," said Bantam, but he made no move to do so. A couple minutes later he pulled out his fourth beer, cracked it, tossed the cap in the back with the empty bottles, and lifted it to his lips. As another car appeared ahead of them, approaching from the other lane, Bantam's left hand came up toward the wheel, deliberate yet slow.

Like a Thanksgiving turkey, thought Jasper, tensing, but the hand went to the stereo, not the wheel, and a moment later the other car was gone behind them and their own vehicle was filled with the sound of Seventies classic rock.

"Bad company," sang Bantam. "I can't deny, bad company till the day I die...."

97

"Oh shit, oh Jesus," Scarlett was whispering in the soft breathy voice of someone getting a good fucking. She had to deliberately concentrate on not calling out anything louder or more aggressive. She was a screamer, was Scarlett Hamm, and when the need to squeal out in ecstasy finally came she ended up pressing her mouth violently against Greg Helter's neck and using it to muffle her final gasps of pleasure. It worked, he himself barely heard her. When he too came several moments later he asked her if she was all right... meaning had she finished?

"Yes, of course," she said, barely able to get a breath now at all.

"Good."

She stepped back to look at him. "You couldn't tell?"

"I was... preoccupied."

They'd decided instinctively, and out of necessity, to use the cinematically popular but rarely-utilized-in-real-life standing position. Instinctively, because each of their passions were threatening to erupt violently and this seemed the quickest way to get things going. It was necessity that demanded it, however, because they had chosen for their liaison a location

98

that was also popular in movies but rarely utilized here in the real world: a broom closet. Simply speaking, there was absolutely no room for any position requiring them to lie down. Which was fine, standing worked well. The whole thing took less than seven minutes from start to stop... or from first crushing kiss to last zip of zipper, if you will.

"Preoccupied," she said. "Cute." Then, looking toward the door. "What if they heard us?"

He looked at the door and thought about it. "I don't know." He was straightening his clothing, as much as was possible, but in the exceedingly dim light his tie remained askew. There was a single bare light bulb hanging from the rather high ceiling of this closet, with a chain at least four feet long dangling from it, and that bulb did little to light the tiny cluttered space with anything more than a yellow glow the color of slug underbellies.

"When did you turn *that* on?" Scarlett asked as she too made herself presentable.

"Around the time I turned *you* on."

"Cute." But she giggled, she liked this kind of talk. She was even good at dirty talk herself, when the mood struck her. *Fuck me oh fuck me oh harder*, that kind of thing. This particular mood hadn't struck her here today, but that had more to do with the time allotted and the place available. She could be a kinky girl when she wanted to, but a quickie in a broom closet in some small-town Iowa historical museum didn't allow her full passions to bloom. She needed a bottle of red, perhaps some incense, a space big enough to let her arms flail out and her voice to ring as if in song. Oh yes, a church, that would have been ideal. But you take what you can get.

"All right," Helter said, and he prepared to open the door.

She reached out and took hold of his arm, stopping him. "Wait," she said, then paused, not sure how to go on. She looked into his eyes and cocked her head, searching for something in those dusty green orbs. "You didn't answer my question."

"I turned it on right after we got in here."

"Not that question, the one I asked you earlier. You know, the one you said you had to pull me aside to answer." She almost batted her eyes when she said this. Pulled her aside indeed... took her somewhere secret and quiet and away from those gathered downstairs. The broom closet was on the

99

second floor and the steps that led up to it were roped off. NO ADMITTANCE BEYOND THIS POINT, read the sign hanging there, easily stepped over by a horny and over-tired campaign manager for a third party candidate people were only just beginning to hear about on a national level and—

"Oh." That question. He looked around at the brooms and mops and sponges and cleaning supplies, and the strange amount of old clothes either hanging or lying neatly on shelves, all of it reeking of mothballs. It was a lifetime ago, that question, or at least twenty minutes.

"Come on, I really want to know."

"Why?"

"It interests me, okay? It's a mystery and I want to know the answer."

He sighed and tried to lean against one of the shelves in the closet but the whole thing wobbled and almost fell. "Oh... Jesus, really, right now? We should probably get back downstairs. I tell you what, the next time I get—"

"No, dammit, I want to know now, you promised. First you promised, then you took advantage of me in a broom closet... me, a poor helpless innocent college girl."

"Christ."

She took two steps so that she was blocking the door and looked up at him all sexy-like.

He sighed again. "All right." Looking down at her as she bit her bottom lip in that way girls had that drove him crazy, one incisor pressed carnivorously into the thick pouty flesh, he said: "All right, dammit."

"I'm waiting."

"All right." He paused. How best to tell that particular tale? "Okay. It was back in college, at Birnbaum University...."

Ten minutes later they rejoined the others downstairs, mixing back in easily, grabbing cups of coffee and nibbling on powdered donuts.

"This is a beautiful old building, hey?" asked Helter.

Bantam nodded as he looked around but didn't say anything.

The wood in the place, the frames of the windows and doors, was a gorgeous and dark variety that simply reeked of age. You looked at it and you realized it had taken in the full brunt of more than a century's worth of dusty sunlight and

100

memories. Traditions had been born and followed in this building, lives had been created and taken. It was called the Webster House, named not after the family that had built it back in 1855 but after the family that had owned it last and donated it to the Iowa Historical Society in 1984. The family that originally owned it was named Perry, and though there had been three families since them, the presence of previous occupancy you felt in the place was all theirs. When you took the guided tour of the home (which was a monster, containing eighteen rooms total and covering one full block, with a seven-acre yard cropped from the original forty-plus) and you looked into the bedrooms you could simply *feel* the presence of the Perry's that once lived there. Not ghosts, no, but the very sense of occupancy. People had lived here, had fought and fornicated and slept and dreamed and died here... like Randolph Perry himself, patriarch, dropped by a stroke as he dressed in his bedroom one fine summer morning. You didn't have to be overly sensitive to such things to feel these people... or feel the *idea* of these people. The walls of this house had soaked up their daily comings and goings, like any house does, and it took barely any imagination at all to picture them walking down the halls, the children running down the stairs, the women cooking in the kitchen, the parties that gathered in the front parlor. The idea behind the current décor of the Webster House was to make the place look like it did back in 1855, from the furniture to the clothing left on beds or hanging in open closets. Even the children's toys were era-appropriate, little wooden wagons and ugly dolls with straw-like hair, or the assortment of bells and whistles and other noise-makers seen resting thankfully silent in a corner of the kids' room. The dullest-minded man could enter this building and know immediately how the people back then had lived, could vividly imagine the most basic of their daily deeds, not just from the way the Historical Society had casually placed everything (so that it was as if the Perry's had just stepped out for a bit and might be back at any moment), but from the memory of once-vital lives that haunted the place like an odor.

"We sometimes bake bread and leave it on the kitchen table, with a knife and some homemade butter nearby," explained the President of the IHS. "It makes you feel like you're trespassing, and that any minute you might turn around and see Randolph or Margaret Perry in the doorway."

101

"Did they often have political candidates over for bread and butter?" asked Helter. He thought he was making a joke, but its effect was tempered by the fact that he was looking around hoping no one suspected anything about him and Scarlett, which made him look a bit darting and nervous, mouse-like.

"Oh yes indeed. In fact, it was said that Abraham Lincoln visited once. He was the guest of a guest, I believe, and not an acquaintance of Mr. Perry himself. This would have been in 1865, if I remember correctly. I seem to recall it being not too long before he was killed."

"President Lincoln slept here," said Helter.

"We need another Lincoln like we need a hole in our head," added Bantam.

"Where have I heard that before?"

"Does anyone need more coffee and donuts?"

Helter turned toward Scarlett. "You want some more coff—"

She was just standing there staring with a half-open mouth at Jasper Callister, who was doing his best to imitate a stone statue in the far corner of the room.

And goddamn if she didn't look sort of... intrigued.

"Shit," whispered Helter. He didn't like the look in her eyes, it frightened him with its lustful corruption and decadence. What did I just make love to? he wondered. She had seemed like a normal girl until this moment, and now she struck him as something else entirely. A symbol, maybe, but of what? Something dark and rancid, that was all he knew. Something dark and rancid and foul.

And don't be foolish: that was not love you made. Far from it.

He tried to remember when she said she had to go back to school, and he hoped it was soon. He felt ill at the very thought of her... and at the thought of the secret he had revealed.

"You all right?" Bantam asked, looking at him.

"Never better," he answered, and then he left the old house for some fresh air.

*

"You know," Bantam said to Jasper. "My folks owned about seven acres of the most gorgeous oak trees I've ever seen. I used to love those trees, I'd go out there and spend hours around them, climbing around, or just sitting on the ground and staring up to where the branches pricked the sky. And then…" He lifted his fifth bottle to his lips. "And then my dad died, my mom remarried this shmuck, and this shmuck went and sold them and they were all cut down. You know what's there now? Four houses. Four goddamn houses. How the hell can you put four houses on seven acres? What kind of living is *that*?"

Jasper shook his head. He didn't know, he was just the driver. The designated driver, apparently. The whole interior of the car smelled like beer and whenever they took a corner the empties in the back would clank against each other like a dull-toned wind-chime.

Bantam, apparently not feeling the alcohol at all, was pontificating freely now, a sometimes wild and sometimes flat improv of a speech which to Jasper alternated between interesting and dull every other sentence. Take this, for instance, this rap about oak trees. Who gave a shit?

He looked out at the sudden thick stretch of woods they were passing, and which had inspired Bantam's oak tree memory. An ancient wooden fence, run through with sagging barbed wire, stood on the far side of the ditch, and then the woods began, trapping shadows and leading the eyes onward and inward towards a seemingly ever-spiraling labyrinth of dark designs and periodic little splatters of sunlight. It was hypnotic, driving down this suddenly ragged stretch of country highway and looking into those gnarled and scratching trees as they flashed past between darkness and light, darkness and light. If a man wasn't careful he might lose control completely and go flying off the asphalt. The wire of the old fence was tight in some places, but mostly it hung low, even fell to and below the ground, like the strings of a maligned guitar, and he found himself watching and waiting for it to rise up again from the dirt. Careful boy, careful… you'll stare out there too long and get lost.

103

"Flag burning, for Christ's sake," Bantam was saying. "Would you believe there are actually people out there who think that's a serious issue? Like someone burning a piece of cloth died red white and blue is a matter of such importance we need to alter the Constitution? Like that means anything compared to starvation, disease, the poisoning of the air and water we put in our kids' mouths? The day someone stands in front of my face and tells me eye-to-eye that that is an issue which matters as much as *those* is the day you see me break someone's goddamn head open."

Can a man be driven to madness by the act of driving? Likely. Endless asphalt, stretching unwinding spreading ever onward... it was always *there*, always in front of you. There was always *more* of it, you couldn't turn your head without seeing a line of it, black or gray or turning slowly to cracks and weeds but *there* nonetheless, every square inch of our planet streaked with the stuff. You'd think mankind wouldn't be happy until every single last corner of the earth was accessible. Screw green space and wilderness, who the hell needs *that*? Who the hell needs woods, prairies, simple goddamn *fields*? Did it make any difference if a kid grew up with access to trees for climbing, hills for sledding, fields for running, or would he turn out exactly the same surrounded by roads and highways and concrete and steel? Well fuck yeah it made a difference. A kid who grows up knowing the joys found in secret dark woods stands a better chance of staying sane and rational than the kid whose playground was pavement and who climbed nothing other than fire escapes. People who have never experienced (or who have forgotten) the pleasures found in a simple little corner of Mother Nature are worthless, soulless automatons, and that was a pure scientific proven goddamn fact. Except....

Well, yes, of course, except the kid who grew up in a rural area would most likely go insane when he realizes that every year, every day, there was more and more asphalt everywhere he looked. So was it better to remember the green and no longer have it, or to have never known it and miss it not at all?

For his part, Jasper looked out at the asphalt in front of him and cursed it. He'd take the memories, of course, all those sweet days of tree climbing and playing in the swamps, but he knew damn well the thought of someone looking at, say, these fields and these dark woods and thinking nothing other than *What a great place for a mall/subdivision/parking lot* was enough to cause his mind to sour. It certainly wasn't the same mind he'd had as a child. It was bitter, coarsened, maybe not quite fully sane....

He thought of suburbia stretching outward, spreading like a plague over the land. Urban sprawl? How do you stop urban sprawl? It was simple: first you take a gun....

"Let me ask you something," Bantam said.

"Shoot."

"Would you vote for me?"

Jasper sighed. Jesus.

"I mean it, honestly. If it was me or Keith or me or Parsons, would I get your vote?"

Jasper looked down at the two six-packs on the floor by Bantam's feet, one of which now held only one bottle. Then he looked at Bantam himself, who was looking back expectantly, his face unshaven, his skin slightly tan but apparently in need of a deep cleansing, some good and solid wrinkles by his eyes suggesting a life spent outdoors. Dorito crumbs hung in the corner of his mouth, the smell of beer floated on his breath.

"Yeah," Jasper said. "Sure, what the hell."

Bantam smiled. "Am I the lesser of two evils?"

"You're the lesser of many evils. I'd vote for you, you could do the job. Look at the idiots and assholes who've done it in the past, what harm could you possibly do?" He thought a second. "What would you do about urban sprawl?"

"Urban sprawl is phallic displacement," Bantam said simply. "Real men don't need to piss on everything like mangy pathetic insecure dogs. Real men and women know when enough is enough, and have the strength and intelligence to say so. 'Growth!' some people say. 'We must grow and develop and get bigger!' Why, though? They never say why. Because there is no reason. The kind of growth they want, which is not at all an intelligent or long-sighted sort of growth, is a hideous mutation of the meaning of the word *progress*. It's a distortion. An ugly deformity."

Now why should that make Jasper think of his old buddies in upper management?

"Look at us," Bantam said. "Two Midwestern boys driving down an Iowa highway, not a care in the world, peacefully discussing the issues of the day and how we plan on fixing them. This reminds me of when I was a kid, driving around the countryside with some beer, some tunes, maybe a girl or three

105

in the backseat, buzzed up and rocking like there was no tomorrow. You remember those days?"

Jasper didn't answer, he was thinking of something else entirely now. Nothing good, you know. Nothing good.

*

The burial went fairly quickly, just the digging of a suitable hole, the placement of the body, and then the filling in of the grave. Only one small little moment of silence was had with bowed heads after the sheet-wrapped body had been set in its final resting place, otherwise there were no speeches, no prayers, no songs. Apparently this is what the dead man would have preferred. It would never be remembered as a beautiful ceremony, by either the family or the strangers present. The afternoon sky was a dreary Poe-gray, there was a new cold thinness to the air that threatened to crack the bones, and a strong smell of manure came from the closest field, ripe and alive in the nostrils. It was a utilitarian burial, no frills attached.

"That's done," said Ricky when they were walking away. "I could use a cold one." His mother gave him a look. "What? He woulda wanted me to have a beer in his name."

The widow sighed and kept walking. The three anonymous men had offered to drive her out in the pickup they'd used to haul the old man in, but she said it was their dad who was dead not her and there was no way in hell she couldn't walk across a damn field. Bury *me* the day I can't, she said.

We'll take you up on that, said Tapper. You break your leg in a furrow and we'll throw you in there with him.

"Thank god the ground was thawed," Ricky said, kicking at it a little. "We'd never have been able to dig a hole a few weeks ago."

Helter and Lisa and Hamm stayed back a little, taking this all in silently. They hadn't wanted to take part in the burial but it was impossible to say no, so they'd gone, stood there reverently, felt like idiots for not helping with the shoveling (their half-hearted offer to assist was turned down in unison by Ricky, Tapper, Uncle Jim, and the other three anonymous men who'd shown up), and paid their respects to both the dead man and his widow. Now they were each wondering how to respectfully get back on the road.

"You know, he once ran for President himself," Ricky said, looking back at them. "Kinda half-assed, of course, just a big joke, but he did."

"Ricky," his sister whispered, like she was going to chastise him for bringing this up, but then she simply kept walking in silence, watching where her feet went on the field and keeping close to her mother.

"Had to be back in '80," Ricky continued. "I was just a kid. He put up flyers at the bar and around town, put up a huge sign in the front yard, had some high-school kid make up a pamphlet with all his positions in it. Hell, he even got mentioned in the *Des Moines Register*. I remember when this newspaper guy came to the farm to interview him. They sat at the kitchen table and Pa told jokes the whole time. What the hell ever possessed him to do that for, Ma?"

"Your father was like that," was all she said.

"What were some of his positions?" Helter asked. It was pretty much the first time he had spoken since they'd started out for the burial site.

"Oh hell, you know, pro-farm stuff. Agriculture things. Against gun control, against us meddling all around the world. Parades, goddamn I remember parades too. Pa loved parades and one of his things was he wanted there to be a law requiring every community to have a parade once a week. Crazy things like that. He said nothing bad happens when there's a parade, so this country should be filled with them."

"Tell that to Kennedy," Hamm whispered to Lisa.

"It was all just a joke, just to rile folks up. He musta been bored that year, wanted to get known as the local kook, I guess."

"Your father always did things his own way, for his own reasons," said the old woman. "That's all there was to it." She was walking amazingly well now, quickening her pace. "A man like that doesn't come around all the time. He's the last of a kind."

"Amen," said Ricky.

"The mold was broken the day he was born," agreed Uncle Jim.

For his part, Tapper spat down to the ground, then squinted up at the gray sky and said nothing.

After the claustrophobic and insular world of the car, walking in this open field under the gigantic gray sky was like

107

being set free after a prison term. Both Helter and Lisa were looking around at the immensity of the openness around them, the field stretching back what seemed like miles until it touched the strips of dense woods that outlined it, the farm they were walking to looking small, Fisher Price small, and the highway they'd been on not too long ago resting benign and quiet in that whole other world way over there. The quiet of the open air, too, was odd after the constant hum of the car. There was a wind, yes, but it had died somewhat and now only blew into their faces every few minutes. It was rather shocking to be walking here in this open landscape, surrounded by nothing, under a sky thick with clouds but as open as interstellar space. For Helter it was familiar from all the friends he'd had who lived on farms. For Lisa it was as familiar as home.

Hamm kept looking back at the burial site, which was at the crest of a small hill that swelled out from one of those runs of thick woods and which overlooked not only the largest field but the entirety of the farm itself, including Flotsam Creek. It had been a peaceful place, a good site for a grave. One imagines it would be an ideal meditative and reflective place come crisp sunny spring days. Zen-like, even. Perhaps the old woman would go there, set some flowers down, have private conversations with the man she'd been married to for more than forty years.

"What will they do when this area becomes a sub-division?" Hamm said softly. "Dig up the old coot or let the bulldozers find him?"

"Shhh!" said Lisa, giving him what was becoming known as the Look.

Helter said nothing but looked back at the site. There was a tree there he hadn't noticed before, a medium-sized thing he thought was a young oak... but he didn't know trees. It looked like an oak, thick trunk, branches widening out into a complex tangled mushroom cap of sticks. With no leaves it was impossible to say for sure. It sat twenty feet from the sight of the grave itself, far back enough to be unnoticed as they'd stood there but close enough to be a significant addition to the place of burial, a necessary detail in that small, personal landscape. As he looked at it he could now completely visualize someone (the old woman, Ricky or his sister) sitting under its shade as they contemplated mortality and fate and whatever else it was people thought about at gravesides. There were worse places to

108

be buried, he now realized. In a cemetery you are just one among many... they were like subdivisions for the dead. A place like this, something private and secret and away from the rest of the living and the rotting, seemed so much more ideal. When you visited a cemetery it was all about *How do my flowers compare with the others? Does this grave look cared for?* A place like *this*, on the other hand, was made for thought, reflection, contemplation. There was really no comparison.

Ricky had turned and looked back at Lisa. "Did I hear right before... you grew up on a farm?"

She must have been deep in thought herself because she looked momentarily confused, frowning at him like he'd asked her the strangest question in the world. "Yeah, that's right. In Illinois."

"FIB, huh?"

She smiled politely. "That's right."

"Only the B doesn't stand for Bastard," Hamm said.

She again gave him the Look, snapping her head back and glaring at him with slitted eyes.

"Cow?" asked Ricky.

Lisa's head spun back to glare at *him*. *"What?"*

"What kind of farm? Cows? Produce?"

"Oh... oh... we had some cows. Dairy. Other stuff, too... Dad tried all sorts of things over the years."

"He still farming?"

"No." She looked like she was going to add more but did not.

"I didn't see any animals on your farm," Hamm said to Ricky. "You don't own any?"

"No, we do. Look," and he stopped and pointed off to the left. They could just make out the corner of a field there, and several dark shapes standing motionless in the middle of it.

Hamm stopped and squinted over. "Oh. When do you milk them?"

Ricky laughed a little. "Shit, the closest we come to milking them is when we swallow 'em down with a *glass* of milk." He and Tapper laughed at this. Uncle Jim paid it no mind.

The old woman must have heard something, even though she was quite a ways ahead of everyone else except her daughter, because she stopped and looked back at her son.

"You stop messin' with those folks," she said.

"I'm not messing with anybody. They're not city folks, Ma. *She's* a farm girl, just like you." He looked at Lisa. "I'm sorry... I forget your name."

"Lisa."

"Lisa's a farm girl," he called up to his mother, but she was walking again. He sighed. "Shit, she never cuts me any slack. I might as well be ten years old."

"She's going through a lot right now," Lisa said.

Ricky stood there watching his mom walk off, then he shrugged. "Yeah, I s'pose." He kicked at the ground a bit and started walking again. "I s'pose...."

Lisa looked at Helter, but Helter was again staring back at the burial site, this odd melancholic yet hopeful expression on his face... she would later write that he looked like he was "dreaming of such a place for himself."

She was dead on.

There are worse places to be buried, he was thinking. It's something you don't really ever think about, unless you happen to be that sort of depressed or gloomy type of individual. He remembered being a kid and visiting his grandparent's graves... with his grandparents. They had picked out their sites several years back and every now and then would take the half-hour drive to the Holy Trinity Cemetery just to take the short walk back to the peaceful far end of the place and gaze upon the little nondescript plots of lawn where some day they would both rest. Kind of odd, he remembered thinking. There were headstones in place already, engraved with their names and birth-dates:

MARTIN PAUL HELTER 1912-

LUCILLE LYNN (THOMPSON) HELTER 1915-

It was that last space following the dash that always bugged little Greg Helter the most, that unwritten fateful year lying somewhere *out there*, just waiting for them, like a black cloud on the horizon, a great dark shape hovering over their heads. And yet it never seemed to bother Martin or Lucille themselves. Indeed, when they stood looking down at their future burial sites they always had smiles on their faces... small, strange smiles of satisfaction, like this was some grand accomplishment. They're actually saving us shitloads of money, his mom said on more than one occasion. Funerals and burials can be such pains in the ass. And for years Helter had always thought that was the reason for the looks of satisfaction

110

the old couple always wore, but he knew better now. There was such mystery to death, such overwhelming uncertainty about the whole process, so it had to feel good knowing there was at least *one* thing they could control. They might not know how or when they would go, but they could be certain exactly where they would eventually be laid to rest.

And they'd be side by side, together forever, and blah, blah, blah.

"You okay?" Lisa asked him.

"What? Yeah, yeah, of course." He came back to the present world of the living with a slight sense of vertigo. Thinking about death on such a gray afternoon was fitting and appropriate, of course, but afterwards, realizing that that had indeed been what you were doing, was kind of unnerving. The living should rarely think about death. Leave thoughts of dying and rotting to the priests and nuns and Goth kids of the world, the rest of us should simply *live*. Death will get here soon enough. It's the only thing that never misses its appointments.

"What are you thinking about?" asked Lisa. She seemed honestly interested... but she was a journalist, remember, and Helter wondered if his thoughts of death and suicide were things he wanted her writing about.

"I should try Bantam," he said, and pulled out his cell-phone. NO SIGNAL, the screen told him. "Shit."

Soon enough they were back at the farm, and the burial site was nothing but a vague area off in the distance ("way back there a bit," as Ricky had originally put it).

"Anyone want coffee or something?" Ricky's sister asked, turning to look at everyone.

"We should probably get back on the road," Hamm said, and he looked at Lisa and Helter for back-up. "Right guys?"

"What for?" Tapper asked. "Road's not going anywhere."

The new widow didn't stop to listen to this conversation, she just marched right on into her farmhouse, as steady and strong as ever, as if this day was no different from any other. A steady, defiant, proud, independent woman, was Mrs. Withers, perhaps more so now than even that morning.

Ricky's sister (and goddamnit, what *was* her name?) was smiling at them, but the men were looking at the three out-of-staters with vaguely aggressive expressions.

"Theresa makes a mean cuppa joe," said Tapper. "Gotta cut it with a knife. You look like you could use some."

111

Theresa, that was it.

Uncle Jim stood with arms folded over his chest, his white shirt, tie, and pants spotted here and there with dirt and grass stains. Burial is a dirty business. "You need to stay, have some coffee. We've all been through a lot today, we're all sharing in this. Stay and visit."

Voice quavering a bit as he looked at Helter, Hamm said: "Well...."

Lisa looked up at Helter too: "Shouldn't you get in contact with Bantam? Don't we have to meet him somewhere?"

Helter was thinking about that *burial is a dirty business* phrase. The words *like politics* seemed to naturally want to follow it, so much so that he wondered if that was indeed already some well-known quote, something by Jefferson, Franklin, Rousseau, maybe Voltaire. And this thought opened up a whole host of sudden ruminations on the nature of modern day American politics, all of them swarming his mind at once, crashing in on his brain in one cacophonous firestorm, no single one of them able to be grasped but each calling out to be looked at, considered, pondered, like bratty, needy, attention-starved children in desperate need of a quick Ritalin fix. And they were all bad thoughts, of course, every last one of them. If he'd learned anything in his short time working in American politics it was that very little good could come from being involved in it, at any level. It blackened things, rotted them, at the very least ran them down. Look at him, hooking up with Hamm's sister like that, that was something he would never have done back in the real world, it just wasn't his nature. This thing called Politics was nothing if not a force for dulling and muting and—

"Well?" Lisa asked.

Helter came out of his thoughts and looked at her and the Iowans. "I'm sorry," he said. "I guess I zoned out there for a moment."

"I was saying you should come in for a cup of joe, talk a little," said Tapper.

"Oh," Helter said. Thoughts of an electric coffee jolt zigzagged before his mind. "Oh. Sure. Sure, what the hell."

So in they went, and within ten minutes were each sipping cups of the hottest, blackest, thickest coffee they'd ever had. The house no longer smelled of manure and cigarettes and old woman's perfume, but the woodsmoke odor was still there,

112

spicy and comforting, bringing to mind a dozen or so memories in all three out-of-staters. There was just something about the smell of burning wood to make you feel at home, safe and secure and warm, your parents in the livingroom, a cat dozing on the sofa, a dog lying on the floor, everything right with the world. Helter for one would take deep sniffs of the coffee whenever he brought it to his mouth, just to keep from getting used to the woodsmoke smell and losing it forever. One doesn't want to get acclimated to an odor like that, one wants to taste it with every breath. When he took the mug from his nose the warm smell of burning wood would be new again.

They were back sitting in the livingroom, each of them on the couch, staring at Tapper and Uncle Jim, who were in the other chairs. Ricky was standing in the doorway to the kitchen (again), while the other three men had gone back to their own farms. Work never ends for a farmer, though it might get pushed off a bit for a burial.

A long time went by with no one speaking. The only sounds were the sipping of coffee and the clearing of throats. What the hell do you say in a situation like this? The only thing was to ask about the dead man.

"How old was he?" asked Lisa.

Tapper frowned. "Who?"

"Your...." She hesitated and then looked at Ricky. "Your father."

"Seventy-something."

"Seventy-seven," said Tapper.

"Nine," added Uncle Jim. He had his tie off now, and his dirty shirt was unbuttoned disco-low.

"Seventy-seven, goddamnit," Tapper said.

"Seventy-nine and don't make me prove it."

"Prove it."

Uncle Jim sighed but made no effort to stand.

"I think he's right," Ricky finally said. "Seventy-nine sounds right."

"When was he born?" asked Hamm.

"Jesus, who the hell knows?" answered Tapper.

Ricky shrugged and stared down into his coffee. "Thirties."

"I seem to remember him saying just last summer that he was seventy-seven. Jesus, when *is* his birthday?"

"September 12."

113

"Yeah, that's right. It was in August, and he said he was gonna be seventy-seven. I remember because he said if seven was lucky, double-sevens oughta be *really* lucky."

Uncle Jim sighed again. "He didn't know how old he was himself, then. He was seventy-nine."

"Did he grow up on this farm?" Lisa asked.

"His folks had a place just up the road a ways. It's not there anymore."

"Foundation is," added Ricky.

"This place went up in the fifties, I believe. But yeah, he spent all his life in these parts. I'm not even sure he ever left Iowa."

"He never wanted to. Said all he ever needed was right here, if you can't get it from your friends and neighbors it ain't worth getting."

"He went to Wisconsin once," Uncle Jim said. He was picking at the dried bits of earth on his pants. "A wedding or something back in the early Eighties. 1983."

"How do you remember all that shit?" Ricky asked him.

Uncle Jim just looked over calmly, with the unblinking eyes of a statue, though there was a devilish little smile lifting his mouth as well. "It's called brains."

"Brains," Ricky huffed, and went back to gazing into his coffee cup.

"Seventy-nine years all in the same place," Lisa marveled.

Tapper shrugged. "More common than you think, I bet."

"It's an old-school attitude," Uncle Jim said, looking over at her. "You were probably raised to think the opposite."

"She was raised on a farm like this," Hamm said.

Uncle Jim's eyes lit up. "That's right, I forgot. So you must know people like old Frank."

She shrugged. "I guess, yeah."

"What kind of farm, again?" asked Ricky.

"Dairy," she said, and sort of slunked down in the couch.

"Dairy. That's right."

"Your mom makes excellent coffee," Helter said, sitting forward suddenly and looking at Ricky.

"Folgers makes the coffee," Ricky said. "Ma just adds the water."

"It's the well water you're tasting," Tapper said. "You must be used to all those chemicals in city water."

114

"Chlorine, Fluoride," said Uncle Jim, and when Ricky looked at him he added: "Brains."

"Water here is sweet and pure." Tapper lifted his cup to his lips and drank the rest of his coffee down. This done, he sighed and looked toward the kitchen. "Where *is* that woman, anyway? She and that sister of yours working somewhere?"

Ricky looked into the kitchen, then shrugged but said nothing.

"Jesus, even the death of her husband can't get that woman to sit still for a minute."

"You sit still you die," said Ricky dryly, and at that Uncle Jim and Tapper started laughing.

"Shit, *yes*, that's something he said all the time. You sit still you die."

"Words of wisdom from Frank Withers."

"How about: useless as tits on a motor?"

"That's right," Tapper said. "Or: you got to dance with what brung you?"

"Up and at 'em."

Tapper leaned forward and whispered: "Drop your cocks and grab your socks."

Ricky nearly fell out of his chair. "Oh sweet Jesus...."

"All right," said Uncle Jim. "All right, there's a woman present." He looked ashamedly at Lisa, who wasn't paying attention anyway. She was writing in her notebook. "You taking notes on all this nonsense?" he asked her.

She looked up. "I'm sorry?"

"You writing a book on all of us?"

She glanced at what she'd been writing, then looked back at him with nearly the identical look of mild shame he'd just worn. "Just going over my notes on the whole day."

"Ahh." He nodded, then looked at Helter. "So tell us about what you guys are doing. Must be something, traveling around doing all this political nonsense."

Helter sighed. "Yeah, it's something."

"Must be interesting."

"Not really. Mostly driving. Going here, listening to a speech, going there and listening to a speech. I don't recommend it."

"Beats workin' for a living," said Tapper.

Helter just nodded.

"So... what's the name of your man again?"

115

"Bantam. John Bantam."

Uncle Jim shook his head. "Never heard of him. Republican, Democrat?"

"Gadfly."

"Gadfly? What the hell is that?"

Helter shifted himself on the couch, looking uncomfortable. "It's his own party. A third party. It's just... it's just his party."

"What's he closer to, Republican or Democrat?"

Helter shrugged. "He's somewhere in between."

"Playing it safe in the middle, then."

Helter started to say more, then settled for: "Sort of."

"Well hell," said Tapper. "Tell us what the bastard believes, then. Maybe we'll vote for him."

Helter looked at Lisa and Hamm. He was the campaign manager, yes, but all of his energy for the job had gone out the window... or into the grave with the old man, perhaps. He thought of the phone conversation he'd had with Hamm back when he'd first talked Hamm into joining the campaign.

I have an opportunity for you.

I have a job....

That web shit isn't changing the world. *This* will change the world.

Porn?

No, goddamnit. Listen, I'm joining a Presidential campaign.

A *what*?

A Presidential campaign.

Okay, interesting. Washington is... well, it's no New York, but....

I want you to join with me.

What the fuck for?

Dissemination of information.

What about... artificial dissemination? Isn't that how you came along?

I'm serious. You know people. You can be our Manager of Info, or something.

It's not... it's not *you* who's running?

Of course not.

Thank god. So who you working for? Parsons? You seem like a Parsons guy.

No. Bantam. John Thomas Bantam.

116

Okay, okay, hang on. (There was the sound of shuffling papers, keys clicking on a keyboard). I'm Googling him right now, hang on, let me check this guy out....

You won't find anything. That's part of the problem.

There's a John A. Bantam in... New Mexico.

No....

John William Bantam from Mobile?

No, listen, he's a nobody. You won't find anything on him.

Sounds like a real winner you've picked. Good luck with that.

It's not that kind of campaign...

Now he looked at Hamm and Lisa and saw no opportunity for support there: Hamm had a deer-in-the-headlights look and Lisa had gone back to her notebook, perhaps writing down this very conversation word-for-word to be used in a particularly awkward chapter of her book. Shit.

"He's a..." he began, and then yawned, a great gaping yawn like a snake readjusting its jaws. Coffee or not he felt exhausted, so beaten down it might as well be him lying out there in the cold Iowa ground. It was catching up to him, he realized. He'd gotten what, a half-dozen decent nights of sleep on this adventure? That was no way to live. It was bound to catch up. Like Death itself. Like... like politics? Shit, he was losing himself here, his mind was turning to mush, odd things swirled in his brain, meaningless sentences (*mine is a mind of mishmash and manure*), half-formed thoughts (*really need to call him*), memories (*there's this guy who beat up my sister*), and any one of them, spoken now, aloud and into this room, would make these people look at him and think—

"You look like one tired sombitch," Tapper said.

Yeah, and there was more to it than that. The world seemed to bleed and melt and ooze out its viscera of color. Was he about to pass out? Sure felt that way. The far wall of the livingroom came at him suddenly and then flew back away, a million miles... and the faces of the farmers grew large and small. Something smelled like a freshly washed pillow case brought in from the clothesline. Gramma, can I help? You run along dear, you go play. Something else smelled bad, like shit. Mom, Buffy made a mess in the hallway again.

He felt himself nodding.

"You okay?" Lisa's voice, and her hand on his knee.

117

"He should lay down," said another. "Take him down the hall, he should lay for a while."

"I...."

Within a shifting moment or two (watery, blurring, like rain on glass) he was down some dark hallway and lying on a bed that smelled of sweetness and mothballs, the side of his face against a pillow so soft it was like (*look at the clouds, Greggy, see how they look like animals?*) it was like (*that's it, just hold it there, we got to keep the bleeding down*) it was like air.

One last voice following him down into darkness: "Jesus... what have you folks been doing to yourselves?"

Sleep now, pumpkin. Sleep and dream well.

There were an ugly series of blood drops leading into the building and down the hall, and no matter how hard the janitorial department of Birnbaum U tried to remove them those stains would stay, to some degree or other, for years to come, fading only slowly into the carpet, dulled by dirt and dust and merging effortlessly into other stains like puke and liquor and all the assorted essential liquids of college life. On this night the blood was fresh, bright and evil looking, thick half-dollar-sized droplets every two feet or so. They looked big and thick enough to have been audible when they landed, though it was two in the morning when they were created and there would have been no one around to hear them, other than the bleeder herself.

She sat in her dark dorm room for twenty minutes, until the door opened and the light was flicked on.

"Oh my fucking god!" said the young man in the doorway.

"Turn the light off," she said, consonants swollen and vowels thick from her fattened lips.

"Susie—"

"*Off!*"

He killed the light and went to her.

119

"When I was a much younger man I saw a guy with his head split open," Bantam said. "Some other guy had hit him with a bat. He was lying in this bar, under a pool table, just lying there in a big pool of blood. I remember thinking that if he stayed there too long that blood might coagulate and he'd get stuck to the floor. Then I thought: where the hell does a guy find a bat in a bar? Where *are* we?"

Jasper was barely listening, and the fact that that last question was directed at him went unnoticed. He was staring out at what looked like a much different Iowa than the one they'd been in just a few miles back: this one here was less open, was rather thick with woods, in fact. A sudden blossoming of trees had swelled on either side of them, partially hiding the old houses that sat within. The ditches were deeper and looked wet, and the road itself was older, less visited, heavy with crows' feet at its center line... which was itself practically nonexistent, just a pale yellow memory fading with each moment into the asphalt. He liked roads like this, their slow decay, their neglect, the patience with which they sat and took in the passage of time, the deaths of deer and possums and coons and humans they occasionally saw. This wasn't the highway, they'd left that a ways back, but when? And why? He couldn't say for sure. And though he knew exactly where that highway was (over there to the right) he wasn't so sure he knew how to get back to it.

"Where *are* we?" Bantam asked again.

"Iowa."

"When did we leave the highway?"

"1846."

"What?"

A bit of trivia from school, remembered now for no reason, recalled like it meant something: Iowa entered the Union in 1846, a free state. Meaning, it fought on the side of freeing the slaves in the Civil War. Meaning... nothing. History was history, that was all. What good was it to know that some states fought *for* slavery and others fought *against* it? What good was it to know any of that out here, in the middle of the country, driving aimlessly down rotting old roads with a nobody-candidate for President in the passenger seat and the

120

smell of beer hanging thick in the air between them? Some things were useless to know, that was all.

The road curved, then rose on a hill, the trees thickening even more... and my god this would be beautiful when the leaves came, a good goddamn little forest, with those half-hidden homes adding just the right quaintness to reek of *Americana*. When the hill ended they came across a river, wide with snowmelt, a cold dark blue in the fading afternoon light... soon to be black, of course, flat and without depth or weight. Jasper slowed as they crossed the bridge and looked up the river, seeing where it curved and disappeared. There was such mystery in rivers, such myth. He recalled a young woman in his hometown who jumped off a bridge just like this, killing herself in the name of love. Rumor had it she'd left a note that said she was giving herself to the heart of the river because she knew it would accept her, unlike all the boys she'd known who had pushed her away. Crazy what people will do. Once a man climbed the water tower and threatened to jump off, only to be talked down hours later by his mother. Once some kids entered a high school and started shooting people. Once a madman took out a President, and another took out his brother, and yet still another started a war that brought forth the end of the whole goddamn world.

"What does 1846 mean?" Bantam asked.

Jasper shook his head. Iowa. He thought of Iowa. Could he live here? He thought about Milwaukee and everything he had waiting for him back there and he realized he had nothing tethering him, he could probably live here as well as he could live in Milwaukee, New York, Paris, Amsterdam. Bantam had called him a Wisconsin boy and it was true, sort of: he was *from* Wisconsin, yes, but he was not *of* Wisconsin. And right now he knew the world was open to him, he could pack up his meager belongings (or just leave them altogether) and head out, make a new home in some distant town or city, set down roots if he wanted or just stay there for a while and then move on again. He could do anything he wanted, and for a moment he felt the hot-cool rush of freedom shivering through his spine. Yes, he was free, maybe for the first time ever. And yet... Jesus, was anyone ever free? It seemed highly likely that he would just end up in another town, working another goddamn stupid job and pissing off yet another set of asshole bosses. Then he'd be fired again and forced to move on, perhaps

121

ending up once again thinking these same thoughts in some place just like this one here. Jesus, how many Iowas *were* there? How many Iowas could he stand? A person might go nuts traveling the world finding nothing but the same old Same-Old everywhere they went.

His knuckles were aching now, reliving old memories, old wounds... not all of them his own. For each ache in his curled fingers there was a corresponding ache in someone else's face or gut. He took his left hand off the wheel and made it into a fist, finding it hard to do so without the whole hand trembling and the joints feeling like fire. He forced the fingers into a tight fist and once it was made the aches and trembling subsided. The fist felt good, comforting, pleasurable. Natural. He glanced at it and saw a series of scars running over the skin, including a few deep and wide ones he thought he could remember making. Good times? Not all of them. Some of those times were simply necessary. Sometimes you had to break something or someone just to get by, just to make yourself get through one more miserable day. He looked at the fist again and wondered which one of those scars had led him to this bodyguard gig in the first place, which one had tied him, however loosely, to Greg Helter from Birnbaum University. If it wasn't for that one night all those years ago he wouldn't be here now, feeling depressed and misplaced in the heart of Iowa, driving a doomed Presidential candidate around in a rental car filled with empty beer cans. Violence giveth and violence taketh away. He thought it was the zig-zag scar running away from his ring finger, but he really had no way of knowing.

He looked over at Bantam and remembered something Helter had told him long ago: Bantam was a guy who would change everything.

Yes, but for who?

The radio was still on, so low Jasper couldn't hear it (not over the sudden ringing in his ears). He realized it was on only because Bantam was singing softly to some mid-Seventies soft rock piece of shit ballad about mountains and girls and open spaces and everything that really didn't exist anymore. Things like freedom, love, openness, sun-dappled leaves, youth and health and optimism and happiness and the future like an ocean before you. Maybe that was something Bantam actually believed could be had again, maybe he saw himself as a return to all that. And maybe he had honest hopes that he could do it, that he could lead the charge and be a fresh face and fresh voice for a better future. He spoke off the cuff, yes, he spoke freely and openly and often coarsely, but there was always a positive tone to his words. He bitched about the uber-rich and the standard cookie-cutter politician types who have choked the country for far too long, yet with each statement of bitterness and anger was, of course, an implied corresponding love of its opposite. He was without doubt a good man, a thoughtful man, a man of passion and dedication... but could anything really be done to change the way things are, even by such a man? Jasper thought about this and couldn't see how it was possible. There was too much apathy, too much anger... and yet not enough, really, not enough to spark a revolution.

This should be a time of change and rebellion and the blossoming of freedom and joy, but it wasn't, it couldn't be. This was just like yesterday, just like all the yesterdays that had ever been.

By the time Bantam asked his next question Jasper was again no longer listening. What was the point in listening anyway, you miss a question now and it didn't matter, the same one would be asked later... because nothing changed and nothing was ever resolved.

His knuckles ached. His chest ached. Every goddamn scar on his body ached like they had something they wanted to say.

*

Hamm and Tapper were getting drunk on Milwaukee's Best. They were alone in the livingroom, everyone else had ditched them. It's not my beer, said Tapper, sneaking off to the kitchen, but what the hell. He brought in six right off the bat and they started drinking quickly, eventually getting to the point where they were talking like old buddies, getting all giggly and loud, their language degrading minute by minute, the empty cans at their feet like dead dogs. From somewhere in the distance they could hear (though they weren't listening) the sound of sawing and hammering. If they'd really been paying attention they'd have heard the sound of Helter snoring down the hall, passed out at last, lost in a dream.

(*killing the light and going to her. And blood, so much blood, so much blood you could hear it hit the floor, so*)

"Life is strange," said Tapper philosophically, examining his beer can the way you study wine in a glass.

"How so?" asked Hamm.

Tapper looked over at him. "It's just... strange. Strange *strange*. You know?"

"Strange *strange*?"

Tapper nodded, sucked on his beer, opened another. After a good long sip he saw Hamm looking out the livingroom window, studying the farm and the fields.

"I hate farming, myself," he said.

Hamm looked at him. "Huh?"

"Can't stand it." He shook his head like the very thought of it put a bad taste in his mouth. "I grew up with that shit. Bring in the cows, milk the cows, feed the cows, milk the cows, take care of the cows. Bale hay, drive a tractor, drive a combine, clean up the barn, kick a cat." He shook his head again. "Nope, not for me. By the time I was seventeen I'd had enough. Dropped out of school and went to work for Mein's. That's a cheese factory ten miles North. Worked there for a few years, until I had enough of that shit too."

"So now what do you do?"

"Manager of Dave's Hardware." He said this like Hamm would recognize the name. "I get up at a decent hour, none of that before daylight shit. Farmers have to have a certain craziness to do what they do, keep the hours they keep, for the pay they get. Which is usually nothing, really, just enough to keep going... sometimes barely that."

Hamm nodded, finished off his latest beer, set the empty on the floor, looked out the window again.

"Getting dark," he said.

Tapper sighed. "No sir, I keep human hours now. Banker's hours, they say. Healthy hours, I call them."

Hamm nodded, only half listening.

"Life is strange," Tapper said again. "Strange *strange*."

Hamm looked at the darkness.

*

The shadows at dusk crawled over the sidewalks, dark reaching fingers on the concrete, spreading out to grasp the night that was already pooling in the yards. The sky bid farewell to the sun with great splashes of color, bleeding rips in the blue flesh of the day. It was the best time, Helter knew. He would sit out on the front steps and watch night come in like a tide. That neighborhood was peaceful back then, quiet to the point of silence, as motionless as a graveyard. On some evenings in the heart of summer you could hear televisions being clicked on, the distant but definite sound of news or game show themes. A few hours later it was Johnny Carson.

There were no kids in the neighborhood then, so he played alone mostly. On the rare occasion he played basketball with his brother, long games of one-on-one or Horse, tossing air-balls toward the hoop over the garage. Once upon a time there had been a net with that hoop, but it had lost its battle with time and rain and even now was probably still rotting under those front bushes.

Those front bushes were still there, too, he saw them the last time he passed by the old house, gnarled and thick old things that didn't take to pruning too readily, that seemed to grow with chips on their shoulders, hugging the house like guardians or captors, relinquishing nothing. As a very young child he used to hide between them and the house, just barely fitting in there and trying not to laugh as his mother called his name or his brother ran around with a water balloon with his name on it. He would lie there until well past nightfall and then crawl out scratched and dirty and wander in late to supper, facing not wrath, no, but his mother shaking her head and saying: Gregory Allan... what will we do with you?

You can't get those times back, of course. That is why all life is a tragedy.

Later there were kids, a few new families moving in and bringing new faces with them. Sweet little Mindy Berg, his first crush, running around that hot June day in her new white dress, falling to the grass in a fit of laughter and letting him get a good look at her underwear (like a glimpse into eternity). And her two brothers, older boys, getting little Greg Helter to smoke old and crushed cigarettes out behind the Wagner's shed. And Missy White pulling up her shirt to show him her titties, and *her* brother Marc holding Helter down and pummeling him for no reason whatsoever. And then there was *Mr*. White, a beaten and bloated man with skin like leather, reeking of alcohol at every hour of the day, his eyes wide and focused but bitingly red, like the eyes of an animal glimpsed in the middle of the night. Stay away from them, Helter's mom

125

would say, don't go near them. But of course that was the house that interested him the most because it was so odd, so different than any he had ever known. The atmosphere and dynamics of that home and family were mysterious and dangerous and intriguing, and he would go over there like an anthropologist studying some primitive tribe, making mental notes on their fights, their conversations, the clutter of their livingroom, the unflushed toilet (gotta save water, said Mr. White). He always felt like he might get hurt over there, that at any minute the whole family might turn on him, pounce like beasts. But no, it was only Marc White who did that sort of thing, friendly to Helter one minute and then punching him hard on the arm the next. And still he went to their yard, hanging out with Missy, making up stupid little skits and plays. It was the weekend before Halloween when she pulled up her shirt. He'd kept that image with him ever since, and now here it was again, rising up from a million others all vying for attention in the mysterious muck of this Iowa dream.

There was a monster in that dream, too. It looked like a mad werewolf the size of a whale, and stank like a cow. He was running from it at one point, lost and alone in the dark hallways of his old elementary school. *Tap, tap* went his tennies on the old uneven floor, the hollow sound echoing back to the beast. He ran until he came to the gym, and when he went inside he found the Lincoln Monument sitting smack dab in the middle of the basketball court, old Abe looking down with stone eyes on a young boy shaking and shiny with cold sweat. He didn't know what was worse, that out of place statue or the werewolf behind him... which, when it grabbed him, turned out to be nothing but his Gramma Helter pulling him back from the highway where a caravan of horses was passing in a violent thud of hooves and where the faces of the riders looked familiar to him, folks lost through the years, old classmates, people he worked with, eager eyes glimpsed here and there on the campaign trail. You can't go out there, Gramma said. You'll get hurt. They *want* to hurt you, it's what they do.

It became a sex dream, too, him fucking Scarlett Hamm in the broom closet of that museum. She was hot like sun-baked limestone but didn't grip him quite the way his first girl had all those years ago. Oh to be seventeen and lying prone and sweating on the bench seat of an old Ford pickup, a girl named

126

Tabitha moaning softly beneath you, like a Catholic beast full of guilt, wrapping her legs around you the way she'd seen in movies, her breath on your neck smelling of Doritos and beer, her body hot against you, gripping you with a steamy sweetness that was almost unbearable. It was her first time, she'd said. Of course it was. Yours too. Oh to be seventeen again. Back then it was so new you were inventing it yourself.

In the dream the feel of her inner thighs on the outside of his legs was hot and smooth, satin-smooth, and slightly fleshy, though she was a fit girl who ran track and swam obsessively in summer. Nevertheless, he could feel that part of her legs wobble a bit each time he pressed himself down and into her, and it seemed each time her legs opened wider and yet her soft sweet tender female flesh took hold of him like she didn't want it to end. The dream was exactly as he actually remembered it, the truck off completely, no dash lights to throw a green glow on her face, just a darkness alive and fertile. No radio, no sounds save the hum of crickets through the cracked window. They were parked on some dead old gravel road of the sort that formed veins all around their town, a ragged woods on one side and an even more ragged field on the other, the summer sky pulsing with stars and planets. Now and then he lifted his head to look around and check for approaching cars, and more than once found himself gazing through the window and past the field and into that sky. The feel of her hot softness gripping him as he pressed tight and safe against her, then pulled back, then pressed down and against her again, the subtle give and take of her belly against his, and the look of that eternity blossoming out there the way it had always done, unconcerned with him or the petty doings of *any* man... it all seemed connected. He was a young nobody fucking another young nobody on a young nobody planet somewhere on the outskirts of a nobody galaxy, that was all. That blackness out there loomed down on them without care, and he should have felt small, should have felt insignificant, a speck of dust floating separate from all that... and yet he felt the opposite, he felt like a part of it, at one with Jupiter and Mars and Andromeda and the trillions of other planets and galaxies just like them. Why? Because they too were small and insignificant, *everything* was small and insignificant, nothing mattered anywhere. When he looked out at the night sky with that young woman moaning and breathing deeply beneath him he realized that that was

127

exactly why it was all so precious: the very fragile trivialness of everything was what made it all priceless.

Hey, says a voice in the dream. Hey, you never answered my question: what were you doing that was so important?

When?

Just now. Right then. When you were thinking.

I was trying to talk to the gods.

The gods of what?

Iowa.

Iowa? But you never answered my question.

What was it?

Same as it always is: Why?

Why what?

Just... why?

And it was Scarlett Hamm again. They were done screwing and were standing somewhere in the middle of a desert, a half-dozen saguaros around them like the Secret Service.

Why? Why *him*?

Why him? Why him....

Don't go out there, says his Gramma, perched on a saguaro like she might ride it off into the sunset. You'll get hurt. They *want* to hurt you, it's what they do.

The dream shifted, melted, became something else again, and he along with it.

*

The Withers Farm had the look of a place that had never been well-taken care of, which was the way most such small farms look: there was never time to tend to crumbling foundations or leaning barns, there were far more pressing concerns to deal with. When you lived on a farm you were always working, and that constant hard work did little but keep you in a steady state of *just making it*. You never got ahead, and you knew you never would. This was a state of mind Lisa knew well, of course, she had not only felt it herself she had seen it written clearly in the faces of her family. Being a farmer was very much like being a hamster running in its wheel.

She was wandering slowly around this Iowa farm, trying to take in as much as she could in the fading light of the

128

afternoon. Every single inch of the place brought back memories and images from her past, even though the Yates family farm had been better cared for than this one here. That had been her father's obsession, keeping the place looking clean and solid. That was his word, *solid*. Some folks' places look like they might fall down with the next good wind, he used to say. So when his long days were over he would still find the time and energy to go out and fix barn beams, clean up the landscape in the front yard of the house, work on building a new patio out back... anything he could find to make the place look like somewhere people *lived*, and not a dying old farm rotting slowly into the scenery. Lisa thought of the energy and motivation this must have required, to say nothing of the sheer force of will, and could feel nothing but admiration and awe. Her own life was far from hard, but at the end of the day she barely had time to cook herself a decent meal. Lots of Chinese for her, and lots of leftovers. Lots of staring at gargoyles and wondering when they'd come to life.

Maybe he ran himself so hard because he knew he didn't have much time.

Bullshit, she thought. And if that *was* true it made him an asshole: if a man feels like he won't have much time left on the earth and chooses to spend the time he does have *working* and not with his family, then that made him an asshole, pure and simple. She didn't believe there was any other way to look at it.

She tried not to think of his body decaying into the ground in the Shawnee Forest, but it was hard not to. Every day she lived with the idea that maybe, just maybe, some kid or hunter would stumble upon his remains and the Yates Family would get a call and there would be closure at last, and yet every day passed and there was no phone call. There was nothing, just more doubt, more uncertainty, more terrible mystery.

She thought of the Yates farm now, not so well-cared for, everyone too busy with the work of *just making it*, no one around to give it that extra special love and concern that Jack Yates had given it. Even Ma, she didn't go out and go the extra mile, she barely worked on her flowers anymore, she spent all of her time in front of the television. There were game shows to watch, reality shows to keep up on. The front yard of the Yates home was starting to look like the front yard of every

129

dying family farm everywhere. It was just a matter of time before it all went the way of weeds or rot or subdivisions.

There were three barns on the Withers farm, each a different size, but it was to the largest that she wandered. The biggest barn had been one of her favorite places to hang out back home. She used to go up to the loft on cool afternoons and drift off into a light sleep, her dreams influenced by the smells of hay and old wood and barn cats and, floating in from outside, the omnipresent odor of cattle, that bitter-sweet soft smell that symbolized for her everything fresh and pure and innocent... home. As she came up to the Withers barn she paused, admiring how it stood solid yet fragile before her, those two things in perfect balance. One part of its roof was missing, and here and there on the outside were gaps in the planking, like missing teeth in an old man's smile. The color of the big building was a gray that appeared flat and dreary from a distance but which was full of intricate textures and patterns up close, and she stood there staring at it like it was a work of art. At her feet was a calf-high run of grass that faded as it came closer to the barn, giving way to bare earth, and there were footprints in the dirt, human and beast. Everything was just like the barn she knew back home, except for the color. The big Yates barn was a muted red... but it had been a vibrant red once upon a time. Nevertheless, if she closed her eyes and inhaled and listened she felt like she was right back there, waiting for her father's voice to call out for her: *Lisa come help your brothers*!

She turned and looked around, feeling watched. It was officially evening now, the sky was a dark slate-color, with the western horizon only slightly pink from the setting sun. The quiet was heavy around her, and though the wind of earlier had faded the air was cold, crisp. The windows of the old farmhouse let out the barest glow but it was tempered by yellowing curtains, making the whole farm look empty and alone, the sort of place glimpsed in old Southern movies. When seen from a distance such places made you think: *Americana*. When seen up close you thought: *Texas Chainsaw Massacre*.

On most farms there was a light over the area between the house and the barns, usually perched on a pole or strung from a tree branch, but on the Withers farm there was nothing, the thin glow from those windows doing little to stop the progress of the shadows that were spreading over the gravel drive just as they were already spreading over the fields. She listened for the sound of voices or laughter from the house but heard nothing. She'd excused herself by saying she needed to get some fresh air and no one had protested, but it wasn't air that she needed. She didn't know *what* she needed, really, other than solitude and memories, but she was suddenly very conscious of the fact that she felt fragile and tender in a way she hadn't felt, really, since earliest childhood. Sitting in that livingroom with those people she had suddenly realized that she was a stranger among them, that each and every one of them was unknown to her. Not two weeks earlier and she had never even heard of Helter and Hamm, and now here she was sitting in an old house with all these *other* strangers, barely an hour or so after burying an old man in an illegal ceremony. The realization made her feel vulnerable, and though she'd tried to get past it the feeling grew, so she had no choice but to claim a need for air and get out into the coming night.

You're alone, that's what it is.

She knew that was true. She was alone, perhaps more alone than she'd ever been. She was, after all, so far from home, both the one she used to know back on the farm and the one she'd made for herself in the City. But coming outside didn't do much to change this feeling, in fact made it stronger: the darkening sky and fields made her feel small and lonely and lost. She looked up to see the stars but there were none, just an expanse of muted gray that reminded her of old chalkboards or decaying sidewalks in forgotten neighborhoods. And looking to the fields she saw only the distant woods, dark and without detail now. She wasn't even sure where the old man's grave was anymore.

Without giving it much thought she finally turned and entered the big barn, finding herself in a dark space with those same old familiar smells she remembered: hay, cats, ancient wood. She ran her hand along the closest wall and found a switch. She flicked it up and brought forth a weak but serviceable glow from a series of naked bulbs that had been strung from the ceiling to run the full length of the barn. This wasn't a barn they brought cattle into, it was an open space in which a tractor or two could be parked or overflow hay could be stacked. Indeed, against the wall to the right stood a little maze of hay bales, a couple dozen of them piled in random

131

columns six and eight feet high. The rest of the hay would be up in the loft.

She stood there for a moment admiring the barn. It was cleaner than she had expected. Perhaps the old man had had a thing for clean barns, keeping them neat and orderly the way her own father had done. On the wall to her left were hung a series of tools, rakes and shovels and scythes and mallets and axes, all placed deliberately according to type and size. She stepped into the middle of the barn and looked down to either end. On the far right was another door leading to that section of the barn, on the far left was what looked like an old car underneath a light brown canvas tarp. The latter was a familiar sight on farms, she knew. Her father kept the first car he'd ever owned under a tarp in a corner of his middle-sized barn. A 1962 Nash. Why don't you fix that up? people were always asking him. Fix it up, sell it, make some cash. That car will go to the grave with me, he would say. Too many memories for me to give her up.

When she was a little girl she used to sneak into it and play in its backseat. On more than one occasion he would scold her because she'd left her Barbies in there... but the only time he really yelled was when she left half a sandwich and some potato chips in it. Mice'll get in and eat up the seats and wiring! he said. Is that what you want?

The truth was she didn't care. She liked mice, they were cute.

She debated going down to have a look at the car under that tarp, but instead she went right, towards that closed section of the barn. Most likely it would be another storage area, probably more tools, maybe a little museum of ancient farm implements like those always found in such places: wooden planes, rusted axes, plowshares, bridles, saddles, yokes, and so forth. When she got to the door she stopped and listened again, not feeling quite alone. Had she always been this paranoid, or was that something modern life had given to her? She cursed herself for placing her notebook in the rental car, wishing she had it now to write down the thoughts and feeling that were coming to her. If this whole trip didn't make for a good story it might at least serve for decent therapy. Paranoid? When did you become paranoid, Miss Lisa Yates? Tell us about it, tell us how it makes you feel.

132

She grew acutely aware of the silence around her, it was a silence that hung like fog in the air, not even the faint rustling of swallows in the rafters. She couldn't recall if the old Yates farm had been this still. Likely not, there was always something going on, kids screaming and laughing, motors running, some piece of equipment being beaten into submission, a dog barking... if not their own then the Shackley's dog next door, that old hound howling in the night at phantoms and shadows. Then again, how often had she gone out to the big barn in the early evening like this? She would have been inside, helping her mother with dinner or dishes, or doing homework, or drifting off into the sort of waking dreams she'd been prone to back then. Perhaps if she'd gone out there she would have found the world of the Yates farm as deathly quiet as this one. Maybe. Now she would never know, she so rarely went back there.

And why is that, do you think? The therapy voice again. Why is that, Lisa, why don't you go back home?

She always told herself it was because her life in the city kept her busy, but she knew damn well what it was: there was something about that farm now that haunted her. It was the presence of her missing father, the great gaping hole that existed and which had once been filled by him. She'd felt it pushing on her, an unendurable weight, the very last time she'd been home. She didn't like going back because going back made her way too conscious of the fact that he was gone, never to be found, just another in a long line of missing persons. It was better to stay away and never feel that goddamn ghost at all.

Ah, but the guilt this creates must be worse, must weigh on you just as heavily.

This was shit she didn't want to think about. She reached out to open the door to the next section of barn and—

*

"Having fun yet?"

Jasper Callister looked down at the young woman standing in front of him and never changed his expression: it was the same old scowl he'd been wearing all day.

"Scarlett," she said, holding out her hand. "Scarlett Hamm."

133

He nodded and at first made no movement to take that hand, but eventually he sighed and brought forth his own, engulfing hers completely but giving her a rather limp shake.

"Hamm's sister," he said. The words were the first he'd spoken in close to two hours and his voice was rough and deep.

She shrugged. "Yeah, Hamm's sister. What a great way to be known."

He grunted and looked off at the other people milling around. They were in a high-school auditorium, which had been hastily and sloppily converted into a sort of impromptu convention space. Bantam had just gotten done speaking, having followed Parsons by several hours. There were a lot of people, however, various cross sections of the local citizenry, all of whom had likely hung around to hear this John Bantam fellow talk. Bantam? Yeah, you know, that guy that says whatever the hell he wants? That guy.

A benign crowd, but Jasper was keeping a close eye on all of them nonetheless. Nowadays you can't rely on any benign-malignant instincts you might have, there were psychos everywhere, absolutely *everywhere*. Any one of these people here might just reach into a back pocket and pull out a knife and plunge it deep into the heart of Bantam, who was standing about eight feet from Jasper and talking closely with an old man with a hunched back and a walker. Like that guy, you even had to watch that guy. He might just fool everyone, swing that walker up and try to brain the candidate. Yeah, it was best to look at everyone with suspicion. Everybody everywhere was a sniper, a lone gunman, a disenchanted voter, a passion killer, a nut-job with a grudge. That was the nature of life in modern America, baby: trust no one over three.

Bantam, for his part, had been rather benign himself at this speech, saying nothing overly venomous or divisive, and had not even attacked Parsons or Keith by name. He *had* referred to the "main parties" as "corrupt as the devil's dick," but no one in the crowd had seemed to even understand what he'd said or meant, and the phrase had fallen flat. Nevertheless....

"I can't tell if you enjoy this or not," Scarlett Hamm said.

He ignored her, continued to study the crowd, in particular the people gathered around Bantam. Still that old guy with the walker, and some lovely white-haired ladies whose faces looked powdered and whose eyes seemed to flash out at Bantam with what might have been considered lust in women forty-plus years younger. Beautiful blue eyes, naughty blue eyes, they stood out like gems from their snow-white faces and hair. But even they could pull out .57 magnums and blast open Bantam's head. Oh yessir.

"I would think it would be boring," Scarlett said.

"Don't you have something better to do?" he said, his mouth barely opening.

"Like what?"

"Like anything. Can't you see I'm working?"

She laughed. "You're not working. You're just standing here wishing someone would pull a knife or something so you could break their head open."

He glanced down at her.

She smiled. "See, it's true, isn't it? You're just *itching* for it, aren't you?"

"Fuck," he grumbled dismissively, and looked over her head again.

"How many people have you beaten up?"

"None today."

"I mean ever. Come on, how many?"

"Go away."

"How many?"

"Go away before I pick you up and *throw* you away."

"Oh, the tough guy. What kind of man would that make you, Mr. Callister? Harming a sweet little innocent girl like me?"

"Sweet and innocent," he said with a snicker.

"What does that mean?"

He said nothing. That guy with the walker looked like he had something tucked into the front of his pants. A gun, a grenade, a bazooka, a colostomy bag.

Scarlett kicked Jasper playfully in the shin. "What does that mean, huh? What are you trying to imply?"

"Nothing, go away." He was looking for Hamm himself, or Helter, someone who could get over here and take this annoying kid somewhere else.

"I've heard stories about you," she said. "But you're not that tough. I can tell: you're just not that tough."

"It's true. I'm a phony, now go away."

"I heard about Birnbaum," she said.

He resisted the urge to look at her. Better to not show any emotion.

135

"Yep, I heard all about it. The big tough knight in shining armor, defending the honor of some poor little college girl. Why'd you do it, for money?"

He said nothing.

"Just for fun? Or did you secretly like her? Come on, just tell me, I want to know."

At this point Helter was approaching, passing through the crowd with an odd half-smile painted on his mouth. Damn but the guy looked tired... exhausted. Which probably explained why he'd opened his mouth to this silly little girl in the first place. Not that Binrbaum was, or needed to be, some big secret, but still... some things just did not need to be spoken.

"Hey," Jasper said when Helter came up. "Could you take this kid away from me?"

"Kid?" She looked mortified. "*Kid*? What the hell does *that* mean?"

Helter took her by the arm. "Goddamnit, stop bugging our security guy."

She shook free of him but kept smiling up at Jasper. "You need to learn some manners," she said. "Ever heard of having a conversation, huh? Ever heard of *talking*?"

He ignored her, kept looking for assassins. They were always where you least expected.

*

Later she cornered him in an unlit hallway away from everyone else. The shadow they were in was ghostly, a flat slate-colored thing that pooled over the floor and lockers and made him think of mine shafts. To their left was a bolted and windowless door (leading out to the rear parking area, he believed), while down to their right was where this hallway met another in a very faint wash of yellow light. It was quiet here, they couldn't hear a thing.

"You're such a naughty boy," she said, looking up at him. "Bantam could be getting killed right now."

"Fuck him."

She laughed. "Maybe later...."

He sighed. "Could you go away?"

"I could. I won't."

He could have pushed past her of course but was enjoying this brief but sweet moment away from Bantam and Helter and

136

the crowds... away from what he was starting to view as the oddest job he'd ever had, and he'd had plenty. The girl was a nuisance, but a minor nuisance. Certainly there were worse things in the world.

"Little gnat," he said.

She laughed. "That's all you got?"

He hadn't seen lockers in years, hadn't been inside a *school* in years. All sorts of memories tried to come to him but they were overshadowed by almost everything else in his life now, which was just as well. He looked up the hall, saw and heard nothing, and then closed his eyes. What was the point of memories? They only got in the way, they only messed with your mind.

So, you fell down? the counselor had asked him.

Yes Maam.

You fall down a lot, don't you?

I guess so.

Is there anything you want to tell me?

No Maam.

Nothing you want to tell me about home, about your parents?

No.

Are you sure? Because I'm willing to listen. I'm always here and I'm willing to listen and I don't judge and I keep secrets. Okay? So if you ever need to tell me something I'm right here, you can come see me anytime. Understand?

Yes Maam.

"Penny for your thoughts," Scarlett said.

"A penny's not enough."

"How much, then?"

He frowned at her. "You couldn't afford my thoughts."

He closed his eyes again and rested his head back against the locker he was leaning on, ignoring whatever it was she said next.

From the other side of the school, echoing emptily through the halls, came the sound of laughter. The speech was over but maybe Bantam had said something funny. He really shouldn't have slipped off like this but sometimes you had to, that was all. Like he'd had to slip away from the factory... like he'd had to slip away from most of the things in his life.

137

If he hadn't taken *this* gig he wondered where he'd be right now, right this very moment. Not working, no, not yet. He was still nursing the bitterness he'd cultivated at the factory.

Duties as assigned, said that priggish fuck Daniels. It was the way he said it that made Jasper almost instantly want to smash his face in... no, it was the way he said *everything* that made Jasper want to smash his face in. He'd wanted to smash the fuck's face in the first time he met him. Some people do that to you, particularly management types... particularly priggish management types who looked like they hadn't ever done a lick of work their whole life and who walked around like their khaki pants and white dress shirts made them better than anyone else and gave them the right to do whatever the hell they wanted. Yeah, particularly *that* type.

I won't do it, was Jasper's answer. Just like that, as calm as could be: I won't do it. There was no room for debate in those four words, they weren't open for discussion or interpretation.

You know, we can make you.

You can't make me do anything.

Certain obligations come with being an employee here.

And at that Jasper had thought: What the fuck does *that* mean? He wasn't sure, but it sounded ominous. It sounded like something a man ought to fight, to protest, to argue with, to avoid at all costs. Obligations? *Obligations*?

I'm only obliged to do what I was hired to do, he said. No more.

And by this point Daniels was seething, you could see something ripple under his skin as he clenched his jaw and tried not to show his anger. His eyes flashed with annoyance, though, there was no hiding that. He might have been the smaller man but he wore *khaki* goddamnit, and that gave him certain powers here.

Enough of this, Callister, he'd said. You'll do it or—

Oh Jesus, you just don't say things like that. Jasper knew he needed to hit the guy as soon as the word *it* was out of his mouth, it was instinctual, reflexive. His fist connected dead-on with Daniels' mouth, he could feel the man's teeth with his knuckles. It was a satisfying hit, too, and made a good sound. Daniels, for his part, didn't hear a thing: he went down to the floor immediately, like the proverbial sack of shit. He landed flat on his back and his head hit next, with all the subtlety of a

138

brick. The few other workers nearby, all of whom had already stopped what they were doing to watch the initial conversation, looked like someone had just hit *them*: they were open-mouthed, wide-eyed, as motionless as figures in a photo. No one said anything for what felt like several minutes, they just stood there staring at Daniels as he lay on the floor, with only an occasional glance to Jasper. And then finally Jasper's buddy Stockton walked over slowly from his own workstation and looked Jasper in the eyes. You should disappear, he said. He said it softly, calmly, like he'd been in this situation before and knew what the best course of action was. And perhaps he had, it wouldn't have surprised anyone, Stockton was that sort of guy. A good guy.

Jasper just stood there, however, not saying anything, not thinking much either. He looked down at Daniels and then at his co-workers and then at the factory around them all. Lots of people have the wrong impression of factories, they think they're the worst places to work, that the folks who make their living in them are of below-average intelligence and below-average skills. Bullshit. Factories were just another place to work, no better and no worse than any other. They certainly beat slaving away out in the hot sun and bitter cold, and they definitely beat a goddamn office. If you got the right position in one (say, operating a molding machine), and you were a person with intellectual inclinations, you would find that you'd been given ample time to sit and daydream or work on philosophies or come up with theories about all sorts of things. If you were a smart guy and you played your cards right you'd find a factory to be the ideal place in which to indulge your intellectual desires. It was mindless work, most of it, which for the clever thinking man meant it was perfect. If you were *not* a clever man, you'd still find it was perfect. A real win-win situation.

You should disappear, Stockton said again.

Right, but to where, and for what? He'd done what he'd done, there was no reason to run from it, to hide like a child ashamed of his actions. Hell no, he was rather proud of his work. Look at that, he'd laid out the priggish motherfucker with one shot and got nothing in return but a minute cut on his fist. Which was starting to ache, by the way, and itch a little too. What the hell had the guy been wearing on his lips? On his teeth? Numzit for a toothache? Lip gloss to look pretty?

139

You should disappear.

Maybe, but he just stood there, immersed in the moment and yet above it as well. Duties as assigned? Surely they weren't serious.

He remembered looking at Stockton and holding his eyes for a good thirty seconds before the other suits came running up. Word travels fast in a factory, that was one bad thing about them. Stockton looked worried and sort of sad. He really means it, Jasper thought. Maybe he knows something I don't... maybe disappearing is exactly what I should do.

Holy shit, someone said. It was Beakins, Daniel's peer. Behind him was Taylor, their boss. Taylor was *true* management, he'd been there for something like fifteen years and was connected to the owners via family ties. Beakins and Daniels were supervisors, Taylor was next in line for VP, a fact he wore like a halo. Cocksucker walked around like he crapped diamonds. There was only one way this scene could go now.

Jasper turned to face them, looking down at their soft-cheeked pampered faces with his own hard and coarse one. He was pretty sure he was showing no emotion, but he was wondering if he could take these two should the situation go the one other way it might possibly go. Of course he could: Taylor was pushing fifty and had developed middle-aged fat sometime around the fifth-grade. Beakins worked out, but more for looks than strength... certainly he did not have the stomach necessary for violence, you could see that in his eyes. Management eyes, soulless and without passion.

They looked at Daniels and then at Jasper... and they looked at Jasper with more than a little fear in their eyes. Fear was good. Fear was exactly what you wanted to see in the eyes of upper management. When you saw fear you knew the playing field was level. Finally.

"Come on," Scarlett said, breaking these thoughts. "I'm bored, let's have some fun."

"No. Go have fun by yourself."

"I'd rather have fun with you," and she reached out and touched him between the legs.

He grabbed her wrist and twisted her arm up, staring down into her face in a way that made her flinch.

"Never touch me," he said.

She looked for a second like she was going to smile and laugh the whole thing off so he gave her wrist a little squeeze so she knew he was serious. Don't smile, he was thinking. Just don't smile.

"Fine," she said finally. When he released her hand she shook her head. "You're a weirdo. You know that, right?"

"Whatever."

"It's okay, I like weirdoes. And you interest me, you know. I bet I could write a paper on you. I should change my major to psychology."

"Do what you gotta do."

"Maybe I should give up following *those* guys around and just stick by you, find out what it's like to be Mr. Bodyguard-for-hire."

"You wouldn't like what you'd find."

"Gotta be more interesting than this political bullshit."

"'Bout the same. Now go away." He was suddenly nervous, expecting someone to come around the corner any second now and see them there. It might look like they were up to something, and any sort of *something* was bad in a racket like politics. Certainly someone could read into this little scene anything they wanted, and then spread their theory out to the mass media in such a way that the Bantam crew might not appreciate: GADFLY PARTY EMPLOYEE CAUGHT IN PUBLIC SEX ACT, or some such nonsense. Not that it mattered, it wasn't like Bantam was on his way to victory or anything. Still....

She leaned forward like she was going to try and touch him again.

"Would you vote for him?" she asked.

"Who?"

"Bantam."

He sighed and looked down the hallway. "Go away," he said. "Little gnat."

*

In the middle of a dream Helter came half-awake, stirred by some sound outside the window. It could have been any window, the one on the Iowa farmhouse, the one back home in Illinois, the one *way* back in Birnbaum, or the one way, way, *way* back in that hometown he once knew out there in Never-Never-land. Remember that window, the one that faced East so each morning you'd put your head around the curtain and let

141

the bright golden rays of that first sun touch your face as you looked out at the dew, crystal-brilliant and fragile on the branches and leaves, and think that that was how it would be forever and ever? Remember that? The good old days. And remember how at night you'd look out and it was the opposite, all dark blue and gray, formless, the house next door visible only as a black wall between the skeletal silhouettes of shadowed branches? Which view suited you best, do you think, the brilliant morning or the amorphous night? Or neither... and is that why you moved on?

The sound was not repeated and he slipped back into his dreams.

*

"You need another beer," said Tapper. Hamm looked at him, not sure if that was a question or a statement, but Tapper was just staring down at the floor, no expression on his face.

"You offering?" Hamm finally asked.

Tapper did not move, just sat there stone-still, cheeks slightly flushed, this look of vague mournfulness in his eyes... until he suddenly cocked his head and looked toward the room's big window.

"You all right?" Hamm asked.

Tapper raised his hand for silence and kept his head cocked, listening, hearing something Hamm could not.

When Hamm turned and looked out that window he saw only his own buzzed reflection surfacing from a metallic darkness. He listened, heard nothing. He looked back at Tapper.

"What is it?"

Tapper was motionless and quiet for nearly a half-minute, just listening to whatever it was he had heard, attuned to the sounds of his world the way wild animals are, sensing when normality was breached, when strange things were afoot. At last he shook his head.

"Nothing," he said. "Nothing. Just the night...."

"I think if we can get away with it, time-wise, we ought to slip back over to Des Moines and tail Keith some more," said Bantam. "Sooner rather than later. Get a bit further under the bastard's skin. What do you think?"

Helter nodded weakly, distractedly. He was thinking of other things lately. Just... other things.

The weather had changed a bit, at least sun-wise: the gray skies that had been around for what seemed like years had broken slightly this afternoon, that thick wall of cloud now less strong, less thick, showing brilliant swatches of blue underneath, blue like island waters, a blue so shocking in its contrast to the gray as to look surreal and slightly mad, the blue of a crazy girl's eyes. That kind of blue, yes. The first time he noticed the gray breaking up, dissipating like smoke, he'd found himself staring at it, as if not quite believing what he was seeing. It was like there'd been a crack in the order of things, a fracture in reality revealing another reality underneath. He stood there thinking of worlds within worlds within worlds within worlds. Russian nesting dolls. Puzzles.

He was about to step away from Bantam now when he felt the big man's hand on his shoulder.

"You letting this crap get to you?" Bantam asked, leaning in close so he could lower his voice. There were people milling about on the sidewalk around them, some looking eager to talk to the candidate but unwilling to just force their way over. Polite people, these Iowans.

"What crap?"

"This. The whole thing. The campaign. You letting it wear you down? You look beaten, like you need a good twelve-hour nap."

Helter shrugged. "I'm fine. Just working, that's all, isn't that what I'm supposed to be doing? Isn't that what this is all about?"

Now Bantam shrugged. He stood straight again and looked around, making his own study of that alien blue up above. When he finally looked back at Helter there was a different sort of smile on his face, a more casual, friendly smile.

"We're just having fun, aren't we?"

"I thought we were changing the world."

"Can't we do both?"

Helter was walking away a few moments later, looking back to see Bantam chatting up a few locals, mostly men. Behind him stood Jazz, vaguely sinister and deeply focused on the work at hand. Jazz was standing with his arms straight down at his sides, a posture that was misleading: Helter knew the man was coiled like a snake, just waiting for someone to do the wrong thing, to make any threatening gestures. Helter pitied the poor fucker who might try such a thing, because he also knew that not only was Jazz ready for it, he was also *waiting* for it. Hoping for it. Perhaps praying for it.

He studied the tableau for a little bit longer (the candidate, the security guy, the interested voters) then turned and continued walking, moving down the sidewalk until he was away from the chatter, finally taking a left down a decaying old side road that ran alongside some quiet businesses (two bars and a bakery, each with parking lots that were crumbling like Egyptian temples). He pulled out his cell phone, dialed a number, waited.

"Hello?"

"Susie?"

"Ah, Mr. Ambassador mon," she said. The last time they'd talked she'd said that if Bantam became President he, Greg, should ask for an ambassadorship. To where? he'd wondered,

144

and she'd suggested Jamaica. Good pot and a suntan, everything you need. "Do you be jammin', mon?"

"Not much jammin' going on. Not much of anything going on."

"Where are you?"

"Iowa."

"*Where* in Iowa?"

He thought a second. "Honestly, I have no clue. Does it matter? Iowa is Iowa."

"So, what's up?"

"I just wanted to see how you were doing."

"I'm doing good. Except the other day this kid asked me if I was a pirate. Made me wish I had a fake eye so I could pull it out and throw it at him."

"Not funny."

She sighed. "Greg, you all right?"

"Why, don't I sound all right?"

"Actually, no. You sound... tired."

"And beaten, too, I suppose."

"Maybe you should take a break from all that. A little vacation."

"Yeah, maybe." A vacation? Can you take a vacation from changing the world?

"How is it going there, anyway?" Susie asked. Her voice was always sweet to him, full of warmth and innocence. He remembered when they were kids and they used to go running like idiots through the fields just north of town, chasing butterflies and playing tag and hiding in the wildflowers. He thought of her crouched down below the thistles and coneflowers, her big honey-brown eyes looking out at him, waiting to pounce when he passed. Just little kids, left alone to themselves by parents maybe far too trusting... but what the hell, those were different times, softer times. Back then you never thought about losing your children, about psychos and abductions or even accidents, you sent them out to play and forgot about them until supper. And they were little kids, and the world was so huge. But the world was out *there*, always somewhere far away, a place so distant as to be alien. The world the brother and sister inhabited was always so small and insular and yet full of wonder, and they lived in it like they would know no other.

"It's going fine," he said.

145

"I was reading about you in the paper. Sounds like you're gaining some momentum."

He wondered if she remembered all of that. She was younger, and she'd been through so much, her memory might be hazy.

"We've made a little dent," he said.

"You're getting mentioned on real news shows now. CNN did this whole thing on the history of third-parties in America. Oh, and one time they showed you. You were talking to some reporter down there, some woman. I don't know where it was."

The image his mind had seemed to grasp onto now was of sweet little Susie running through those fields, startling insects into flight, chasing killdeer, laughing her head off with her hair out behind her like a halo. When he thought of that image he couldn't help but think of it as the ideal portrait of youth and health and optimism, something they might use in commercials, an image of innocence so powerful it was still emotionally moving decades later. There goes Susie Helter, running through the wildflowers, a little girl with nothing on her mind but that very act of running, of laughing, of seeing how many insects rose up on papery wings as she passed.

"Greg?"

If he could go back he'd tell her to stay there, never leave that field, just stay there forever, there was nothing good for her outside of it.

"Greg, you still there?"

"Yeah, sorry."

"I thought I lost you."

"I'm here."

A long pause from her, and he could imagine her biting her lower lip the way she did, formulating the words in her head, wanting to say something but not quite sure how.

"You take care of yourself," she said. "Don't run yourself into the ground."

"I'll try."

"Try hard."

"I will. And Susie?"

"Yeah?"

He heard something behind him and when he turned he saw Jasper on the main street looking over to him with a dead look on his face. He felt suddenly paranoid, threatened. He could read nothing in the big man's eyes, he always looked like

146

he could be thinking, at any given moment, of absolutely *anything*. A smart man. A smart head-cracker. But he also trailed this aura of... of what exactly? Hard to say. A predatory aura. Something not to be trusted. Helter thought of a cat he and Susie had had as kids, and how it had always looked so cuddly... until the day he saw it take out a bird, and then he knew what it was capable of doing with claws and teeth and from then on he looked at it differently. Hard to pet a cat warmly when all you thought of when you looked in its eyes was glistening innards and black blood.

"What is it?" Susie asked.

Her voice in his ear was close but distant.

"You take care of yourself, too," he said.

*

"If I could just get into one of the debates, with either of them, I could at least stir things up enough to make a crack in their facades, to agitate and frustrate them enough so that their true selves would show through, and people would see them for what they really are."

Bantam looked at Jasper to see if there was a response and there wasn't, the big man didn't even look like he was thinking about this prospect and what it might mean for the future of American Politics. Bantam turned his eyes to the road in front of them.

"Why are we off the highway, anyway?" he asked. Secret little sections of uber-rural Iowa were passing them by at country highway speeds. It was better scenery than on the interstate but he frowned at it before looking back to Jasper. "You know a short cut?"

The big man didn't appear to hear, he just kept driving. The road they were on led up and over gentle little hills surrounded by woods that would be dense come summer. Straggling barbed-wire fences ran up to surprisingly lovely homes nestled amidst the trees, but there was no one in the yards, no one working on cars, not a dog in sight.

"What day is it?" Bantam asked.

Jasper looked like he wasn't going to answer, and then shrugged. "Tuesday?"

"Tuesday?" Bantam frowned. "That can't be."

"Maybe Thursday."

147

Bantam looked at the clock on the dash. "Where is everyone at five o'clock on a weekday afternoon? Eating supper?"

Jasper turned his head and glared for a second at his passenger. Just a second, turning away when Bantam looked over to him.

"Still working?" he suggested.

"Working?" Bantam repeated. He said it like it was the strangest suggestion he'd ever heard, and turned his attention once more to those houses out there, the ones so silent and lonely. You'd think they were empty just by looking at their outsides. Some had no lights on, but even those that did looked haunted by emptiness.

"This is actually not so different from where I grew up," he said somewhat quietly, his face turned towards his window. Soon it would be dark enough for his reflection to show in the glass. Remember being a kid on all those long drives across country and sitting in the backseat with your face against the window, looking at your reflection like it might tell you a secret? Remember late at night, long after they thought you'd fallen asleep, and they up there in front talking about things they never wanted you to hear? All those long drives over Idaho, the Dakotas, upper New York, the abysmal inhuman stretch over the top of Texas.

Jasper's curiosity was peeked: he suddenly sat up straight and changed his grip on the wheel, expecting, perhaps, either some long and involved tale or a short and quick revelation about the life of John Thomas Bantam.

"Really?" he said. "Where'd you grow up?"

"We lived on the edge of town. That's where I fell in love with snakes. I'd catch them all the time, all these beautiful animals. There's something both outrageously beautiful about a snake but also something so subtle."

"Where was this again?"

"They rival birds and butterflies for beauty, but they have a modesty to them. And an honesty. A snake never lies."

"What town did you say?"

"And they never stab you in the back. 'He's a real snake in the grass' is among the stupidest things a person can say. It makes no sense. A snake in the grass is an honest creature, incapable of betrayal. The next stupidest thing is 'if it was a snake it would have bit you.' Sheer stupidity. Snakes are

148

noble and majestic creatures, and there aren't enough of those kinds of things to go around. We need more."

Jasper sighed and looked out the window, studied the landscape they were in. It looked familiar to him, too. "What part of Wisconsin did you say you were from?"

But Bantam had fallen silent, and he remained silent for the next dozen or so miles. They continued up this gray-veined country highway, over a few more hills (some more rolling than others) and alongside several more streams of varying width, all the while with the light fading out in the west in a hazy purple-red glow they could only see here and there between the trees. Only once did they see another human being, someone walking slightly hunched across the road in front of them, retrieving their mail from the box on the other side and then crossing back and disappearing down a driveway. Both Bantam and Jasper watched this guy in their rearview mirrors, but neither of them said anything. It was impossible to tell the age of that man, or even if it *was* a man: there was nothing about the shape of that body that told of either sex or age, it was square, chunky, and lacking anything resembling grace in its movements. Didn't matter, either. Both men returned their eyes to the road ahead.

After those dozen or so miles had passed Bantam suddenly stirred in his seat and looked at Jasper.

"Where are we going?" he asked.

*

In a dream-within-a-dream, Helter was standing behind a podium and speaking to a gigantic crowd of people. He wouldn't remember it when he woke, but this is what he was saying into the microphone:

"I do solemnly affirm that I will faithfully execute the office of President of the United States, and will to the best of my ability, preserve, protect and defend the Constitution of the United States."

And as he said it, in this dream-within-a-dream, he believed it, the words came to him naturally, unforced and with depth and power. They were words he'd been born to say, words he was *meant* to say at this hour and this moment. No other man had ever spoken them with greater integrity, no man had ever given that oath as if it arose fully-formed from his

149

own heart and mind. No other man had ever been a *real* President, a true President, a President of Destiny. Only Gregory A. Helter. President Helter. GAH.

Ah, but it was only a dream-within-a-dream. In the real dream he was just a lonely small town kid playing in the shadows of a darkening front yard, with the smell of supper rising on the evening air, that sweet steamy smell of mother's pot-roast mixing and competing with the scent of fresh-cut grass from the yard next door. The town was quiet, the neighborhood peaceful and still in its post-Fourth of July slumber, but he began to grow aware of a sound far off in the distance, at first a slow rumble, like a train, and then, drawing closer, a definite rhythm.

"Gregory Helter, time for supper!" His mother in the doorway.

He ignored her. Listened.

"Gregory Helter, get in here this instant!"

He turned and looked at her. "Don't you hear it?"

"It'll get cold!"

"Listen," he pleaded, and turned to look up the road. It was louder now, the higher-pitched sounds more clear, the deep thundering bass more pronounced. He squinted into the growing gloom and spotted something rounding the corner several blocks away, out where the street curved as it left town.

He could hear music clearly now. Marching music. He nodded his head to the drum's ostinato and recognized the melody the brass was playing from every marching band he'd ever seen. His mother was still in the doorway behind him and he heard her singing:

"Oh the monkey wrapped his tail around the flagpole, to watch the grass grow, up his asshole."

"It's coming!" he shouted happily into the evening.

"You really should come in and eat, that parade will be here when you get done."

"I'll miss it."

"It'll be here forever, you can't miss it. It'll be here forever." And then she continued singing, the music louder now, every note crystal clear: "Oh the monkey wrapped his tail around the flagpole, to watch the grass grow, up his asshole."

And here it was, a marching band dressed all in gold and red, moving in perfect syncopation, machine-style, down the center of the previously quiet street. The tubas and trumpets

150

and trombones and saxophones all shone brilliantly in the thickening darkness, the flickering streetlights starting to reflect in them like starshine on a midnight lake. None of the musicians looked at him, they just stared straight ahead. The baton-spinning girls were beautiful but even they didn't look at him. They were all focused on the marching and the music.

Behind the band were three big black convertibles moving slowly along the asphalt. They too gleamed in the evening's pale light, reminding him of fish swimming in black water.

He glanced once more at the band before looking to those cars again, mesmerized by how patient and slow they were moving. As the first car came close the driver turned and gestured at him with his index finger: *naughty-naughty*. This man was dressed in a black suit with a black tie and his hair was plastered tight to his head.

In the back of that first car was a beautiful woman in a white dress, the sort of dress one might wear to a fancy party, low-cut and frilly. She looked at Gregory Helter and her eyes were sad and dark.

The music began to fade, to blur, at first naturally and then raggedly, skipping and burping as if it were being deconstructed electronically... or like a radio being slowly lowered into water. The second car was coming now and the boy looked at the driver. He expected another *naughty-naughty* gesture but was instead given a cheerful smile that was all teeth, teeth as white as sun-bleached ribs. The boy didn't like that smile, he felt a chill run up his spine as soon as he saw it. There was no reason for that man to be that happy, no reason whatsoever. After all, look what was in the back of his convertible:

It was a man in a blue suit sitting nice and tall and straight. He had a peaceful look on his face and a vicious gaping jagged hole where the left side of his head had been. This hole was oozing blood thick and black as oil, and there were already flies caught in it, while others flew above his shoulders in zigzagging holding patterns.

"Is he dead?" the boy asked.

"They all are," his mom answered from the doorway. "Sorry, honey. They all are."

151

"Oh my fucking god!" said the young man in the doorway.

"Turn the light off," she said, consonants swollen and vowels thick through her fattened lips.

"Susie—"

"*Off*!"

He killed the light and went to her. She didn't allow him to touch her, not at first, turning away from him as far as she could, and then he reached out for her anyway and she turned too far and gave a little gasp of pain.

"Goddamn!" he said, over-loud in the little room.

"No," she said, "no… shhh…." Like she was comforting *him*. She finally allowed herself to be hugged and he felt her tears and blood on his face.

"What the hell happened?"

"I…" She started to cry, shivering there in his arms.

"What the hell happened, Susie?" He was practically yelling at her.

"I had a date," was all she said.

A little less than an hour later he was in a hospital waiting room, pacing like a troubled tiger in front of a television tuned to CNN. After his hundredth-or-so pass an older man on one of the couches said:

"I'm kinda trying to watch this."

And Greg Helter told him to go fuck himself. Go fuck yourself, he said. Go fuck yourself.

*

"Find anything interesting?"

Lisa was so far gone into her own little interior world she was not aware that someone had entered the barn after her, and at the sound of his voice she gasped and spun around, fists already tight and poised, her right leg ready to knee a groin should the need arise. When she saw the figure of Uncle Jim standing fifteen feet behind her, strangely lit by the barn's dim bulbs, she sighed and smiled.

"You scared me," she said.

152

He smiled too. "Apparently. I would think any woman capable of living on a farm *and* in the big city wouldn't frighten easy."

"I was... lost in thought."

He nodded and just stood there with his hands in his pockets, looking around at the barn, studying its walls and ceiling. After a moment he looked back at her.

"You folks seem to get lost in thought easy," he said.

"There's a lot to think about."

He frowned and cocked his head. "Is there?"

"Well, yeah. A man died today, for starters. That's something."

"I suppose. A good man, too."

"And..." She found herself way too close to saying some of the things that were on her mind and of course decided against it. No need to tell him that. No need to tell *anyone* that.

He added a suitably vague ending for her: "Just, other things, right?"

"Right."

He looked around the barn again, like he'd never seen one before. She thought how natural he seemed in the surroundings, despite his decidedly non-farm-friendly clothes. He reminded her of the men who would come to the farm back home and sell her father seed, fertilizer, various farm equipment. Men like that might not feel out of place on a farm but they certainly never quite belonged, there was just something about them, a certain sense that they were above the actual labor to be found there. She tried to see Uncle Jim's hands but he kept them in his pockets. No matter, she doubted they would have been rough and calloused, he just didn't have that look to him. She wondered what he did. A banker, approving loans to farmers? A seed salesman? An accountant? Impossible to tell, of course, people didn't trail their jobs around like auras to be read by those sensitive to such things. In fact, she'd always believed that what a person did for a living had absolutely nothing to do with the sort of person they were, that it was in fact the least interesting part of someone. Look at her, a technical writer by trade but not in any way by nature. Yeah, then what are you? A journalist. Well, maybe not, she certainly had yet to actually *journal* anything about this here Bantam campaign. That left her a writer, just a writer, and

153

what was wrong with that? Maybe she was a writer, period. And maybe when this was all over she'd write something about this stupid Presidential campaign bullshit that would have something important to say, a theory to espouse, a statement about modern American politics she could claim as her own. Or, barring this, how about a simple tale to tell about simple men out doing what it was they were called to do. Or shit, a quick and easy piece of supermarket fluff someone might read during an afternoon at the beach. Whatever.

Uncle Jim looked at her. "I do wonder, though, what sort of stuff a pretty lady like yourself has in her pretty little head."

Oh Lisa, you're losing it, you missed the subtle little shiver that just ran up your spine.

"You wouldn't want to see in there," she said, and laughed a little nervous schoolgirl laugh.

Now he was walking towards her, still with his hands in his pockets and a weird little smile of his own stretching his mouth. He did not blink.

"Oh," he said, "oh I bet there's something interesting way deep down."

She shrugged. "Not really."

He was on her.

*

Helter opened his eyes and found himself in darkness. Darkness, strange surroundings, odd smells, the works. He lay there a moment thinking, wondering where he was and what might have led him here. What leads a man to darkness? The lack of light, of course. Jesus, he wondered, where the hell am I?

In the dream he'd just woken from he'd been a child back in that sweet old golden-green town of the past, and even though something hadn't been right there, even though something had been *off*, it had still been a place he was comfortable, a place he felt safe, a place he knew and loved... whatever it was that was causing the uneasiness was just passing through from other distant lands, a visiting abnormality. So where in the hell was *this*? And then it came to him, and all of this strangeness became suddenly familiar, all of this oddness suddenly made sense.

"Iowa," he whispered, and his voice was dry like the dead.

154

Part III

Out of the darkness a dog runs across the road, just a quick blurred shape moving from blackness to blackness, washed for only a fraction of a second in the headlights. Jasper's foot instinctually goes for the brake but it's not needed, the dog is gone, slipping away to the strange night-world of the ditch, hot on the trail of a rabbit or cat. Jasper exhales and looks over to Bantam, who is sitting with eyes closed and his head against the window. Sleeping at last. How many beers did you have? Jasper wonders. He hears the empties knocking around gently, almost melodically, on the floor. Was Bantam a good man? Probably. Presidential material? Sure, who the hell knows. What the hell was *Presidential* anymore? Bunch of self-righteous assholes with dollar signs in their eyes and gigantic machines of entitlement and tradition behind them. There hadn't been a great President, a man who truly *should* have been President, in... shit, I'll get back to you. Jasper could think of a few good and honest people throughout history who, in a better and more just world, would have been President... but even better, he believed, would have been *no* President. Rule by the people. True anarchy: rules, but no rulers. If we were indeed a great nation, and our founders great men, this is the road they would have taken. Instead the founders were men

156

with dollar signs in their eyes and entitlement in their heads. They were men who thought they *should* be rulers. American monarchists, despite all pretenses to the opposite. Men of wealth and property and intellect, each of whom believed more than anything that the common man should have as little say as possible in how things were governed. Hence the Electoral College. Hence the absurd idea of *representatives*. You can't send another man to represent you, there's no guarantee, no assurance. The only way you can be sure you'll get what is best for you is to represent yourself, with a gun if needed. Was a time not so long ago when a simple man could walk into the White House and discuss these things with the President. Not anymore. Pointless psychos ruined it all for everyone. There were indeed good reasons to kill a President, but all those pathetic nut-jobs had soured the populace on the very idea of assassination. Shit, assassination could be a useful tool. When the common man believes it's the worse sin imaginable to threaten his "leaders" with a gun, then that is the day the common man has lost.

Jasper hears Bantam starting to snore lightly and he frowns. What sort of dreams does a Presidential candidate have? Dreams of ascendancy, oaths, secret meetings, red buttons?

Maybe not for Bantam. Bantam was different, he wasn't coming from an established line like all of those other fuckers (Keith with his multi-generational tradition of Senatorhood, Parsons with his entire family history going all the way back to the fight for Independence). Bantam might be a mystery but he was certainly not a man of entitlement, he wasn't backed by a secret machine with a history of "public service." He might be rich but he wasn't *rich*. He was running to be a pain in the ass to those other candidates but not necessarily to win. And that was noble. And yet, what if he won? This thought comes to Jasper just as he sees another shape in the night, a rather large figure off the road on the left side, a sleek but thick shape with glowing eyes. White tail. The deer stands there as the car passes and does not move a muscle. Jasper looks back in the rearview mirror but can see nothing, only a faint sketch of road. When he looks ahead again he sees another deer, this one dead and bloated on the shoulder, all broken neck and legs and a belly split to the stars.

So, what if Bantam won?

157

It would change him, Jasper knew. He'd be ruined by the power of the position. The people that would surround him would sour him on everything he believes. His eyes would fill with dollar signs, his heart with blackness. Everything he is saying now, out here on the stump, would be forgotten, repudiated, maligned. The power and history of the *Presidency*, of American politics and tradition, would take hold of him and make him one of them. One of *them*....

And that wouldn't be good for anyone, not for Bantam and not for the American people. Imagine a man like Bantam trying to talk the country into buying things that were no good for them, things that were deadly and evil. Imagine a man like Bantam becoming just another run-of-the-mill asshole President like the rest. Just imagine it....

Jasper looks over to the sleeping man next to him. Just imagine.

*

The hallway was dark but there was a faint and ghostly yellow light at the end of it, throwing shadows that were deep and long. Helter moved down it slowly, headed for that light, thinking of the smell of this place (woodsmoke, manure, other faint and sickly-sweet odors) and knowing it was time to move on. They had business to conduct, things to do, people to meet, and it was already way too late for most of it... which meant there were calls to make, apologies to be made. How long had he slept? Felt like only a half hour or so but it could have been a day. Everyone was telling him that he looked exhausted, and apparently it had been true. This was a tough line of work, draining and deadly. And for what purpose? To change everything, to make a difference? Well, what difference does a difference make?

He wondered what Bantam was thinking right at this particular moment, when it seemed his whole support staff had deserted him.

BANTAM CAMPAIGN FALLS APART. Good headline. Catchy. Maybe inevitable. Shit.

Having gotten a little sleep (or a lot, who knows) he suddenly found himself able to look at this whole thing with fresh and clear eyes, despite the muddled feeling of a post-nap daze. It was one thing to work so hard on a Presidential

158

campaign of this sort, and to lose yourself in every detail and every moment, but quite another to ponder life afterwards. Certainly Bantam would never win. Well, he *could* win, but most likely, when it came down to it, when it came right down to those last little sad-faced suburban women with the tight lips and the tighter purses, there was no way Bantam would get the necessary votes to actually step through the front doors of the White House and lead the nation into the future. The American voter might flirt with him, throw winking and seductive looks his way, but in the end they would vote as they always did, safely and predictably. Nothing more cautious than the American voter. John Thomas Bantam would be a crush they might have a brief fling with, but in the end they would return to the safe and secure arms of that which was known and familiar. Bantam would fall back into the same realm as the typical Other Man: a pleasant memory, a secret smile, a diversion, a bit of harmless fun back in the good old days. A roll in the political hay.

By the time he had come down the hall and was about to enter the livingroom he was thinking he might just quit all of this. Quit now and beat the rush, head east and live out the rest of his life without drama or nonsense. Hamm knew people, Hamm could get him work. He'd always said that, right? Come out to New York and I'll find you a job. Maybe now was the time, put all of this nonsense, this playing around, behind him, embark on another life, something that might actually prove satisfying.

Sure. Maybe. Why not?

He started to imagine that life, some safe yet satisfying job, nine to five, nice people, a fair boss, and afterwards a long walk down the New York streets, past all those smells and sights, the hustle and bustle of city life, the barking of car horns, screeching of tires, eclectic odors of various exotic restaurants settling like fog down the sidewalks. Then, an apartment somewhere, high above it all, where he could sit cocooned in his own little world surrounded by glass and concrete and quiet, where he could put on some jazz and sit around sipping wine and contemplating a visit to the Guggenheim that coming weekend because there was a traveling exhibit of all these old sketches by Rembrandt, or maybe a collection of rare and priceless manuscripts like the original hand-written *Moby Dick* or *Alice in Wonderland* or the first few biblical pages to roll hot

159

off the Gutenberg press. Whatever it might be it was supposed to be good, everyone was going, and maybe he'd meet a woman there who might—

He didn't know if this was a good fantasy or not, if it was a life he'd really enjoy or not. It was always worth trying, but how long can a man go on trying different lives? How long can he go on starting over? How old does he get before he's too old and he just becomes a sad spectacle of himself, starting lives and stopping them a year later, never putting down roots? At a certain point he just becomes a functioning transient, a successful bum. A perennial hobo.

Ah, yes, Mr. Helter, but there was a woman in your little scenario, true? And a man with a woman cannot be a hobo, or a transient... not in the traditional sense, and anyway he wouldn't really be pathetic. In your little fantasia you would be a man of restless energy, constantly changing, constantly seeking new adventure and new inspiration, constantly evolving. And that is not and never will be a bad thing.

Evolving, right. But the point of evolution is to get to the next best level of existence, to adapt to new situations and environments... maybe to get better, too, to become a better man. And would constantly starting over make me a better man?

These were the thoughts Helter was having as he made the short walk from the dark bedroom down to the ghostly yellow livingroom. They all came rushing at him at once, making him feel dizzy. For the last few steps he shook them away and cleared his mind and tried to become once again the responsible head of a political campaign. A *Presidential* campaign, for Christ's sake. He couldn't have these nice people here see him as frazzled and exhausted and sick and tired. No way. He rubbed at his eyes and put on a smile and came into the livingroom expecting to say "thanks for the nap, I needed that, but it's time to move on, we thank you for your kindness and we're sorry for your loss and—"

He found Hamm passed out on the sofa and Tapper (it *was* Tapper, right?) passed out in the recliner. Several neatly arranged but empty beer bottles sat at each of their feet.

"Oh Jesus," he said. Hamm was snoring loudly, deeply, but Tapper opened his eyes a fraction and looked at him. "Where's everyone?" Helter asked.

Tapper blinked. "Everyone...?"

160

"Everyone. The others. Lisa, the kid... Ricky? Your mom?"

"...she ain't my mom, she's...." The eyes closed, the mouth stayed open.

"Oh this is just great!" He walked over and kicked at Hamm's legs. Hamm didn't move. He kicked again and the snoring stuttered for a moment, paused, and then resumed. "Hey, goddamnit!" He kicked harder.

Hamm jerked awake this time and did as Tapper had: opened his eyes a sliver and regarded Helter sleepily. He mumbled something, then started to close his eyes again... but Helter wouldn't have it, he kicked him once more in the legs.

"What?" Hamm growled.

"Where's Lisa? We should get going, we should...." He sighed. "I can't believe you."

"...you can believe me, I'm right here...." His eyes closed.

"Goddamnit!"

"I can't believe it's not butter," Hamm said, and Tapper, eyes closed and mouth open, started to laugh.

"Oh for fuck's sake..." Helter turned and looked in the kitchen, went down the dark hall and checked the other bedrooms, even opened the door to the basement and called out to the dampness and the cobwebs. Finding no one, he went back into the livingroom and once more kicked Hamm in the legs.

"Dammit," Hamm mumbled.

"We're leaving," Helter said. "Soon as I find Lisa we're leaving, we have to get going. We...." Frustrated, he went to the front door and opened it, looking into the night, listening.

"I heard something," Tapper said.

"What?"

"I heard something."

"What?"

His eyes still closed, Tapper shrugged and turned his head toward the wall, getting himself comfortable for what was probably not the first drunken recliner sleep he'd ever gotten.

"Same thing it always is," he said, and then he was out.

Helter sighed and went out the door and into the night. He walked out to the driveway and squinted into the darkness, thinking that maybe the women had made another trek out to the gravesite for another prayer session or something. Jesus, leave the old man alone, he thought.

161

Seeing nothing, he turned his attention to the rest of the farm. His eyes settled of course on the barn, that hulking wall of graying wood over there to his right. He'd always found something vaguely threatening in barns, something uninviting, off-putting. He couldn't recall if he'd ever even been in one. But there was a light on inside it, he could see a sliver of it through the crack of what had to be a partially closed door. It was a much more pleasing light than the one in the livingroom, a softer yellow, a much more organic glow. Hopefully he wouldn't open it and find the others inside drunk off their asses. Jesus, what happened while he was asleep? He'd have to have a serious talk with Hamm. They couldn't have that kind of behavior, they just couldn't.

He did wonder, though, as he made the walk across the dirt and gravel to the barn, what Bantam might have done this evening had he been here. It was quite possible he would have been right in there with Hamm, boozing it up with the locals. Could one really know Iowa without getting drunk with the salt of Iowan earth?

"Shit," Helter muttered. That sounded exactly like something Bantam would say.

Just before he got to the barn he heard something off in the distance... or felt it, rather, more than heard it. He stopped and listened. At first there was just the whispery rush of a soft breeze through the chilled air, and then it came again, a deep heavy resonant hoot, rising and falling in pitch and without echo, loud at first and then fading into the quiet. It was a sound that made him think of childhood, of childhood's midnight dreams, of Halloween and bare skeletal branches and dead leaves shivering in moonlight. He was pretty sure it was an owl, but he did not necessarily think *owl* when he heard it. Instead, he thought of a town and faces so distant as to be mythical, and felt an emptiness somewhere deep inside him where he had not known he was empty, even though that call (there it was again) was full of things, mystery and life and hope and longing and maybe death for some lonely mouse or mole that had made the unfortunate choice to take a walk across the lonely and barren late-winter fields.

It came a fourth time, a rippling semi-musical tone from an unseen predator, and though he stood there listening for some time it never came again. There was only the breeze, his own breathing, and the soft exhalations of the Iowa night. He turned

162

to the door on the side of the barn and slowly opened it. Might be folks working inside, one never knows. These were farmers, honest and hard-working people, the salt of the earth, and he had no idea what sort of work hours they kept. For that matter, he had no idea what hour it was at all, period.

He blinked a little at the light inside even though it was weak, the result of a row of naked bulbs suspended from the ceiling, and then he stepped through the doorway into the smell of hay and dust and wood. Fresh smells, clean smells, surprisingly inviting smells. He didn't feel threatened by this barn, he was surprised to find, he felt rather welcome.

He walked in slowly, listening for anything that might suggest someone was inside, but at first he heard nothing but his own soft steps on the wood floor, a gentle thump with a scraping after-sound, the result of the fine layer of dust and chaff and dirt that covered the wood. He looked around, admired how clean the place looked, saw the stacks of hay bales to his right. He walked over and touched the bales, felt their prickly dryness, thought of the phrase *a roll in the hay* and wondered if anyone had ever really done that. It didn't seem like it would be much fun to make love on hay: too dry, too much like lying on little needles. And yet in movies and books people were always up in hay lofts getting it on. Crazy. You'd come out with skin pocked with little red marks, and probably more than a few breathing problems from all the dust and chaff. Nothing romantic or exciting in any of that.

He was standing there feeling the hay, his mind wandering off on all sorts of tangents (like how exactly did a hay baler form these perfect squares?) when he finally noticed the door on the wall. Must lead to where they bring the cows, he thought, having the image in his head of Holsteins lined up in stalls with a milking apparatus on their udders. Might somebody be in there? Jesus, Lisa, where the hell did you go? It was going to be hard enough to get Hamm awake and sober enough so he could walk out to the car without passing out or throwing up, he didn't need to spend hours looking for a young woman who was wandering all over a farm remembering her childhood. You can take the girl out of the farm but you can't—

There was a sound behind the door, a very soft shuffling followed by a thud. Helter thought for a moment that it might be some sort of animal, and that maybe it wasn't in his best

163

interest to open that door, but his need to get the hell away from the farm and back into his normal life (such as it was) was stronger. Hoping it wasn't some pissed off beast (bull, goat, mangy farm cat), he reached out and slowly opened the door.

"Get the fuck out of here!" a deep and angry voice said from the darkness, and the door itself seemed to come alive and fly back at Helter. He tensed and made to turn around, and would have run right out of that barn if it hadn't been for Lisa's voice, partially muffled but unmistakable:

"Help!"

He stood for a moment, confused and worried, and then turned back to open the door again. He had to, something wasn't right. The door only opened a few inches before being blocked by something.

"Goddamnit, Ricky, get the fuck out of here!"

"Who's in there?" he called out, and immediately all shuffling sounds stopped, replaced by very faint but heavy breathing. A couple seconds of that and then more frantic noises, the jangle of a belt buckle, sound of shoes clomping on the floor.

Helter pushed on the door again, harder this time. It moved a foot or so before stopping.

"Hey! What the hell's going on?" he asked. "Lisa?"

"Greg—" Her voice was clear for that one syllable and then was silenced. However, in that one syllable he detected fear, anger, panic.

"Lisa, you all right?" He put his shoulder to the door but it wouldn't budge.

"Why don't you just turn around and head back inside?" said the man.

"Is that Uncle... Jim?"

"Just go back inside, pretend you didn't hear anything, okay Chief?"

"Open this goddamn door!"

"You don't know what the fuck you're doing, just go back inside."

Helter tried to shoulder the door open again but it wouldn't go, so he took several steps back, deciding to rush it. Just before he took off he noticed the tools nailed to the wall to his right. He had a choice to make, and maybe just seconds to make it. Weapon or no weapon. Some situations elevate to levels they shouldn't simply because someone decided to—

164

He chose a small hatchet, then ran for the door.

It opened with only a little resistance, as he felt whatever had been blocking it get thrown backwards violently with his weight. What he found inside was a tiny dark room, lit just enough by the bare bulbs behind him so that he could make out the shape of Uncle Jim with the writhing and smaller shape of Lisa underneath him. It had been Uncle Jim's legs that were keeping the door closed, but no more: with the sudden inward force of the door opening Uncle Jim's legs had been pushed to the left at an awkward angle, and it took him a few clumsy seconds to try and stand.

He never managed it. Helter reached down and grabbed him by the back of the shirt, pulling him off of Lisa easily.

"Motherfucker!" Helter shouted.

Lisa slipped out from under the man and Helter saw she was still dressed, a good sign, and yet one that didn't serve to quell his anger one bit. He threw Uncle Jim against the room's back wall and raised the hatchet... couldn't help but raise that hatchet, it suddenly felt like a hot wild living thing in his hand, filled with power and momentum all its own.

"Kill him!" Lisa said. "Put that fucking thing in his head!"

Still he hesitated.

"Do it goddamnit!" She began to reach for it herself, grabbing at his wrist.

"Stop it!" He pushed back against her but her own fury and fear had combined to make a supernatural strength and he found it hard to fight her, she was like a fish on a line, a wild thing caught or trapped, all muscle and energy. Now would have been a good time for Uncle Jim to lash out or go bursting past them out the door but when he saw the hatchet he slunk down to the floor, closed his eyes, and started to throw his arms up in the air crazily, like he might get lucky and blindly block the blade when it came toward him. He looked pathetic, like a crab flipped upside down, its legs flailing madly, hopelessly, at the sky.

"Kill him!" Lisa said.

And part of him wanted to, part of him knew it would have felt great, maybe the best feeling in the world. As he looked at that squirming excuse for a man before him he couldn't help but see every other man just like him, bullies and rapists and molesters and every other variety of asshole he could think of. This man here was a symbol, he stood for everything

165

oppressive and violent and smug and evil, and wouldn't it have been sweet to feel the heavy old dull blade of that hatchet make contact with his skull, with his neck, with his chest, sinking in deep, deep, deep? Wouldn't it have been just what he, Helter, needed?

Indeed. As he fought off Lisa he could picture it, could feel it, and as a result he began to fight her less and less. Let's kill him, he thought, let's just do it and get it done with and never speak of it again, it has to be done and why not us and why not right here and now? Now is the time, everything's perfect. Strike a blow for justice right in this big old Iowa barn. It would feel good, too, oh yes, sweet and pure and the holiest thing in the world, just sink this blade right down deep into his sad little skull.

But no, he gave one final pull and had the hatchet away from her. She looked at him with fury in her eyes but he kept her back with his other arm.

"No!" he said. "Enough!"

She stood there panting, then looked at Uncle Jim cowering against the wall. Just like that her rage seemed to subside, and she was looking at him with disgust and pity.

"It's done," Helter said. "It's over. Lisa, look at me." When she did he reached out and touched her shoulder. "Go to the car, we're leaving."

She looked back at Uncle Jim.

"Lisa, go."

She sighed, then nodded and turned away. Helter listened to her footsteps fade across the barn and then he looked down at Uncle Jim.

"You know how lucky you are? You know how badly I want to hurt you?"

Uncle Jim said nothing.

"I'd love to cut you up. Cut you up and watch you bleed to death. I think it might be...." What was the right word? Ah, yes: "Beautiful. It might be beautiful."

He thought a moment, then knelt down until he was at the same level as the other man and looking him straight in the face.

"Why did you do it?" he asked. "Honestly, I need to know. Why would you do it?"

"I didn't do anything, I don't know what—"

166

"Don't lie to the man with the hatchet." He ran his fingers over the handle for emphasis, almost lovingly. "Why would you do it? What drives someone like you? Come on, honestly, tell me. What's going on in that brain of yours, what happened to you? Were you injured as a child? Did you fall on your head? Do you think you're better than everyone else and can do whatever you want, take whatever's not yours? Tell me, this is very important to me, I need to know."

Uncle Jim just blinked and was silent.

Helter sighed. "Please...."

*

A knock on a door, a couple of half-hesitant, half-intense raps with shaking knuckles. Otherwise silence, and that weird yellow light that seems to exist only in the hallways of cheap off-campus apartment buildings on cool crisp midnights.

A few more knocks.

A muffled voice from inside: "Go the fuck away."

A mouth pressed close to the crack between the door and the frame. "Dude, it's... me."

"Who the fuck is *me*?"

The lips move closer, the voice is hushed but a bit stronger: "Helter."

Pause. "Skelter?"

"Yeah. Let me in."

"What do you guys want?"

"It's just me."

"Where's Randy and Skink?"

"Just let me in."

A moment later the door opens and Helter appears from the darkness looking ragged and tense.

"What do you want?" Jasper asks, his eyes instinctually glancing around for their mutual friends and then, realizing they're not there, frowning down at the guy standing in the hall.

"Can we talk?" Helter asks.

The big man rubs at his face, eyes, forehead. "Now? Why?"

"You have anyone else in there?"

He sighs. "No, not tonight." Then he pulls his hand from his face and gets a good honest look at the other fellow, sees how ragged he looks, how nervous and troubled as he gives

167

paranoid glances up and down the hall.   "You all right?
Tripping? You look like shit."

"Just let me in, Jazz. Just… let me in."

Tripping, yeah. Had to be. Nothing else makes you look
like that. Dead and ragged, nervous and troubled.

He lets him in.

He had to visit the girl first, if this was going to happen. He made that perfectly clear, despite Skelter's protests. You can't just go into something like this straight off, without any emotional connection to what happened, you needed to look at it, to see it first-hand, to gaze into those broken eyes and see those shattered bones, split lips, broken teeth, bloodied cheeks. He needed to smell that antiseptic hospital smell, see those tubes in her arms, hear the sickening wheeze of machines and labored lungs. He needed to hear the voices of the doctors and nurses in the hallways (their technical talk, their weird feathery whispers, their little jokes) in order to absorb the full depth of what had happened here. Otherwise he was just a man being paid to fuck someone up.

"Susan Helter," he said to the squat-bodied middle-aged woman behind the counter. He'd dressed nicely for this visit, nothing too fancy, just a sweater over a buttoned-down shirt, with wrinkled but passable khaki pants. His shoes had been nice dress shoes once upon a time but now they were beaten all to hell and splattered with mud from the melting snow outside. It was a warm day, Spring was coming.

169

The woman behind the counter looked him up and down. Dressed nicely or not, he knew she had instant doubts about him. He was a big man, and not an overly friendly-looking one. Not today, anyway. He was tired and worried and rather sick, hospitals always made him sick. It was the smell, and all of those ill people. People die in places like this, or they get plugged into wall outlets and fed all sorts of crap so they can linger and linger in perpetual pain, bled dry of money and self-worth. Terrible places.

The woman started tapping on a computer keyboard. "Room 234," she said. "She'll likely be sleeping."

"That's fine," Jasper said. That was in fact just the way he wanted it. He did not want to talk to her, that would have been unbearable. "Thanks."

He thought about the girl as he took the stairs to the second floor. Susie Helter, the cute head-turning lass who now and then came bounding deer-like down the hall to fetch her brother, to tease him, to tell him he simply *must* give her twenty bucks for the movies. She was a freshman but she walked around without any of that freshman nervousness you see in others, the darting eyes, the quick movement from building to building, the half-open mouth that suggested surprise or awe or confusion. No, not this girl, she went everywhere with a confidence that was startling. She would march down the hall of her brother's dorm and not look out of place at all. Did she notice the turned heads, the lecherous eyes? Likely, but she wouldn't have cared. Why should she, she was young and in college and finally at the beginning of life's great journey, she had everything ahead of her, the world was open and waiting. He remembered seeing her sitting Indian-style on her brother's futon, could picture her being sassy and smart-mouthed when she was a kid, the annoying younger sister tormenting her brother and his friends. There had been a movie in the union once, and Jasper remembered her tagging along with the group. He thought of how she and Skelter seemed so close, like they could still share secret codes, private little raps on bedroom walls in the middle of the night. Must be nice to have a sister. Must be nice to have anyone.

When he came to the second floor he was nervous. How bad is she? he'd asked Skelter.

The doctors said she was going to lose one eye, and the other would lose some degree of sight. Seven broken ribs, a

170

collapsed lung, multiple cuts to head and face, a broken nose, and a concussion. She was lucky the blow to the nose had not killed her, they said. They asked me if I knew who did it.

And you said you had no idea, right?

I said I had no idea.

When Jasper walked down the hallway of the hospital and stood at last before her room he did indeed have a name in his head, it was just sitting there, waiting patiently.

The room was dimly lit and he knew she was sleeping. He stood there in the hall for a moment, took in some deep breaths, looked around, saw a nurse pushing a cart into another room, its wheels squeaking softly like baby birds. God-awful place. From a PA system came a page for a doctor, some sort of code. Not a Code Blue, not now, though eventually there would be, of course. You can't escape a Code Blue.

At last he found the strength and stepped through the doorway.

The figure on the bed looked ghost-like under white sheets and a light-blue spread. There was a dim light coming through the closed shades, a pinkish glow that hurt his eyes. Various machines were humming and breathing around the bed, each with its own lights: flashing greens and reds and yellows. One of them had a digital counter but he couldn't quite see the numbers, let alone know what they would have meant. Blood pressure, perhaps. Heart rate.

Once he was inside the room he hesitated again, then took a few more steps so that he could see her face. He needed to see it, he needed to—

"Who are you?" she asked. Her voice was weak but clear.

"No one," he said, and started to leave.

"Wait, please, who...." She started to sit up.

Jasper turned back and raised his hands. "Don't move, you don't need to move."

"Who are you?"

Should he tell her? It seemed wrong to do so, but it seemed worse not to. "Jasper," he said.

She said nothing for a moment, then appeared to nod. "Big guy. Friend of Greg's."

"Yeah, that's right."

"Thanks for coming."

He nodded.

"Why?"

171

"Why what?"

"Why did you come?"

"I...." And what to say to that? He should just walk right out. "I don't know," he said. "I wanted to see how you were."

"And how am I?"

"I'm sure you've been better."

This made her laugh, though that wasn't his intention, he just didn't know what to say, had no idea what she might want to hear.

"I'm not going to die," she said. Her voice sounded weaker, like it hurt to talk.

"No, of course not." He stepped closer to the bed. "I'm sorry I woke you, I should get going."

"I was dreaming. I was dreaming about an old house. It was burning, but no one seemed to care, they were all standing around it smiling, not really noticing it at all. Playing, I think some of them were playing with a football or something. It was cold out, winter, and everyone was wearing hats and gloves and big coats. No... some people cared, there were some old people, old men, who were running around crying and asking for help. I was up on a hill, just sitting there, watching it all. Then I was sledding down and the air was cold on my face and I was happy, I think. I think I was happy." She lifted her head to look at him. "What do you think that means?"

"I don't know."

She put her head back on the pillow. "I don't know either." She said nothing for a long time and Jasper thought she had fallen asleep. Then: "It's a strange world, you know? Nothing ever turns out the way you think it will."

"No," he said. He thought about that, about how true it was, and didn't realize she had fallen silent again. When he finally shook himself out of his thoughts and looked up he saw she was sleeping for real, her breathing deep and steady and strong in the quiet room. He hoped she'd have better dreams now, with nothing burning, nothing cold, and then he slipped out and away.

Within three days a senior named Mark Rogers was in the same hospital, two floors up. He was in much worse shape than the girl and would not be able to talk for a month. He would never be able to play baseball again, and he would never be able to use his right arm. He would lose a testicle and ten teeth, and for some odd reason seventy-five percent of his sense

172

of taste. It must have been the head injury, the doctors would suggest. Blunt trauma to the front of the skull. Repeatedly. Blunt but *precise* trauma. Do you know who did this? the police asked his parents and friends. No, no idea, they said. Mark Rogers himself would say the same thing when he was finally able to talk again. Not long after that he dropped out of Birnbaum, six credits shy of graduating.

"What did you do to your hand?" someone asked Jasper Callister.

He looked at it as if he had just noticed the cut and bruised knuckles, the swollen fingers, the blood.

"I hit something."

It wasn't too much later that he dropped out too. No more playing at being a student, at using this academic route (never a good fit for him anyway) to hide from all the things he needed to hide from, the crap back home, the vicious black thoughts that rumbled and rattled around in his head, the feelings that sat stewing in his heart. So long, Birnbaum University, it's been good to know ya, he thought... and then he entered the world.

*

Outside the realm of their headlights there was only darkness, nothing visible but the faint edges of barns and fences and homes and cars that were glimpsed for brief moments as they passed, a silvery etching of bumper here, the soft rotting corner of a shed there, perhaps the ghostly outline of a cow standing at the edge of a field or the flash of yellow eye-shine from a ditch. Otherwise the world out there did not exist, there was only the old gray road ahead of them, slowly doing its dance of decay.

Helter had turned down the dash lights so the inside of the car wasn't bathed in the influenza-green glow of tachometer, speedometer, gas gauge, and though he didn't look over to see for sure he thought Lisa might have been sleeping. Sleeping or just taking deep breath after deep breath. Either way, she was slumped down in her seat angled away from Helter with her head on the door, and she hadn't moved in miles.

The road signs offered little guidance, only numbers that meant nothing, flaring up in the headlights for a few seconds and then immediately lost to the darkness again as they sped past. Where are we? Helter wondered. Where are we and

173

where are we going? You could get lost out here following old highways forever and ever, slipping past cornfields and hills and rivers and lakes, all of it looking the same, nothing different anywhere, the country as a whole swallowing you up as it sends you down the long twisting vine-like spines of its roads and highways and avenues into the deep dark depths of itself, nothing to mark your way but farms and small towns and little roadside vegetable stands run by children. It was a danger, yes, but it wouldn't be so bad, getting lost here was better than getting stuck in subdivisions and strip malls and the stinking shadowy back alleys of cities. And the sun would come up, this black impenetrable night would end, a golden crescent would peak over the horizon, over those cornfields and hills, and light you up all nice and warm. You'd still be lost, yes, but lost in sunlight and blue skies, not driving without aim through such heavy dark stillness, watching for eye-shine and dangerous curves, hoping some bored farm kids hadn't removed all the stop signs in their county and put you on a collision course with some late-night semi driver hauling logs or hogs or steel. Helter remembered long drives like this as a kid, crossing landscapes in the backseat of his parent's cream-white Buick, the soft hiss of an eight-track tape playing Elvis or some K-Tel collection (*Golden Country Favorites!*) through cracked and dusty speakers. He would curl up on the seat or the floor and slip off to a hazy hesitant halting sleep filled with hazy hesitant and halting dreams, rocked all the time by the play of the car on the road, sung into dreamland by the engine, the tires, the music....

The land was so open back then, the fields stretched like seas of grass and corn and wheat and wrapped themselves over the horizon past farms and silos that rose here and there like they were part of the land themselves, set down by nature or god or both, unobtrusive and beautiful, surrounded by the jittery dry buzz and rattle of grasshoppers and crickets and cicadas, the slow gaze of horses and cows, the effervescent eternity of the sky, the gentle nodding wisdom of prairie-smoke and goldenrod, the evening burst of impassive stars and planets. Barns sat eternally rotting, suspended in their decay, leaning either bored or dreary at the sides of roads, with boy-tall grasses all itchy and dry stretching up their cracked and hollow sides and pigeons perched on what was left of their roofs. A tired dusty old hound lying dreamless and dull on a shadowy

174

patch of gravel drive, and an even older farmer crossing a yard with a paint can in one hand and a warped piece of wood the size of a coffee-table book in the other. Later, passing back this way, they would see the simple sign he'd made: VEGGIES. And maybe they'd stop and buy tomatoes or corn or pumpkins or peas or radishes or onions, perhaps the rare jar of honey or maple syrup fresh from the back acres of the farm, and the dog might wander over and the boy would pet him, or maybe he'd walk off to the closest fence and watch the cows stare out at the world like they'd seen it all or seen nothing and didn't care either way. A simple breeze would come in, soft and sweet, pulling with it the soft sweet smell of hay, horse, and hollyhock.

Why think of this stuff now?

"Why did that all come to you then?" Lisa would ask him later. She would be sitting there with a tape recorder pushed in front of him and a look in her eyes like she thought this all might mean something. He would pity her, of course: this meant nothing.

"I don't know," he would say. "Except, it's all gone, you know. There might be a dog like that, a veggie stand, and an old farmer, but there's something else with it all now, like a disease or a plague of insects."

"What do you think it is?"

And he would say: "You know. Everybody knows."

Onward through the Iowa night, searching for a way off this old highway, headed Eastward, searching for the tell-tale sign of an interstate or the glow of a town in the distance. He wondered what Bantam and Jasper were doing, and after a time pulled out his cell-phone. It was pushing eleven-thirty. He dialed a number and there was no answer. He tried again a few minutes later and his phone died.

And now he knew Lisa was sleeping. She was beginning to snore lightly, the sound soothing in the little dark womb of the car. He wanted to reach over and touch her leg, to reassure himself if nothing else... but reassure himself of what, he didn't know. Maybe that there were still things that were soft and warm and alive. The fear, though, was that he might touch her and find her cold, stiff, as dead as that shape back there on the side of the road, some cat or dog or raccoon smuckered two or three weeks ago and continually flattened by cars, trucks, tractors until it became part of the asphalt, a dried out

175

meaningless *thing* wasting away in the sun and moonlight. No, he kept his hands to themselves, gripped the steering wheel tightly, watched the road.

In the backseat Hamm was staring out at the ditches, likely seeing nothing but staring out there nonetheless. Helter could see just the barest outline of his neck and shoulders in the rearview mirror.

This was all wasted time, he knew, every moment between now and when he'd left Dreary. He'd been caught up in the excitement of something that, when he looked at it now, wasn't really that exciting. Bantam? Bantam for President? Please. He'd have been better off staying with the union work, or heading somewhere else, taking Hamm's suggestion and checking out the city.

Same old thoughts again. And there, there's a sign for a highway: 13. Did he want Highway 13? He wasn't sure, but he knew if he slowed to take it he'd wake Lisa and she sounded peaceful snoring in her seat next to him. The turn came closer and closer and finally passed on by, he didn't even give it a glance. She might even be dreaming now, her foot kicked out now and then and her hands looked like they were twitching. He hoped they were good dreams, something safe and peaceful to slip into, an escape from this world here, from predators in old barns, from Presidential campaigns and whatever else she might have to fret over. He looked over to her but could not see her face, she was turned away from him. He hoped there was a smile on her lips, that it was a dream of puppies and clouds and sweetness and hope that swept her up and sent her off and lifted her away to enchantment and mystery.

A little while later she said something in her sleep. He wished he'd caught what it was, but she only mumbled it once and then fell silent again. It sounded peaceful, though, not a word or phrase spoken in pain or fear. Please be a good dream, he thought. One of us deserves to have them.

Enough of this, he told himself a moment later. Whatever the next highway is I'm going to take it.

He didn't, though. He started thinking about Susie again and that was that.

*

"Hey Susie, come here and meet someone."

176

Hands were extended, shaken.

"Susie, this is Mark, Mark this is Susie."

Susie did not blush (she was above blushing) but she bit her bottom lip and cocked her head and looked at her brother.

"Are you trying to set us up?" she asked with a smile.

"No, not at all," he said, all the while thinking: Mark's a decent guy, he seems pretty cool, maybe it'll work out, a bit of fun if nothing else....

*

"Fuck!" Hamm said.

Helter was jerked from his thoughts. "What? What's wrong?"

"I think I'm gonna puke."

Helter looked over to Lisa, who hadn't stirred.

"You sure?"

"Yeah."

"Goddamnit." He rubbed at his chin nervously and then decided it was better for Lisa to wake up from him stopping than with some idiot puking on her. He braked and pulled as close to the side of the road as he could get.

Hamm jumped out before the car was stopped and immediately headed for the ditch.

"What's going on?" Lisa asked. Her voice was cracked and thin.

"He's throwing up."

She sighed and stretched before pulling herself up to a full sitting position. She looked out the window at the night.

"Where are we?"

"I don't know. Iowa. You doing all right?"

"I'm great." She yawned. "I need some air." She opened her door and slipped out.

After a time Helter killed his headlights and followed after her. The sound of Hamm retching in the ditch greeted him.

Lisa was standing in the middle of the road doing little stretching exercises, apparently not distracted by the awful violent sounds coming from the darkness.

"Fucker's still drunk," Helter said. He leaned back against the car and looked up and down the road for signs of traffic.

"He's drunk a lot," Lisa answered. "You never noticed?"

177

Helter ignored this, instead took a moment to turn his eyes from the road and up to the sky, where a million shiny things sat sparkling and dead. Cassiopeia, Canis minor, Gemini, Leo, Cancer, Lynx, Orion, Taurus. An eternity of darkness and dust, and the cold dead light of cold dead stars. Meaningless, he thought, meaning himself and everything on this planet. Under such immense space we all had to be meaningless, insignificant, destined to fade out in the face of all the never-ending minutes and seconds and hours that had passed and were yet to come. The Universe was expanding all the time, they said. It was growing outward, getting away from us as fast as possible. Maybe that meant something. It was humbling if nothing else.

He remembered that Susie had been interested in astronomy, it had been her favorite class. I'm no good at math, she said, otherwise I'd pursue it more. But she loved to go out at night and look up at the sky and get lost in all of that silver and gold. He wondered if she still did that. He hoped so, and he hoped she found comfort in them, that she didn't stare up there and think of all the things that might have been.

"Oh Jesus Christ!" Hamm said from the ditch.

Helter shook his head and looked at Lisa, who was standing about five feet away in the middle of the road. He noticed that she too was looking up to the sky, lost in thought.

"What's that?" she suddenly said, and in the thin glow of the parking lights he saw she was pointing straight up.

He looked and saw a tiny but solid silver light making a steady, easy course overhead.

"Satellite."

"Oh." She gestured with her chin to the ditch. "Is he almost done?"

"You almost done?" Helter called out. The answer was something only marginally similar to a human voice.

She sighed. "Jesus..."

"You want to talk about what happened?"

"No."

"Because I'll listen. I mean, if you just want to—"

"I said no."

He nodded, let maybe only a minute go by, and then said: "It wasn't your fault, you know."

"I know it wasn't my fault. I'm not an idiot. You think I'm an idiot?"

178

"I was just trying to help."

"I don't need help. It's over." Then she turned and walked off down the road. He watched her silhouette fade into the dimmest of shapes before it was lost completely in the darkness and he was alone with the sound of Hamm puking and, further off, the faint songs of some very early chorus frogs. Spring was coming. And then what?

Good question. Was he done with this campaign bullshit?

"I'm dying," Hamm gurgled from the ditch.

Certainly he couldn't go all the way through now, regardless of what happened, even if Bantam were to become a viable, realistic candidate. He doubted he could survive that long. He looked over to where Lisa had wandered down the road. He doubted *any* of them could survive that long. He looked around at the night, saw nothing but formless darkness, a dreamscape without detail or texture. Where are we? Indeed. Where was anyone?

We're drowning, he thought. We're drowning in something without a surface and without a bottom, something endless and black, and each of us is floating away from the others and we will never come together again.

The sound of Hamm retching rose once more through the quiet, silencing the rhythm of the frogs.

The sun was far from coming up but they could feel its presence burning and itching in their eyes. Helter saw the weak neon sign before the others (FOOD) and was momentarily confused, since there didn't look to be a town anywhere nearby, it was just a spectral yellow-green FOOD rising without context from the depth of the night. Only when he slowed for the place did he see the dark shape of the town buried beyond it in the muck of the predawn darkness. The proverbial sleepy little village. The smaller unlit sign above FOOD said MA'S. Of course.

The place was open but there were only two other vehicles there, a compact little broken dwarf of a car and a new but dusty pickup with extended cab and dually wheels. Helter turned off the engine and the sudden silence was grating, he'd gotten so used to the hum of the engine, the gentle rhythmic thumping of the tires on cracked asphalt. He looked over at Lisa, thought about asking her if she wanted to talk again, and decided against it.

"Where are we?" asked Hamm as he opened his door.

Helter sighed. "Ma's."

"Where the hell is Ma's?"

"Everywhere."

180

They went in and took a booth near a window that looked out at the car. From here they faced east, and if they stayed long enough they could watch the sun climb out, a slow subtle blossoming of faint light over the houses and fields that made up this corner of the world. Their waitress was a pleasantly pear-shaped middle-aged woman who smiled at them in that friendly but distant way which seems to come to every waitress naturally. She took their orders for omelets and coffee and orange juice and then left them alone.

Helter and Lisa were on one side of the booth, Hamm on the other. Lisa had the inside and was looking out the window, watching.

"When we get to the hotel I'm gonna tell Bantam I quit," Helter said.

Hamm looked at him. "What? Why?"

"I'm done. I need to go home."

Hamm frowned. "Where's home?"

"I don't know."

Hamm looked at Lisa, expecting her to ask the same questions, but she only gave Helter a brief glance before turning her attention back to the window.

"Well that's just great," Hamm said. "You make me come out here to join this goddamn thing and now you just up and quit. I mean, this isn't exactly my idea of a great fucking time, but... Jesus, Greg, I took a huge risk leaving my job."

"They'll take you back."

"Well, yeah, they'll take me back, that's not the point. I...."

Their waitress came over with the coffee, poured each of them a mug and set the pot on a small little scorched pad. When she left Hamm looked at Helter, then sighed and put his hands around his coffee. "Shit...."

They sat there in silence, and over the next several minutes more people started to come in, locals and late-night truckers. Farm-looking dudes in overalls and jeans, and one pleasantly plump dough-faced woman in shapeless slacks and a flower-print blouse. They all took booths and tables and a few gave the three campaigners a glance and a nod, but otherwise they were ignored.

Doesn't anyone sleep around here? Helter wondered. He tried to look into each of their faces to see what he might find but gave it up when all he saw was something at once familiar

181

and so different from himself it was scary. He sipped his coffee, thought it tasted bitter and thought he could feel it doing bad things to his stomach. He wondered if he was getting an ulcer. Likely.

"Shit," Hamm said again, mostly to himself, and drank from his mug.

"Bud, you still driving that piece of crap Ford?" said a man a few tables over. He was an older guy dressed all in dark denim, and he was speaking to another guy one table over, this guy also dressed in dark denim but with the addition of a baseball cap on his grizzled head. The cap had an enigmatic and boldly red C written on it that appeared more than vaguely threatening, though the face it rested over was pleasant enough, a typical Midwestern worker sort of face, the kind that belongs to someone who's been a Midwestern worker for more than half a century.

"That thing'll be running long after you're dead and buried."

"I keep eating here that won't be long at all."

"Careful," said the waitress as she passed by.

"You know I'm kidding, I love this place. It's this food that'll keep me alive forever."

"Heaven help us," she said.

"Oh Clara, I know you love me."

"You know nothing of the sort, Gene. You gonna have your regular?"

"Of course."

Lisa didn't take her eyes from the window. Something that looked like a cat had slipped underneath their car.

"Is Jeffrey cooking in there today?"

"You got a problem with Jeffrey?"

The older guy in the denim leaned back in his chair and put his hands up defensively. "Not at all, Jeffrey's good. He makes a mean Denver. I just like Carl's Belgian waffle, is all."

The waitress, who was also quite possibly Ma, took the rest of the orders and then slipped out of the room. She returned a few minutes later to give the other people coffee and then came over and smiled at Helter.

"Your food should be ready shortly. You need anything?"

"We're good," Helter said.

"Glass of water," said Lisa.

182

"Water, sure." And just before she turned away she gave them all a peculiar look that made Helter wonder what they must have looked like to her, coming off the night they'd just had. He turned his head to study Hamm and then Lisa but Lisa had gone back to staring out the window and Hamm... well, Hamm didn't look like anything other than an exhausted and nerve-wracked creature of the night. A bad salesman on a super-slow day. When he saw Helter watching him Hamm said:

"Come out and join me, you said. We'll change the world. That's what you said. A noble adventure. A once in a lifetime chance."

"I was wrong."

"What about your beloved candidate? You're just gonna abandon Bantam like that? Isn't he the last great chance for change in American politics? Or do you suddenly no longer believe that?"

Helter shrugged.

Hamm shook his head.

"How's old Stewie doing, anyway?" This was a voice from those other tables. Helter had half an ear on them, just listening to the cadence of their speech, the friendly verbal jousting, the playful abuse. If political debate in this country could be done like that then things might get done. As it stood there was far too much paranoia, too much anger, too much distrust. With good reason, too: anyone, anywhere, was perfectly willing to stick a knife in you... from the back or the front. Either way. As long as it went in good and deep.

"Last great hope, you said," Hamm was saying. "A new sort of politician. A voice of honesty and integrity in the modern era."

"What do you think?" Helter asked. "About Bantam, what do you think?"

"I think it no longer matters." He refilled his coffee.

The waitress came with their food, set each of their plates in front of them and asked again if they needed anything.

"Water," said Lisa.

"Oh criminy, I forgot. Sorry 'bout that, I'll get it right away." She left.

Helter turned his attention to his food, his cheese and ham and onion omelet with toast and hash browns. He slathered the toast with grape jelly and refilled his coffee and glanced over at

183

the other people in the diner. The food was as he expected, good and honest and fat with taste. When the other customers got their orders he saw a stack of pancakes that made him wish he'd gotten those instead: they were thick and beautifully brown and when the man covered them with deep amber maple syrup he had to look away. Best to stick with what you'd ordered.

"Do we know where the hell we're going?" Hamm asked after a few minutes.

"Yes."

"Do we—"

"Look," Lisa said. She was pointing out the window.

Hamm and Helter looked and saw that the cat was now perched on top of their car, just sitting there looking around, gazing at the world from its new perspective. After some time it began to clean itself, licking its front paws and running them over its head.

"You feeling all right?" Helter asked.

Lisa nodded. "Sure. Never better." She kept picking and poking at her food while staring out at the cat.

Helter and Hamm exchanged looks and went back to eating. What Helter was thinking was that he'd never before in his life felt quite so empty, that he was surrounded by meaninglessness in search of meaning, that everything he was, everything he'd done, everything he stood for, had absolutely no worth in the general scheme of things. He was one among millions in the modern world, a ghost floating on breezes here at the start of the new century. A ghost among ghosts in a ghost world. He felt like he needed something, that there had been promises made and never kept, that there was something he was supposed to have that was being denied him. He wanted to feel that his life had potential and promise but he could not, he felt like he was just sitting in a diner somewhere in pre-dawn Iowa with nothing lying ahead or behind him. He felt like everything, the past and present and future, was a waste. He imagined himself moving out to New York to start a new life and couldn't believe anything would really come of it.

Change happens slowly, like avalanches. One rock, one little pebble upsetting the balance, and everything builds from there.

Bantam's voice. And maybe he was right, and maybe that was how things really worked. But how much time do we have?

"You hear about that Bantam fella?"

This was the guy who'd been bantering with the waitress. Gene. He was speaking to Bud, the man with the C on his cap. Nevertheless, Helter felt his heart jump at the question and was glad it hadn't been directed his way. He glanced over and then quickly away, trying not to appear interested. The last thing he wanted was to be outed as a member of any sort of political campaign. He was over it. It was done. And it was no kind of work for a grown man anyway.

"That guy," Bud said. He grimaced and turned his head sideways like he'd just tasted something bitter. "Kind of a nutball, ain't he?"

"He's got some good points. He speaks his mind, says it clear and without any bullshit."

"No politics in the diner," said the waitress as she walked over.

"We're not talking politics, Clara, we're talking people."

"Less talking, more eating," she said. When she was gone Gene leaned toward the man in the cap.

"You can tell he's a real person, he talks like you or me, not with all that mumbo-jumbo the other guys use."

"Might be so. What kind of chance he got, though?"

"As much chance as people will give him."

"You talking about that new fellow?" someone at another table asked. "That guy that swears a lot?"

"He don't swear no more than you do."

"Shouldn't swear at all. A person's in the public eye they oughta watch what they say. Voters won't go for it."

"They *all* watch what they say, that's the problem with 'em. They watch what they say so much they don't say nothin' at all. Real people with real problems don't watch what they say."

"Goddamn right."

There was laughter, then: "What problems *you* got?"

"Do I know this person?" someone asked. "The one you're talking about?"

"That Wisconsin fella. Bantam, ain't it? The one that said that stuff about Parsons."

"Republican?"

"No, he's something else. What party is it?"

The man in the C hat shrugged. "Can't remember. An independent, though."

"It's gonna be Keith. He'll take Parsons unless Parsons can somehow make a dent in the South."

"Keith *used* to be good, now he's just like all the others."

"This Banter guy's got some interesting ideas."

"Bantam."

"He said something somewhere that reminded me of my dad. He used to tell us: 'never say a good thing if a bad thing is the truth.'"

"Can't win an election on words alone."

"That's right. You need money. And lies. Lies help."

"That Bantam guy seems all right. Saw him on TV somewhere and he reminded me of someone you'd trust. Or drink a beer with. Seemed smart."

Gene nodded. "That's right. I don't know if he can get enough people behind him, but he's not a typical politician. We need someone who can say things like a normal human being. Just come out and say it, say what needs to be done, and stop all the playing."

"You like this Bantam fella so much, why aren't you out working for him?"

"Maybe I will be. Get me out of this damn town and away from you fools."

"You know where the door is."

Laughter.

"Listen, Gene, here's how I see it: if we're gonna put someone in the White House, they better have three things: integrity, sense, and a backbone. What do you know about this guy? Where's he come from? What's he done? What's he like as a person?"

"What are *any* of them like?"

"Are they really people? Maybe they're made in a lab somewhere."

Laughter again.

Helter looked up at Hamm and Lisa but they were absorbed in their food, not taking their eyes from their plates.

"I kinda like that guy," the woman in the flower-print blouse said. "You get sick of the others."

"Ending immigration until we get jobs for everyone. Death penalty for child molesters. Making sure there's no piss and

186

chemicals in the water. Making sure teachers have what they need. Staying out of trouble in other countries. I can get behind all that."

"That's what he's for?"

"That and other stuff."

"I heard he wanted to make snakes the national animal or something."

"Rattlesnakes. Like on the old *don't tread on me* flag."

"Oh, that's right, I heard that. Said the way a snake acts is how we oughta be."

"Well, now he's just crazy," said the woman with a shiver.

"He doesn't want to make them the national animal, he wants to make that whole 'treading on me' thing our policy again. Keep us out of being the police of the world. Don't bother nobody unless they bother us."

"They're bothering us everywhere. We can't isolate ourselves."

"We can keep out of places we don't belong."

"Maybe. And if we get pulled in anyway?"

"Then we go in and do what we have to do."

"I like that he's for guns."

"Who?"

"That guy you're talking about."

"Bantam."

"A bantam's a chicken."

"A bantam is a rooster. What kind of farmer were you, Rodney? Good thing you retired."

"A bantam is a type of chicken. Don't try to outsmart me on fowl."

"A politician don't support the Second Amendment and I don't support the politician."

"Your cousin still has that chicken farm up north don't he?"

"How's he on all the social stuff? Gay marriage and all that?"

"I don't know. How are you?"

"Hell, I don't care what anyone does so long as it's not done to me. Fags want to join the misery of marriage then let 'em."

"It's legal now everywhere anyway, isn't it?"

187

"I like what Bantam had to say about manufacturing. I think it was him, anyway. Said we oughta punish people for sending jobs overseas."

"They all say that. No one ever does anything."

"Punish how? Higher taxes on 'em? How's that going to create jobs?"

"I don't know if it was taxes or what. You might be right."

"He *was* the first guy I've ever heard call politicians assholes."

"They *are* assholes. I say that all the time."

"Ever heard a *candidate* call politicians assholes?"

Clara the waitress had come back into the room with a pot of coffee in one hand and a small stack of napkins in the other.

"Watch the language, Gene," she said. "These nice folks don't want to hear your mouth." And she smiled at Helter.

"Well, that's what he called 'em," Gene said. "There's no other word for them anyway."

"Public servants," someone said, and everyone laughed.

"I think this Bantam guy doesn't have a snowball's chance but I really do like that he has no polish. He doesn't seem to have some sort of public relations guy next to him pulling on a leash or anything. Reminds me of what Presidents were like back in the old days, when you could maybe be a whole lot more real, when there weren't cameras and cellphones and journalists all over the place. I could see him talking to foreign presidents and saying what needs to be said."

"Gotta do what needs to be done, can't just say it."

"I think he could do it."

"Not if he ain't got the establishment behind him. If *they* don't want him to win he won't win, it's as simple as that. You can't go anywhere without the big money behind you."

"I think running as someone who *doesn't* have the big money behind you could get you elected. People would respond to that. They'd like it. They'd like the integrity."

"That might be. That's one thing I really think that Bantam guy has on his side: he doesn't seem like the type who could get bought and sold."

"They can all get bought and sold. Just give 'em time."

"You gotta get behind someone sometime and trust them. Voting just comes down to trust, that's all."

"I thought I said no politics," Clara said.

"Kick us out."

"I might have to. I'll take your money first."

"My cousin saw him speak somewhere. He said he also wants to stop all immigration, from anywhere. You can't win saying something like that."

"Doesn't Keith say that?"

"Something similar."

"Too many people here already. It's getting so you can't take a piss in the woods without looking up and seeing some fool standing there."

Clara frowned. "Who are you talking about?"

"The next President of the United States."

Laughter.

"Bantam," Gene said. "Ever heard of him?"

"Isn't that the guy who said politicians should have to pass a lie detector test when they make a vote, just to keep 'em honest?"

"Something like that."

"That was him," Gene said. "Also said to take the money out of politics, stop allowing the politicians to vote on their own pay raises, stop the endless campaigning. No political commercials, he says, they're all poison. Make it so any regular joe can run for office, not just the millionaires. Term-limits, so none of these idiots are in there for decades."

"I'd go for that."

Everyone was silent, taking this in. Helter caught Hamm's eye but there was nothing to read in it other than slight embarrassment and unease, the same things he himself was feeling.

"A person can say all that stuff," the man in the C cap finally said, "but it doesn't mean a thing unless he can get something done, and no stranger can just come in and make anything different. That's just the way it is."

Gene sighed and held out his mug for Clara to refill.

"If you accept things as they are just 'cause that's how they are and how they've always been," Gene said, "you've done nothing but give up."

"Sometimes you say things that make sense, Gene. Not always, but sometimes."

"I'm telling you, you guys should hear him talk. It might open your eyes a bit."

"We should get out of here," Hamm said, leaning over the table to whisper.

189

"You have awful breath," Lisa said.

"So would you if you just spent the night puking in a ditch."

Clara came up to their booth. "All done? Nothing else?"

Helter shook his head. "Just the check, please."

"It was delicious," said Lisa with a smile.

"Thank you, dear." She set their check down on the table and was about to walk away but Helter stopped her, pulled out his wallet, flipped through the cash inside, and handed her a few bills. "You need change?" she asked.

"No."

"Well thank you much, you folks have a nice day."

"You too." Helter looked at his companions. "Let's get out of here."

They slipped out of the booth and made their way across the diner, floating right past the last few bits of political discussion that were still lingering. Once outside they found the morning brighter than they'd thought, half the sun visible from above the horizon, the whole sky lighter now, a few birds singing from nearby trees. *Morning has broken, like the first morning.* Right. They walked weary and blurry-eyed over to the car. The cat that had been perched on top saw them coming and immediately bolted off, running across the parking lot and disappearing behind the old house there.

"Christ, look at that," Hamm said. He looked sick again.

The cat had left behind the remains of a mouse. It appeared to have been neatly cut in half, with a glistening coil of pink and blue intestines spilled out onto the car and its little naked feet and tail lying useless to the morning sky. The upper half was missing completely, likely right down the cat's throat. An impressive smear of blood was spread across the roof, along with little bloody cat tracks.

Helter looked for a stick and flicked the corpse away. Lisa watched it land and stared at it a moment before looking to where the cat had run.

"Get in the car," Helter said. She didn't move. "Lisa, get in the car."

Hamm had already done so and was lying down in the backseat with his eyes closed.

"What do you make of that?" she asked.

"Nothing. Come on, let's go."

190

"I thought the little bastard was just up there getting warm, looking at the world, keeping an eye on things."

"Are you all right?"

She nodded slowly but never took her eyes from the old house. Helter looked at that house too and frowned at its slanted and rotting back porch, the overgrown scraggly bushes, the dead yard, the flaking paint. Hard to tell what color that paint had originally been, it looked dirty now, dulled and sullied by age. Might have been white. Could have been yellow.

"They shouldn't let him out," Lisa said. "Outdoor cats get killed."

"Probably a stray."

"They eat songbirds, too."

"Lisa."

"A farm cat, now, that's a different thing. Entirely different. Farm cats are made for killing, it's what they do."

"Maybe it was a farm cat out on a stroll."

"That was no farm cat, you can tell by the eyes. And the fur is…." She made a gesture with her right hand, moving it oddly in front of her chest and stomach, wriggling the fingers a bit to indicate something dirty and matted. She did this for a while before frowning and looking over to Helter.

"Are you all right?" he asked.

She sighed. She looked like she had just realized something had been taken from her, that she had just noticed the new and strange emptiness inside herself, the hole that had suddenly formed there. She nodded.

"Let's go," he said. He went to the driver's side and slid in behind the wheel, noticing right away the cell-phone he'd left charging in the outlet. He picked it up as Lisa climbed into her seat and read the display as she buckled up. "We have a text from Bantam."

Hamm's voice, cracked and ragged and phlegmy from the back: "He dropping out?"

Helter read: "SUPER 8 INDEPENDENCE ROOM 123—COME—B."

A few moments later they were on the road again, cruising through the morning.

"If I remember correctly," Helter said, "there's some sort of event in Waterloo today. I think Parsons was going to be there this morning, a meet-and-greet thing in a diner or maybe the high-school... can't remember. Anyway, I think that was the plan."

"Are you really quitting?" Lisa asked.

That question. He made a face and ran a hand through his hair. "I don't know. Listening to that guy back there I was thinking how much the people who like Bantam actually *like* him, there's a passion for him. Even those who don't like him have that passion. He has no chance in hell of winning, of course, and maybe even little chance of causing change, but... this might be the start of something down the road. This might be the seed of actual honest to goodness goddamn change. Four years from now... eight, ten, twelve. Little things get rolling and start avalanches, it just takes time."

"So you're back in?" Hamm asked. He was sitting up now and staring like a sick dog out the window.

"I don't know. For now." He glanced at Hamm in the rearview mirror. "What else do I have to do?"

Hamm nodded, never taking his eyes from the world outside. "That's what I'm saying."

*

There was nothing quite like the feel of your knuckles smashing into someone's nose and breaking it into an ugly mush. The cartilage sort of gives in, almost way too easily, and there was that tiny little fraction of a second before your hand connected with actual bone... not to be stopped, no, but to send the whole head reeling backwards. It was a great stress reliever.

"You gotta treat women a little better than you have been," he said to that curly-haired monstrosity of a man he was holding down... not that he needed to hold him anymore, the guy could in no way stand on his own. But holding him was part of the fun. Hold with one hand, beat with the other, like a dance. And a one, and a two....

There was no way the guy could understand or respond, but he was certainly getting the point. Hard not to get the point

192

when some big bear of a bastard is in the process of methodically pounding your head into pulp in the middle of an empty hallway which was in turn in the middle of an empty apartment building in the quietist and most impersonal part of town. Somebody would find the guy sooner or later, and the police would come to investigate, but nothing would happen to the man who had done the deed. That was how it was in those days: good things happened to good people.

One more punch to the left side of the head and then the big man stood up, rubbing his aching hands. A normal person might have broken their phalanges and metacarpals on the guy's face, but the big man was odd, his bones unnaturally strong and thick. He took a moment to survey his surroundings, saw no one, heard nothing, and then turned and picked up the crowbar he'd left on the floor behind him. He hefted it, loving its weight, and then turned back to the poor swollen heap of a man below. One bright eye stared out from the blood and bruises, blinking at him curiously. A gurgling moan came from the guy's throat.

"In fact, if I was you," the big man said, "I'd leave all women alone from here on out. I wouldn't date, I wouldn't even look at one. I'd take a vow of celibacy and move somewhere far away. A man like you shouldn't be with a woman. Surely you agree?"

The broken man attempted to shake his head, his eyes now focused squarely on the crowbar.

"Maybe, if I hear you've recovered and moved on with your life and have met someone and decided to get married, maybe I'll come back around, remind you what I said here tonight. What do you think? Maybe I'll join you on your wedding night, try to knock this little lesson back into your head. Sound good?"

Another weak attempt to shake his head and then the man moaned again.

"Hush now. Just think about what I'm teaching you: you should treat people a little better. Especially women. What kind of man puts a woman in a hospital?"

The injured guy opened his mouth as if to speak, and the big man swung the crowbar down viciously to his legs. The iron connected solidly, with a sound like a dropped bag of sand.

"That was a rhetorical question."

He brought the crowbar around again, once more connecting with the legs just below the knee.

"I'll tell you when I want you to answer."

He began to swing the crowbar repeatedly, methodically beating the other guy from ankle to waist. A couple times his aim was bad and he connected with the man's crotch, but oh well, he was batting pretty decently this evening, overall. He paused after a few minutes to listen to the quiet building, then gave a couple quick pin-point blows to the chest area, breaking ribs. There was a distinct cracking sound, like stepping on dead twigs, and then he stood tall and looked down at the dirty results of his dirty deed and thought about how it was nice to do favors for people. He smiled, looked up and down the hallway (and god, was that purple carpet the ugliest thing he'd ever seen) and then bent over the bloody mess underneath him and whispered into his ear:

"Your wedding night, you hear me?"

No response. Of course.

The big man smiled. "Have a good evening," he said.

Then he was out of there.

*

He never took time to sit and contemplate what he had done, he even forgot about it later, when life and all its assorted complexities came in to cloud his mind and further darken his heart. What was the point of going over it anyway? To discover hidden meanings, secret signs, goddamn sub-conscious signals about who he really truly was deep down? Bullshit. Life was lived, and then you marched onward. Those who sit and dwell on the things they might or might not have done in the past were missing the point, and losing out in the end. Life was all forward-momentum. Life was a ride. Life was what you did before you kicked the bucket. It was that goddamn simple. Self-analysis, or the over-thinking of past situations, mind-sets, and actions was in the end worthless, self-indulgent, fruitless. What was the point in going over something you did years ago or even yesterday when you couldn't undo it, when it was part of you, when you probably enjoyed doing it at the time? Regrets? Who the hell could afford to have regrets? What was done was done. Onward

194

now, into the future, raise a glass for history's sake but move on, move on.

He never thought about any of it. Occasionally situations or moods would arise that would light a spark in his mind and reinvigorate a vague and murky image from those old lost times, but he rarely made the connection. He was in the moment, as horrid as some of those moments might have been. He was an animal involved with the serious business of *living*, every second of every day was a struggle for survival, for independence, for substance, for meaning. He lived on nerve endings, bone, and muscle, and tried not to allow the intellect too much say. And it worked for him. He stayed alive day after day, night after night. He remained a vital human being. Dark nights of the soul? Never. Who had the time? He was a creature of instinct, a beast made for the moment, turning off his brain whenever it threatened to rear up and say: *No, you can't do that, that would not be good, that is not the proper course of action, that will get you nowhere.* Better to trust those instincts and nerve endings, better to listen closely to the bristling hairs on the back of your neck, to the tightening of scrotum and fists and eyelids, than to allow the brain to take over like it loves to do. The brain had had its say, it was time now for the rest of the body. And where had the brain ever gotten anyone? Where had it gotten the human race, where had it gotten this little country called America? Think of all the vast and diverse nonsense the brain has thrown into the lives of human beings, draping it over us like the vilest sort of jewelry: the assembly-line, the car, the atomic bomb, the hydrogen bomb, Agent Orange, napalm, draglines, earth movers of all stripes, chemical pollution, pesticides, insecticides, thalidomide, dynamite, Botox, cloned cows, submachine guns, IEDs, chemical and biological weapons, fracking, irradiated food, clones, robots. All of it the brain's doing. When a man goes by his heart and gut he does well by himself and his neighbors. When he goes by the brain he fucks everything up. Like that ancient Chinaman (whatsisname?) said: *think not, only act.* So this is what he did. The days of thinking were over.

Then… he began to wonder: what would happen the day he allowed his brain to take over again, or when it *forced* its way back to the forefront? Would it try to exert as much control as it could over as large a part of his life as possible?

Would it be unbearable in its power-grab? After all, a thing like the brain, with its enormous ego, couldn't just accept a small token of power, an inconsequential arena in which to use its talents and its skill... no, it would have to have it all. Everything. The whole damn deal. And when it took over, when it saw the amount of capital it had... what might it do, and what might become of him?

Depression.

Cynicism.

Or something worse? Madness, maybe. Well, he couldn't risk it, he'd have to fight the intellect as hard as he could, keeping that old hound at bay.

So, onward he went, into life and everything it offered, through the days and nights, feeling more or less alive, feeling bestial and primal, a man-monster moving through the machinery of existence, trudging onward uphill upriver, feeling more and more the resistance of everything coming the other way, pushing against him. And what was this resistance? It was that old hound itself, madness, and it showed no interest in him, instead was focused on the others, the huddled masses marching back the way he had come. He saw it in their eyes, in the expressions they wore, in the way they walked and the way they went about their lives. Didn't they see it? Didn't anyone else see it? Wasn't anyone else free enough, bestial enough, to notice?

No, of course not, because everyone was mad, the world itself was mad, he was moving through the world on his nerve-endings and instincts and it didn't matter because the world was insane, everywhere he looked he saw a raving lunatic asylum full of screams and howls and pointless laughter, the piercing cackles of the crazy, pinwheeling eyes and slack-jaws and brains full of worms. And what goes mad? The mind, of course, not the heart and guts. And he began to suspect that the mind *wanted* to go crazy, that the only thing it sought with passion and purpose was lunacy, that to fall apart into a soft rotten-banana mush was its main and ultimate goal. Everything else it craved worked to that end, after all: reason, logic, learning... they all led to madness. It was reason that led to the atom bomb, logic that gave us Mutual Assured Destruction, learning that allowed men of power to control the proletariat. And noticing this, he began to notice how prevalent Madness had become. It was always there, in the forked-tongue of a state senator, in the perverse ethics of a governor, in the eyes of a mayor, in the vicious and threatening stance of an impotent cop, in the arrogance of a boss, in the twisted and misused and bad-voodoo words of laws and bills and proposals, in the very bloodstream of the System itself. Madness. It was everywhere, and it was always knocking, knocking, violently knocking on his chamber door....

*

"Not so loud," Hamm said. He was past hangover mode now and into full-on desiccated exhaustion, leaning against the wall of the motel and keeping his eyes squinted tight against the unwelcome mid-morning sun. Helter had just knocked on the door of room 123, but he hadn't done so loudly at all, he didn't think. He frowned at Hamm and shook his head.

"You look like Death itself," he said. Lisa stood behind him sighing and surveying the nearby area. She had sunglasses on to keep the sun from her eyes and her face was pale. For the first time in months Helter was the only one who wasn't lacking sleep, the nap he'd taken back at the farmhouse having done much to refresh him. He felt wide-awake, in fact. He figured: get these two a few hours of rest, then get back on the trail with Bantam. Why not? What else was there to do? Might as well follow this adventure as far as it would take them, they were already on it, might as well finish the ride.

He knocked on the door again, and as he did a shriveled old woman came out of a room a few doors down and looked over at the three suspiciously. She said nothing at first, then shut her door, made sure it was locked, and started to walk past them. Helter was just stepping aside when she stopped and looked at him.

"You staying in there?" she asked.

"No, Ma'am, a couple friends of ours."

"Oh." She looked at the door and frowned. "They were very loud. You should tell them to be more considerate of others."

"I will, Ma'am."

She nodded but didn't look like she believed him, giving him a quick little judgmental look-over. She started walking again but after a few shuffling steps she stopped and looked back.

197

"Other people need to sleep. Old folks sleep late. Tell them that."

"Of course. Sorry, Ma'am."

"No one should have to listen to that at all hours of the day."

"Right Ma'am."

"We're paying for a room, too."

"Of course."

She stared at him, then shook her head and moved on. Hamm turned his head to watch her go and when she was completely past he flipped her off.

"Nice," said Lisa.

He flipped her off too.

"Enough," Helter said. "Act fucking professional."

Hamm sighed.

Helter knocked on the door again. "Jazz, John?"

"For Christ's sake, just try opening the damn door," Lisa said. When Helter looked at her like he didn't quite understand she sighed and stepped forward, brushing past him to put her fingers around the handle. She turned it easily and the door opened to the room beyond.

It was dark inside, and smelled of mustiness and breath and... was it firecrackers, that weird yet pleasant odor of burnt explosive powder? The closest bed was unmade, its sheets balled at the foot like they'd not only been discarded but shunned, and there was a warmth in the air that was nearly tropical. Overall, the effect was of a claustrophobic space, an insular space, something hermetically sealed against the cooler, brighter world outside.

"Hello?" Lisa said. No answer. She took a cautious step in and felt for the light switch by the door. She flicked it on but didn't take any more steps.

Bantam was sitting comfortably, casually, on a wooden chair at the back of the room. He was dressed in khaki pants and a white shirt, but no shoes. The shirt was speckled with dark splotches, and torn from the left shoulder to the breast pocket. He looked at Lisa, saw Helter behind her, and nodded. One little nod, meaningless to anyone but him, and then he lifted the pistol he was holding in his right hand and shook it, barrel to the ceiling, as if to say *Here it is, this is what did it, this is what you're looking for.*

"Holy shit," Lisa said simply.

198

On the bed furthest from the door lay the big body of Jasper Callister, a massive stain of blood in a near-perfect circle around the ragged quarter-sized hole in his chest, his eyes staring flatly up to the ceiling and his mouth open just slightly. The bed beneath him was stained as well, a great pool of thick near-black blood that looked like paint or oil. His arms were out from his sides Crucifixion-style, palms up, the fingers curled but not fist-like, just the standard casual half-curl of the dead.

Helter was the next to see Jasper, but he didn't say anything, just stared into the room with his mouth open.

It was Bantam who spoke. He glanced almost absently over to Jasper, no expression registering on his face at all. "He came at me," he said. "He just came at me."

"What's going on?" Hamm asked. "Who is it?" He had appeared in the doorway and was trying to look over Helter's shoulder. Fruitless effort: Helter did not move. Would not move. Could not.

Bantam looked back at them all. His eyes were wide but soft, his mouth lifting into a strange smile.

"Nameless here," he said. "Forevermore...."

F rom *Life and Death in American Politics* by Lisa
Yates, never published:

*The simple fact about American politics is this: it's all
madness, from the top down. Does anything surprise anyone
anymore, is anyone shocked by what a politician does, says, or
is caught red-handed doing? No, because we've all entered the
asylum. And it's worse than this cliché suggests: it seems
pretty clear now that we've all gone there willingly. We're
happy inmates.*

*

The sun was kind and pure, and the world smelled fresh,
the way it always does in spring when everything is coming
back from the long dark days of dormancy. Lisa stood behind
the big barn and stared out over the fields, watching the
shadows of the clouds move slowly to the East. Chickadees
and cardinals called from the tree line, and to her left she heard
the barking of a hound in the distance. On the breeze, every

few seconds, came the sweet, rich, pleasant smell of the cows, that smell she trailed to school on her clothes and in her hair. When the breeze died there was just the freshness of the world itself again, new and joyous, nearly vernal. This was not spring, however, it was late September, summer's end. A long lazy Sunday afternoon in those wonderful days before Autumn.

"See anything good?"

She turned and saw her father coming up. He was smiling and holding the handle of a broken shovel or hoe, and though he looked like he'd just gotten done with some serious hardcore work (stained jeans and shirt, left cheek smeared with dirt, boots scuffed and beaten) he moved effortlessly and with energy, like he'd just woken from a nap. He came up and stood next to her, peered over the fields like she'd been doing, searching for something of interest out there.

"Whatchya got?" he asked, squinting against the sun. "Coyote? Deer? Bear?"

"Nothing."

"Nothing?" He looked out there again, saw something against the very furthest back corner of the field. "Look again: turkeys."

She looked, saw the dozen or so black shapes huddled where the shade of the woods was just starting to enter the field. It was lower land there and she had to stand on her tip-toes a bit to see the birds.

"Missing turkeys," he said with feigned disgust. "You should be ashamed."

She didn't answer, just watched the birds for a while.

"You do what your mother wanted you to do?"

She frowned. "Of course. I always do my chores. I always have, haven't I?"

"Of course. Take it easy." He put his hand on her shoulder. "Don't bite my head off."

"Well...."

"You're just like her. Both so damn feisty it's not even funny. Hard for a man to handle sometimes."

"Whatever...."

He laughed. "*Whatever*. Sounds just like her."

She stared at the turkeys, though they weren't doing much, didn't even appear to be moving.

"So whatchya got planned for the rest of the day?" her father asked. "Wanna help me fix that fence?"

201

"Umm...."

"You could make a new ladder for the little barn."

She bit her bottom lip and said nothing.

He was smiling again. "Ah, let's see... you could take a look at the red tractor and see what's wrong with her? Engine won't turn. You wanna do that?"

"What do I know about tractors?"

"I don't know. You tell me."

"Nothing."

"Might be a good time to learn. Go take a look, climb up there, take my tools and a flashlight if you need it, get your head way in there and...." He saw the look she was trying not to make and laughed. "Just messing with you, kiddo," he said.

"I know. I'm ignoring you."

He laughed again. "See, just like your mother." He watched for her reaction, saw her lip quivering into a smile, and then mussed her hair. "God, you're so easy to tease."

"I am not...."

"And fun to tease, too."

They stood there looking out over the field for a while, and then his eyes happened to turn skyward and he smiled at the blue-black bottoms of the clouds that were moving overhead. Fat lazy late-summer clouds. Beautiful.

"You know what you *should* do," he said thoughtfully. "You know what *I* would do if I was you? I would...." He paused, then turned and looked back at the farm, searching for something, biting his bottom lip just as she had been doing. He looked all around, paying particular attention to the farmhouse. At last he turned back to her. "You know what?" he said.

"What?"

He thought a moment again, then said: "Follow me. Come, hurry!" And he started out toward the field, moving quickly, using the shovel-handle as a walking-stick.

Lisa followed behind without thought, moving with slightly more difficulty through the increasingly tall grass, tripping occasionally on hidden stones or branches, breaking the dried husks of milkweed open to send the cottony puffs of seeds into the air. She'd explored almost the whole range of their property, of course, but had never gone way to the back of the longest field, at least not by foot: she'd ridden on many tractors, sitting on her Dad's lap as he made endless passes while seeding or baling. There was a long line of trees and bushes that stretched all the way from where she'd originally been standing to the woods way out back, these trees and bushes having grown up around an equally long pile of rocks and boulders that had been pulled from the fields over the years. He led her this way, eventually going to the right to follow a sudden natural rising of the land where the grass wasn't quite so tall and the bushes thinned out. It took them a good twenty minutes, and once he was at his destination he turned back to watch her. She wasn't far behind but she looked tired.

"Hurry," he said. "Your mom's probably got the binoculars on us right now."

She came up the little hill covered in seeds and grass and insects and stood there by her dad's side. She looked back toward the farm and it seemed a million miles away, a tiny dollhouse, no movement visible there at all.

"All right," he said, and then he lay down on the hill, stretching out his legs and putting his folded hands behind his head. "Ahh... nice and comfy."

"What are you doing?"

"Looking at the clouds. What else is there to do?"

She glanced up at the sky, then did as he did, stretching out on the hill and staring upwards.

The clouds were heavy and dark-bottomed but carrying no threat of rain. They moved slowly past, hypnotically slow, changing their shapes so subtly you had to really concentrate to notice. A swirl here shifted and became a grasping tendril there, the bottom of one overtook another and became its top. Constant, endless movement as they moved to the east.

A group of thrushes were displeased at first with the presence of the humans, but they settled down in some nearby trees after a while, peeping and clicking to themselves as they bustled about in the branches.

"See that?" her father asked as he stared at the clouds. "Looks like you could reach up and touch one." He lifted an arm toward them and wriggled his fingers in the air. "What would they feel like...?"

She did the same. "Cotton."

"Cotton?"

"Yeah. Cotton."

"You know what clouds are made of?"

She paused. "...umm...."

203

He hesitated a moment, then nodded to himself. "Cotton."

They watched the clouds silently for a few minutes, and then he pointed to one and said it looked like a horse.

"It doesn't look like a horse," she said.

"A horse's head. Look, look, it's changing! What's it becoming?"

She frowned but couldn't tell. "A cotton ball...."

"A cotton ball?" He tore up a handful of grass and threw it at her. "Silly. Look again, what does it look like?" When she didn't answer he said: "The clouds tell stories. They change shapes and tell stories, you just have to know how to read them."

He pointed out a dog, an alligator, a man with a hat. He said the man with the hat used to own the alligator but it ran off with the dog, and now he's looking for them both.

"He'd better hurry," she said, "the alligator's becoming a boat, like Uncle Ted's boat."

"A canoe. I see it."

He watched this shape for a while, then rolled over and looked at her.

"You see how the stories don't always make sense? That's because they're not stories for everyone, they're stories just for you, they're meant just for this moment, just for this little moment before they change and become something else. But they're up there, thousands of stories just for you, if you take the time to sit and look for them."

She stared up at the clouds, a look of wonder on her face.

After what seemed like an hour he finally sat up. "All right, pumpkin, we should probably head back."

"No, just a little longer. Please, just a little longer?"

"All right. Just a bit."

"Yay!"

He smiled at his daughter, then settled back again to watch her as she stared skyward, eventually dozing while the breeze swelled up and the clouds moved silently on.

ABOUT THE AUTHOR

Todd Michael Cox was born and raised in northern Wisconsin and still makes his home in the Dairy State. He received a degree in creative writing from UW-Oshkosh, which is also where he cast his first vote (in the 1992 presidential election). A lover of wildlife and wild places, he has been featured on Wisconsin Public Radio, where he talked about his blog, *Wisconsin Unhuggables*, and is the founder of the Snake Anti-Defamation League, a group dedicated to preserving the reputation of the world's snakes. He is a musician, composer, and sometime-puppeteer. His spoken-word project Ripe For Shaking has been included on *ATTOHO (After They Tore Our Heads Off)*, a CD compilation from the Journal of Experimental Fiction, and has been played on New Zealand radio. He is also the author of the novels *After the Death of the Ice Cream Man, Dizzlemuck*, and *Beast*.

www.ingramcontent.com/pod-product-compliance
Lightning Source LLC
Chambersburg PA
CBHW031953170626
46807CB00006B/2465